Praise for the novels of
Parry "EbonySatin" Brown

Sittin' in the Front Pew

"A laugh-out-loud look at how a family tries to reconcile their memories with their father's secret life."

—*Black Issues Book Review*

"An honest, biting portrayal of disgrace under pressure."

—*Kirkus Reviews*

"A radiant family drama with all-too-real scenarios and deep emotional impact. In her sophomore effort, Parry Brown gives us a ride that is both enlightening and entertaining."

—TIMMOTHY B. MCCANN, author of *Forever*

"A touching story of life, death, and reconciliation."

—*Essence*

"Brown has done a superb job in her debut novel of portraying a strong man doing exactly what he is supposed to do."

—*Booklist*

Fannin' the Flames

"Enjoy while lounging on the beach or by the pool."

—*Essence*

"Brown fills the pages with such richness and suspense that you are forced to slow down and just enjoy the ride. . . . A sizzling read."

—*Quarterly Black Review*

"Brown flawlessly tells the tale of four characters in a story rife with intrigue and deception. . . . An engrossing read."

—*RomanticTimes.com*

What Goes Around

What Goes Around

A NOVEL

Parry "EbonySatin" Brown

ONE WORLD
BALLANTINE BOOKS
NEW YORK

A One World Books Trade Paperback Original

Copyright © 2006 by Parry A. Brown
Reading group guide copyright © 2006 by Random House, Inc.

Published in the United States by One World Books, an imprint of The Random House Publishing Group, a division of Random House, Inc., New York.

ONE WORLD is a registered trademark and the One World colophon is a trademark of Random House, Inc.

Library of Congress Cataloging-in-Publication Data

Brown, Parry A. (Parry Ann)
    What goes around : a novel / by Parry "EbonySatin" Brown.
       p. cm.
    ISBN 0-345-46945-3
    1. Mothers and daughters—Fiction. 2. Domestic fiction.
I. Title.

PS3552.R3275W48 2006
814'.54—dc22

2005055527

Printed in the United States of America

www.oneworldbooks.net

9 8 7 6 5 4 3 2 1

Book design by Lisa Sloane

To my soon-to-be-husband, Neville,
and all my children, Nicolle, Michelle,
Jessie, Nicolas, Shanelle, Krystal, Krysten,
Anjill, Symoni and Nierah

This book is written in memory
of my beloved mother, Colethia Naylor,
and cousin Clifton Brown, Jr., who lost
their battles with kidney disease.

I must first and foremost give all honor, praise and thanks to my Lord and Savior, Jesus Christ, and to God, the Father, for my many talents and boundless blessings. I wish to always exalt Him in all that I say and do.

Readers can be relentless in their quest for sequels. They always want more of the characters in the books they enjoyed. Since 1999, readers have been asking for a follow-up to the lives of the Winstons. Many wanted to know what happened to Ariana and Alisa when they grew up. I'm very pleased to say thank-you to those who never let up in their request. Because of you, we have *What Goes Around*.

To my daughter Nicolle Brown, for reading the first draft so quickly and giving me her feedback and adding just the right touch at the end, I can never express my gratitude enough. You've been there for me with every book.

Pastor T. Ellsworth Gantt, II, his lovely wife, Lady Tofa, and the entire Second Baptist Church of Riverside family, thank-you for the love and support in all that I do. I'd like to thank my editor, Melody Guy, for helping me grow from a budding author to a seasoned writer; and my agent, Portia Cannon, for doing what she does best. No writer could ever make it without her author friends who know the struggle and understand the heartache. Victoria Christopher Murray and Pat G'Orge Walker—you know you're my gurls!

My closest friends, who've done double duty helping plan our wedding, Don and Wanda Wilson, Twania Hayes-Thompson and Glynda Ard, you've constantly made me feel warm from the inside out. My life is fuller because you always show me unconditional love. Michelle Brown is not only the mother to my grandchildren, but a selfless, exceptional person, who just loves me no matter what. My life is less chaotic because you're always there for me. This has been a very special year for me, as I prepare not only for the release of this book, but also for the forever union with my soul mate, Neville Victor Abraham, III. I want to thank him for loving and encouraging me every step of the way, each minute of every day. My life has become so much richer because you love me.

"*I*'m sorry, Ms. Hawkins, there's no other alternative for you at this point. Dialysis is inevitable." The silver-haired doctor spoke very bluntly. "It's the only thing we can do to keep you alive while you wait for a donor kidney."

Catherine Hawkins uncrossed her long, shapely legs and shot from the baby-soft leather chair. She leaned over the desk, inches from the doctor's face. "Let me explain something to you, Dr. Ahmad: I'm a very rich woman. I can buy and sell this hospital in a matter of a few days. So you make this thing happen or you'll find yourself giving puppies shots in some obscure village in your homeland. Have I made myself clear?"

Dr. Ahmad's expression didn't change. "You've made me aware of your economic prowess on more than one occasion, Ms. Hawkins." He sat back with a slight smirk and waited a beat before continuing. "But you see, Ms. Hawkins, there are some things that even MasterCard can't buy. I can't magically produce a compatible kidney. You're on the organ recipient list. The fact that you are a minority only increases the difficulty we'll have in finding a match for you. I've told you many times, your best chance is a donation from a family member."

Straightening her back and squaring her shoulders, Catherine turned her gaze to the picture window overlooking the hospital day care center's playground. She watched the young children in the sandbox, while others climbed on the monkey bars or swung high into the air. A look traveled across her face, and her next words betrayed a rare moment of vulnerability: "I have no family to speak of."

"Then we have no choice but to wait for a match to come up on the list. It will take some adjustment, but you are a woman of strong will and you'll be back to a fairly normal life in not too long."

Picking up her purse, Catherine turned to the man in whose hands she placed her life. Her mouth opened, then closed, and without another word, she made an about-face and walked toward the door.

"Catherine." Dr. Ahmad rose and walked around his desk toward her. "We must set up a counseling session before your first dialysis treatment. We need to schedule the outpatient surgery for the insertion of the shunt, as well. As you can see, there is much to be accomplished in a very short time."

With her back to him, she reached for the door. "Set it up with my assistant. I'm going to get myself a kidney."

*What
Goes Around*

CHAPTER ONE

"But, Dad, we're eighteen. Why can't we stay out all night?" Alisa pouted. "You act like you don't trust us or something!"

"It's prom night, Daddy!" Ariana piped in. "All our friends are going to the after party."

Exasperation drew lines on Terry Winston's face. "And I have to tell you how many times, I don't care what your friends are doing because they're no concern of mine?"

"You know we really don't need your permission," Alisa said, testing the waters of defiance. "We're legally adults!"

Ariana stared at her mirror image in disbelief. She had to think quickly to counteract her sister's temporary bout of insanity. "I think what Alisa means is that—"

"Girl, you are straight up trippin'." The veins bulged in Terry's forehead and neck as he got into Alisa's face. "As long as my name is Terrance Winston and it appears on your birth certificate, my blood runs through your veins *and* you're slipping your key in *my* front door every day *and* driving the car that I make the payments on *and*—"

"Girls," their mother, Jackie, interrupted, "let me talk to your father for a moment. And, Alisa, I recommend you take a few moments to adjust your attitude before this family meeting reconvenes."

Ariana pushed her sister through the arched opening that separated the family room from the kitchen. Alisa jerked away, turning slightly to roll her eyes at her sister. "You're just tryin' to be Miss Goody-goody," she hissed. "You know you want this as much as I do!"

"Just go," Ariana whispered. "If you keep this up, we won't even get to go to the prom."

The two bounced up the wide staircase, splitting at the landing and going in different directions, though their rooms adjoined. "You seem to forget we're grown," Alisa yelled after her sister just before stepping into her bedroom and slamming the door.

Terry sat with his head in his hands, trying to understand where his sweet, almost-perfect daughters had gone and when the imposter who'd taken over Alisa's body had made the switch. In the scheme of things he really needed to count his many blessings. Ariana and Alisa Winston were top honor roll students as they approached high school graduation. They had been accepted by their top three choices of colleges with offers of full scholarships. To everyone's surprise, the girls were contemplating going separate ways in pursuit of their very grand academic dreams, which included environmental design for Ariana and journalism for Alisa.

By anyone's standard, Terry Winston had been a wonderful father since the day he decided he couldn't let Catherine Hawkins, their birth mother, put them up for adoption. He'd brought his darling princesses home from the hospital, determined to be the best father he could be, while Catherine went off in pursuit of her career goals. In spite—or perhaps because—of it all, he knew today as he'd known then that there had been no other decision he could have made. He loved those girls so much that he would have given them the shirt off his back if they needed it. Moments like these, however, made him understand why his temples, mustache and five o'clock shadow bore the distinction of time.

Thank goodness for his wife. Jacqueline Rogers-Winston was the anchor in the many stormy seas of his life. A sense of calm began to radiate through him as he felt the warmth of her touch in the center of his back. "Are you okay?"

"Not hardly!" Terry took her hand and pulled her around to sit on his lap. "When did she get so belligerent?"

"Honey, she's just feeling her womanhood. She *thinks* she's grown. Every girl goes through the very same thing," Jackie said as she slipped her arms around his neck. "Count yourself lucky it didn't happen any earlier."

"Then why is Ariana so different?" Terry pulled back to make eye contact with his wife of seven wonder-filled years. "They look like the same person, walk and talk the same, but when it comes to personality they are as different as sunshine and rain."

"You seem to forget that it's all still weather. But amazingly they really aren't that different. They both work you like a baker kneading dough, but Ariana just has more finesse." Jackie kissed him gently on the forehead. "And then, toss a little estrogen and oxygen into the mix and, voilà, there you have it—women!"

Staring deeply into Jackie's eyes, Terry wondered what he'd done to deserve such a woman. His soul had connected with hers the moment he'd seen her in the supermarket on the rainy afternoon nearly thirteen years before. "What am I going to do?"

Laughing, Jackie pulled back and stood. "Oh, you thought I had a solution?" She walked around the couch into the kitchen, retrieving coffee mugs from the dishwasher. The sound echoed through the large, airy space as she placed them on the counter. She placed her hand on the cool granite and thought a moment before she turned and continued. "This is such a difficult age for everyone. They *are* in fact adults, though you think of them as your little girls. Look at them. They're built like supermodels with beauty to match, yet they still want nothing more than to please their daddy. They have the pressure of friends and adversaries alike to do this or to act like that. You seem to think that you're the only one with a hard job in all of this." Jackie poured two cups of coffee, added a little Baileys Irish Cream in both and moved back toward the family room.

"So you're saying I should let them stay out all night?" Terry wanted to be angry, but confusion won out.

Terry removed two coasters from the cut-crystal holder and placed them on the cherrywood table. Jackie set the mugs down and turned to her husband in the same movement. "Not at all. What I am saying is there should be some kind of compromise."

"I'm their father. I don't have to conciliate with them!" Terry stood, looking down at Jackie. "Teresa Winston never negotiated with me. It was her way or the highway."

"Times are different." Jackie grabbed his hand and pulled him back to the sofa. "And you'd lose your natural mind if Ariana and Alisa decided they wanted to *take the highway*."

"Alrighty then, Ms. I've-got-all-the-answers, what do I

do? No daughter of mine is going to be out all night with my blessings. The only things open after two A.M. are legs!"

Laughing, Jackie found it difficult to be serious. Trying to compose her thoughts for a clever comeback, she gave birth to what she considered sheer genius. "Let's have the after party here."

Speechless and staring at her as though she were an alien, Terry finally said, "Are you nuts? Do you know what a house full of teenagers could do to this place? Look around you. We have beige carpeting and hardwood floors, antiques, fine crystal. We'd have to take out a rider to our homeowners' policy." Terry picked up the coffee mug and blew on the mocha liquid absentmindedly.

Touching his knee and forcing Terry to make eye contact with her, Jackie continued, "But look at the beauty of this. They get to party all night with their friends, doing whatever it is eighteen-year-olds do, with your watchful eye right upstairs the whole time. And even if the floors get scuffed and the carpet stained, isn't that a very small price to pay for their happiness and your peace of mind?"

This woman is as smart as she is sexy. Terry smiled. He had to admit her plan did seem without flaws. "Do you think they'll go for such an idea?"

"In the words of the great don, make them an offer they can't refuse."

"Such as?"

"First find out what the other after party is offering"— Jackie grinned with satisfaction—"then trump it!"

Smiling at her, Terry thought back to the many times she'd been the answer not only to his prayers but also the desires of his heart. "How do you come up with this stuff?"

"Just brilliance, my love, sheer brilliance." She winked. "I think you should call them back down, first making Alisa apologize for her behavior, which immediately puts her at a disadvantage."

Just as Terry was about to summon his firstborn, Michelle, Michael and Terrance Junior rushed up the stairs from the basement playroom. "Mommy, can we have some popcorn?" Michael yelled as he approached his parents.

"Boy, you just had dinner not more than an hour ago. Where do you put it all?" Exasperated, Jackie smiled. "There's a new box in the pantry. I want to see your homework when you're done with the popcorn. Yours too, Michelle and T.J."

"Yes, ma'am," T.J. said with the enthusiasm of a six-year-old who hadn't completed his assigned task.

Michelle beamed with pride. "I'm done. You can check mine now, Mommy."

"Whatever," Michael mumbled in a baritone voice reserved for someone well beyond thirteen.

As the children headed for the walk-in pantry to retrieve an evening snack, Jackie's heart felt full, remembering how the two families had blended seamlessly seven years before. Only those who had known them for many years knew the story of how Terry's identical twins daughters and Jackie's fraternal twins became the loving Winston clan. And the cement that brought it all together was Terry's namesake, Terrance Winston Junior.

"So you think this will really work?" Terry interrupted her reverie. "I mean, how do we even begin to plan a party for teenagers who *think* they're grown?" A serious look crept across Terry's face. "I mean, what do we allow? Do we chaperone?"

Rising, Jackie looked back at Terry and smiled. "You convince them this is a great idea and I'll handle the rest."

Terry watched Jackie's full, round behind as she switched into the kitchen. Opening the door to the built-in refrigerator that blended with the oak cabinetry, she bent to retrieve a fruit drink, and Terry found himself moaning involuntarily. Jackie stirred him in ways he had never even imagined a woman could. He couldn't understand why Jackie had such issues with her size. The thought of her softness, silky smooth skin, round bottom, full breasts, thick thighs, the heat that radiated from her booty as they slept . . . lawdhamercy! The rumbling taking place above his head shifted his attention from the woman with whom he desperately wanted to sneak into the pantry for just a few stolen moments.

"What in the . . ." Terry leapt to his feet and took the stairs two at a time. "I swear, sometimes they act like they're the babies in this house," he mumbled as he reached the landing leading to the east wing of the house.

He stood outside Ariana's room and listened to the two argue before knocking. "I don't need you to talk for me. I can tell Daddy what I mean." Though Terry couldn't see who was speaking, he knew it was Alisa.

"You need someone to keep your stupid behind out of trouble. If you don't stop this, I'm scared we won't get to go anywhere at all!" Ariana's voice had a tone of pleading. "What's the big deal about going to the after party anyway?"

"Everyone will be there is the big deal. How can the most popular twins in the senior class *not* be?"

"Alisa, we're the *only* twins in the senior class!"

Terry knocked lightly.

"Go away."

"This is *my* room!" Ariana yelled just before she snatched the door opened. "Daddy?" Ariana said, taken aback.

With his hand positioned to knock again, Terry said, "Oh,

so you were expecting whom?" He struggled to calm the anger he felt at Alisa at that moment. "May I come in?"

"Sure, Daddy. I thought maybe you were Michelle. She asked me to help her with something." Ariana didn't make eye contact with her father, which was a good sign she was fishing for a believable response.

"What's going on up here?" Terry stepped into the large space decorated in various shades of yellow and blue. The queen-size canopy bed with canary-yellow and cobalt-blue netting draped over the posts showed signs of a tussle. "It sounded like you were coming through the ceiling downstairs." Terry eyed the matching pillows that were tossed about the room.

Alisa turned away from her father, folding her arms. "We're having a private conversation."

"The minute you threatened the structure of this house, it became public." Terry moved to the blue-and-yellow patchwork-covered footstool and sat. "What are you two fighting about this time?"

"She's such a suck-up! I want to go to the after party and so does she, but she's saying whatever it is that you want to hear!" Anger filled Alisa's beautiful face. "You always taught us to be our own person and to stand up for whatever it is that we believe."

"And you believe what about this?" Terry asked calmly.

"I believe we're adults, and legally you can't tell us what we can and cannot do." Alisa eyed her sister, asking for collaboration, but Ariana's stony face yielded little support.

Terry was stoic.

Alisa continued, "I know we still live in your house and with that comes certain rules . . ."

Terry saw Alisa start to squirm and, enjoying the assumed shift of power, he said simply, "Go on."

"But I think you need to relax our curfew." Confidence fleeing rapidly, Alisa lowered her head and voice. "At least on prom night."

"I see." Tension began to permeate the air as Terry turned to Ariana, who stood with her back pressed against the door. "And what do you have to say, young lady?"

As she dropped her head, the only sound that could be heard in the room was the ticking of the clocks representing the four time zones of the United States, each slightly off cadence with the other. "I'd like to hang with our friends after the prom. Could we compromise and go out to eat and maybe come home by four?"

"I would have considered this counterproposal, but your sister's attitude has me more than just a little concerned. Since you're *grown*, then perhaps we need to make other living arrangements." Terry toyed with them. "Grown is as grown does. I think you need to have your own place."

"Daddy!" they sang in unison.

Terry suppressed a chuckle. "Daddy what?"

"When you think you can apologize to me and your mother for that outburst downstairs, you let me know." Terry rose. "Then we can discuss your loss of good standing and what it will mean to this prom and graduation season."

Ariana shot a penetrating stare at Alisa and returned pleading eyes to her father. "Daddy, I didn't do anything!" Unshed tears caused her expressive brown eyes to sparkle.

Though his heart melted, he stood firm. "All for one and one for all! You'd better have a come-to-Jesus with your sister. I won't live in the same house with disrespect, ever!"

Without another word Terry walked to the door, and Ariana moved aside as he opened it and stepped into the hallway. He expelled more air than he contained. It was so difficult to be stern. Deep inside, he'd always felt the need to overcompensate for Catherine's abandonment of them. Even after Jackie had adopted the girls, deep in his heart those feelings never changed. In recent months Alisa had become more and more combative. Jackie assured him it was a long time coming and totally normal. What scared him even more was that Ariana must have just been lying in wait to spring her split personality on him when he least expected it. The thought always made his head ache.

CHAPTER TWO

*T*erry's first thought was to return to the family room, but he needed some time to think about Jackie's proposal and the twins' desire. He walked slowly past the vast staircase into the west wing of the house where he and Jackie retreated to their own private world.

Jackie's scent lingered in the air as he entered the haven, filled with the soft beiges and corals that soothed him. He decided to partake of the comfort of the plushy love seat positioned in front of the window that overlooked the lighted fountain in the backyard. Emotional fatigue weighed him down as he sank heavily into the beige cushion.

Jackie's words rang in his ears: *"She's just feeling her womanhood."* The reality was they *were* women. Terry had protected and nurtured his baby girls with every fiber of his being. The time since their birth had slipped by too quickly. The years leading up to their birth mother returning had been filled with awe.

On the day he'd received the overnight letter stating that Catherine wanted joint custody, their lives had been thrown into a chaotic nightmare. He'd learned in the seven years following his victory in family court never to take his life with them for granted.

He was so caught up in living, he couldn't remember when their miraculous transition into womanhood had occurred. The discomfort he felt in his chest could best be described as paternal growing pains.

After his marriage to Jackie and the bilateral adoptions, Ariana and Alisa received an occasional card from Catherine to say hello. It never ceased to amaze him how these greetings always seemed to follow some great milestone in *her* life. She had shown even less interest in her children's lives since the day she stormed out of court, announcing she had washed her hands of them.

Jackie stepped in, and from the moment she'd become his wife, the girls had accepted her as their mother. The Winston-Rogers clan was very happy indeed, despite the void that was left when Momma C., Jackie's mother, had slipped from labor to reward in her sleep two years before. Clara Rogers was the cornerstone of their family with her down-home wisdom and unconditional love.

Terry smiled as he remembered how she would pray and say, "*Everything is gonna be all right, sugah*" when the battle raged in family court. It was all that he had to hold onto while his best friend, Roland Carpenter, who did double duty as the twins' godfather, came up against Catherine with not only with some of the best legal expertise in the state of Texas but a love that rivaled his own.

By the grace of his Heavenly Father and the love and support of all those who loved him, he'd won what was rightfully his—Ariana and Alisa. Catherine hadn't bothered them since she had signed away her parental rights as easily as she'd signed a check to pay a utility bill.

The one concern he blessedly didn't have was their financial life. Momma C. had left her entire estate to Jackie, an only child. The quiet, unassuming woman had held an impressive portfolio of stocks, mutual funds, bonds and real estate property—both developed and as parcels of land that were just waiting to have a contractor work some architectural magic. Managing the portfolio had turned into a full-time job for Jackie, and she resigned her longtime position as a staff reporter at *The Dallas Morning News*. In the six months since she'd been a stay-at-home working mom, she'd been preparing to take the real estate board exam, which had proven to be somewhat of a challenge.

The fact that Terry was an architect proved to be quite an asset to the family business as Jackie encouraged him daily to leave the prominent downtown firm to open his own with a Winston-Rogers development as an inaugural project.

Ariana and Alisa would split a very healthy trust fund worth well over two million dollars at age twenty-five. In an effort to ease her conscience Catherine had sent a one-million-dollar-check along with the termination of parental rights papers. Though tempted to return the check to her, Terry had placed the funds in trust with very specific stipulations for distribution once the twins had completed college.

But none of that mattered to him as much as the love and peace he felt when he stepped into his home. There was an inexplicable harmony that filled every nook and cranny. Just

Jackie stepping into a space could turn the very place where he sat thinking of his wonderful life into a den of passion. All in all, he knew he'd been touched by God's merciful hand. But with that being said, how would he ever survive his daughters' newfound womanhood?

CHAPTER THREE

*C*atherine paced in small circles despite the vastness of the room. She gulped vodka like a marathoner consuming water at mile twenty-five. There was no way for her to exist on dialysis. She had meetings all over the world and could be gone for weeks at a time.

Illness would show a chink in her armor, and she refused to let any of her allies or enemies get a glimpse of it, especially now. In the past seven years she had managed to build one of the largest conglomerates in the world. The sweeping changes Catherine implemented in the failing companies she'd acquired had increased net profit a minimum of 100 percent.

Catherine Hawkins had a plan. She'd acquire a kidney; there was no doubt about that. Then after a month's vacation, she'd be back at the helm with no one the wiser. Everything had a price. There were those who brokered body parts. Her daughters were her first choice, but she'd built an empire by always having a plan B. With a few phone calls and her connections she was confident a kidney would be hers in a matter of weeks if not days.

Catherine caught a glimpse of her reflection in the beveled mirror behind the bar. She turned and stared. She'd aged. Her illness had drawn dark circles around her eyes that even M·A·C could no longer cover up. Despite her wealth and access to superior health care, there was nothing the doctors could do to stop the ravages of kidney disease.

Perhaps if she had taken the advice of her medical team more seriously in the beginning. If she had stopped drinking and smoking, ate better and taken the medication, she would have been able to avoid these drastic measures. But how did the saying go? "*Hindsight is twenty-twenty.*" "I'm Catherine Marie Hawkins, a mover and shaker. And I *will* shake this thing. I won't be inconvenienced, do you hear me?" She threw the crystal tumbler at the mirror. At impact, the mirror shattered and spider legs ran to the corners of the glass, distorting her image as vodka and ice rained onto the floor.

Dexter, her butler, scampered into the entertainment room. As he entered he stopped short at Catherine's piercing glare. He bowed his head to avoid eye contact. "Madam, are you all right? I heard glass breaking."

"Clean up this mess and make me another drink now!" Catherine yelled.

Dexter's small frame seemed to cower at the sound of her command. "Yes, ma'am." He turned to leave the room.

"Where in hell are you going?" Catherine scowled. "I told you I wanted another drink!"

Never looking at her directly, he scurried behind the bar. "Ma'am, the usual?" Dexter's voice quivered.

"Of course, you imbecile." Catherine lit a cigarette and

blew smoke into the air. "And why haven't you gotten that mess cleaned up yet?"

"I will, ma'am, as soon as I make your drink." Dexter's Haitian accent was heavier when he was nervous.

"I want it done now or I'll have you deported." Catherine smiled wickedly to herself. "How'd you like to go back to that little village that doesn't even have running water?"

"Oh, no, ma'am. I promise I will do better!" Dexter ran from behind the bar, tripping and splashing a little vodka over the side of the glass.

Dexter hesitated and stared at Catherine, his eyes filled with terror. She started to scold him for tripping, but in the recesses of her mind she heard the words *You betta watch your step because one day you are going to trip and fall.* She wasn't sure where they came from, but the words made her change her stance.

"Just give me the drink, clean up the mess and be gone." Her words were stern but her tone less harsh than Dexter was used to hearing.

Dexter was confused. "I'm truly sorry, ma'am."

Catherine waved him off and went to the plush purple sofa and sank into it, reaching for the remote control at the same moment. Had she tripped and fallen? Had the way she treated people her whole life come back to bite her in a place that even she couldn't protect with wealth and power? Had the fates frowned upon Her Royal Bitchness?

Of course not. She believed with all that she possessed she was the captain of her own ship. What happened to Catherine Hawkins, she made happen. In her cockiness she didn't realize how true those thoughts were.

CHAPTER FOUR

"Daddy?" Alisa startled Terry. "May I come in?" Alisa's demeanor had changed drastically.

Terry turned to face her, fighting the urge to smile. "What can I do for you?"

"I just . . . I just want to"—Alisa struggled with the words. "I just wanted to come in here and tell you I'm sorry for acting up."

"Go on." Terry was enjoying her uneasiness. "I'm listening."

"I'm sorry, Daddy. I still think we should be able to stay out late on prom night, but the way I went about asking you was all wrong."

"You got that right!" Terry stood. "Do you know what would have happened to me if I had spoken like that to your grandmother, even today?"

With tears forming in the corners of her eyes Alisa admitted defeat. "You're right and I'm really sorry. Please don't take it out on both of us because I made a bad decision."

"And who should I be taking it out on, if not you and your sister, though I know this was all you? But you've always said 'All for one and one for all.' "

"I know, Daddy, but pleeeaaase. This is our prom. We'll never get to do this again."

"Well, missy, you should have thought about that before you decided to *be grown*." Terry looked stern while smiling inside. "You need to go downstairs and apologize to your mother and then maybe we'll be able to discuss an alternative plan."

"But I didn't—" Alisa caught herself before she went any further and decided to do whatever her father suggested. She did *not* want to ruin the prom for herself, and if she blew it for Ariana, there would be hell to pay. "Yes, Daddy. I'll get Ari."

Without another word Alisa turned and walked from the retreat. Terry smiled, shaking his head. "What am I going to do with them?" He took one last quick glance at the fountain before he headed back to the throng of family activity.

Ariana and Alisa met him on the landing where the east and west stairs met, and the three of them descended. They took several steps down the spacious hallway to the family room. Quiet fell on the room like a snowfall on Christmas Eve.

Jackie broke the loud silence. "Do I gather from this united appearance you've worked everything out with your father?"

"We're still in the *working* stage." Ariana spoke up first. "Alisa has something to say to you, Mom."

Turning her body slightly, Jackie made eye contact with Alisa, who stared hotly at Ariana. "Yes, Alisa. I'm listening."

Breaking her gaze Alisa looked at the floor before speaking softly. "I'm sorry for the way I acted earlier."

"We can't hear you." Terry moved past the twins to the couch where Jackie sat. "Please repeat what you said."

"I'm sorry," Alisa almost yelled. "I still don't think I'm wrong for making the request, but I didn't go about it the right way. We'll do whatever it is you two say on prom night." Alisa looked first at Ariana, then at her father.

"That was a pretty weak apology." Jackie leaned back on the sofa, crossing her arms.

"Mom, I really am sorry for acting out, but please make Daddy understand how important prom night is to a girl." Alisa fell to her knees in front of Jackie. "The only thing that'll be bigger is our weddings."

Terry drew a deep breath as pain shot through his chest at the very thought of his precious *babies* getting married.

"Apology accepted." Jackie turned, staring at Terry.

Terry looked genuinely surprised. "What?"

"Well, *Daddy*, this is a very important night in the life of a young woman." Jackie shot a glance at the twins, winking. "I think Alisa has apologized and deserves another chance to plead their case."

"You do, do you?" Terry refused to let his face reflect his heart. "Little miss thang has to do some tall talking to get me to see why I should let her stay out until the crack of dawn."

"Daddy, I know because our friends are doing it isn't a good enough reason. But we don't want to miss out on all the fun. Some of our friends are going to after parties, others are going out to eat and just ride around in the limos, having fun, and we really want to go. Please, Daddy, please."

"What time do you think would be reasonable for you to come home?"

First looking at Jackie and then at her sister, Alisa whispered, "Six?"

"A.M.?" Terry leapt to his feet yelling. "Are you out of your mind?"

"Honey, calm down." Jackie touched his hands, gently pulling him down on the sofa next to her. "I'm sure that was just a starting point for the negotiations, right 'Lisa?"

"It had better be a joke," Terry steamed. "I was thinking more like one."

"Daddy!" Ariana piped in for the first time. "The prom isn't even over until one-thirty. How about five?"

"I don't hardly think so," Terry stated flatly.

Making a sound of exasperation, Alisa turned to leave.

"Where do you think you're going? We're not done here, young lady."

"Daddy, I don't even see the point." Alisa kept walking. "You've already made up your mind and aren't going to be reasonable about this. We're going to be the laughingstock of the senior class."

"I have a suggestion." Alisa paused and turned to listen to what Jackie had to say. "The whole reason you want to stay out until the rooster crows is to be with your friends, right?"

Alisa nodded, her eyes full of tears.

"Does it matter *where* you spend that time with them?"

Wiping a single line of tears from her left cheek, Alisa asked, "What do you mean?"

"What if we said you could have an after party here?"

"For real?" Ariana asked excitedly. "With music, food and everything?"

"You tell your dad and me what you want, and if it's legal and reasonable you can have it." Jackie smiled, satisfied.

With guarded enthusiasm Alisa asked, "And what time would everyone have to go home? Two A.M.?"

Visually pulling Terry into the decision making, Jackie raised an eyebrow. "Well, Dad, what do you say about the time the party will end?"

Terry felt such relief that the girls were receptive to the idea that he wanted to say the party could last until noon. "I think if we serve breakfast we could say sevenish."

"Oh my gawd! No one's party will last that long *and* have breakfast!" Alisa's excitement was full throttle. "Everyone'll want to come to our party for sure. What do you think, Ari?"

"I think it's da bomb idea." The girls gave each other a high five. "But, Daddy, are you going to be hanging around all the time?"

"Not if you don't want me to. But you know no one can make French toast like your ole dad here."

"Well, I guess we can let you cook," Alisa joked. "But we do like the idea of having our own party," she went on to add without checking with her sister.

"Can we come?" Michael asked as he entered the family room.

"No, you cannot!" Alisa barked. "Daddy, they can't come, can they?"

"No, Michael, this is an adult party," Jackie said as she smiled at Ariana and Alisa.

"They aren't adults!" Michael argued.

"We are, too!" Ariana said with confidence. "At least on prom night we'll be."

CHAPTER FIVE

"Man, I can't believe it. My goddaughters are going to the prom." Roland shook his head as he took a swig from the bottle of Corona. "It seems like yesterday we were assembling cribs, reading books on formulas and sterilizing bottles."

"Man, please don't remind me. I think I need therapy or something to deal with all of this." Terry stepped into the garage to retrieve his toolbox. "Jackie assures me I'll survive, but I ain't so sure."

"I can't even imagine. I'm so glad I have two men-children. Their mama has more hormonal changes than this brotha can stand." Roland finished the beer in one long gulp.

Terry stepped back into the kitchen with the large gray toolbox in one hand and the tape measure in the other, pulling the door closed with his foot. "Sounds like there's still a little trouble in paradise." The toolbox came to rest heavily on the kitchen counter.

"Trouble's a strong word; maybe saying the natives are

restless would be more accurate." Roland moved to the refrigerator to retrieve another brew. "I just can't seem to figure out what she wants. I think I got it and then, bam, the goal changes."

"And you think this is different from any other man how?" Terry chuckled.

The longtime friends high-fived each other in midair as Roland said, "Word, man. It's all good. So tell me, what's this project you want me to help you with."

"Please don't ask me how the women in this house actually talked me into this, but the after-prom party is going to be here." Terry clipped the tape measure to his belt, lifted the toolbox from the counter and headed for the patio door off the family room. "You coming?"

Roland dutifully followed Terry onto the expansive, enclosed space. "Whoa, that's a huge undertaking. What would make you agree to such a stupid thing?"

"Well, they wanted to stay out all night to go to a party. Of course, I said no. Alisa was feeling her womanhood, being defiant, Ariana was looking like her dog died and Jackie thought this would be a good alternative. While I wasn't that fond of the idea at first, it's kinda grown on me."

"You'll be able to keep an eagle eye on them this way. You need me to chaperone?"

"That would be great." Terry began measuring. "But what I need your help with now is building benches. I want to put bench seating all the way around the patio, so the kids have somewhere to sit out here."

"Man, that's a lot of building. Do you see how big this patio is? Rent some chairs."

"We've been talking about adding the seats anyway, and this is a good enough reason to do it. You know by the time we get your family and mine out here we take up almost the whole thing."

"You trippin'. You can get most of Dallas county out here on this patio. So what do you need me to do? You're the architect."

"I've got the design down. I just need the manual labor and I know I can count on my boy." Terry grinned.

"Your boy? This was Jackie's idea—you betta get her out here!" Roland jested.

"Man, come on now. This is carpentry. You know our Lord and Savior was a carpenter. We'll be following in his footsteps."

"I understand all that. And, yes, being a carpenter is quite noble. However, we betta go down to the depot and find us some day labor."

Roland and Terry laughed heartily like the old friends they were. "Come on, man, we can do this," Terry chided.

Roland held up his hands, flipping them back to front repeatedly. "Look at these hands. Do they look like they've touched a hammer this millennium?"

"Man, just get over there so I can measure this out to see how much wood I'll need. Besides, we get to buy tools!"

Pretending to grumble, Roland walked the length of the patio, smiling all the while. "Well, why didn't you say that in the first place?" These were the moments he lived for.

"I THINK WE SHOULD HAVE PIZZA and wings." Ariana bounced on the mountain-high feather bed as Jackie, Alisa and Michelle looked on. "That way we can't go wrong."

Michelle raised her hand as if she were asking her teacher

for permission to speak. "But can you get pizza delivered at two o'clock in the morning?"

"You leave all the arrangements to me. How many people are you inviting and how many will really come? You know your dad is not the only father with a curfew."

"Boys can come, too, right?"

"Of course. What kind of after-prom party wouldn't have boys?" Jackie joked.

"The one Daddy's letting us have," the twins sang in unison.

Everyone including Michelle, who didn't really get the joke, laughed. Jackie finally said, "I get your point. But, yes, boys are invited."

"I'd say twenty people," Ariana volunteered. "What are we going to do for music?"

"I want a deejay," Alisa answered quickly.

"Absolutely not. You'll get us expelled from the neighborhood with a deejay that *starts* playing at two A.M. We can either tune in to the hip-hop channel on cable or play CDs."

"How lame is that?" Alisa pouted. "They'll tell everyone, and we won't be able to show our faces on Monday."

"Lame or not you *will not* have loud music at that hour. The other alternative is no music at all."

"The hip-hop channel will be fine." Ariana eyed her sister to remind her to keep her cool before she blew it again.

Jackie perused her list. "So let me make sure I have this straight: pizzas, chicken wings, sodas, water, chips, dip for twenty people. Anything else?"

"Can we get a karaoke machine?" Alisa asked shyly.

"A what?"

"You know, the machine with the music and the words so you can sing along."

Jackie sat back on the pillows piled high against the antique headboard. "I know what a karaoke machine is. I'm just surprised to hear you ask for one."

"Oh, Mom, we do it with our friends all the time," Ariana answered for Alisa. "It's so much fun and 'Lisa can really sing."

"I've heard her sing and I agree with you. A karaoke machine it is. Anything else?"

"Where will Michael, Michelle and T.J. be? Mom, I swear, if they show their faces, I'll be mortified."

"We'll make sure they're at Auntie Veronica's for the night. She's coming over to see you guys off for the prom, so she'll just take everyone home with her."

"Mom?"

"Yes, Alisa?"

"Thank you."

"For what?"

Alisa's beautiful brown eyes met Jackie's as she began, "We know this is all your idea and that Daddy would've never come up with it on his own. All he wanted to say was no way, no how. But we got what we wanted and you're making us look really cool to our friends. We love you."

Feeling too full for words, Jackie stretched out her arms. "Group hug."

They all piled on top of her and began hugging and covering her face with kisses.

CHAPTER SIX

$\mathcal{C}$atherine sat staring out the window, watching the California sunset. The view was enough to take even the most cynical pessimist's breath away. She slowly turned back to her desk. As she looked through the smoked glass desktop she caught a glimpse of her legs. Her strong, muscular legs had thinned, as had the rest of her. She quickly directed her eyes to the nineteen-inch, flat-panel monitor. She sighed as she toyed with the mouse while she stared at her contact listings in Outlook. Terrance and Jacqueline Winston. How ironic was it that she had to look up the father of her children's phone number in an electronic Rolodex? When was the last time she'd dialed his number?

Had she called the twins on their last birthday or even their last three birthdays? She had sent them diamond pendants for their sweet sixteen. But she couldn't remember if she had called them.

Now she *needed* to call. What would she say? *Hello, this is your mother. Got a spare kidney?* Even in Catherine Hawkins's world that was a bit brash. She needed to cultivate a relationship with Ariana and Alisa before she sprang the news. Sighing deeply, Catherine came to the realization that time was the one thing she was fresh out of.

Though she'd given up her rights several years before and Jacqueline Rogers-Winston was now legally their mother, Terrance had always left the door open for her to communicate with the twins whenever she wished. She'd planned to do it more frequently, but time always seemed to escape her, and one year rolled into the next without so much as a phone call. Terrance sent school pictures every year, and the last ones she'd received showed the two proudly leaning on gigantic numbers proclaiming the year. Would they send her an invitation to their graduation? She'd sent them postcards when she'd landed a new deal or made a major acquisition. Now looking back she wondered how that must have seemed to her children.

Did the words *her children* just tiptoe through her head? She couldn't remember ever thinking of them as her own. Was it because she now needed them? Would they look at her with scorn and disdain, wondering about the years when they had needed her?

Her eyes fell upon the phone number of the Winston household once again. She touched the handset, contemplating her next move. She was startled when the phone rang.

"Yes, Claire?" Catherine answered sharply.

"Rahid MacDonald is holding." The secretary of eight months held her breath while waiting for a response. "Should I put him through?"

"What do you think?" Catherine snapped.

"Very well, Ms. Hawkins. I'll be leaving as soon as I connect the call." Claire spoke quickly, trying to avoid any of Catherine's unprovoked wrath.

"Fine." The next sound she heard was the voice of her first choice for a new second in command. She smiled as she thought of the plans she had for Hawkins International and the vital role Rahid could play. In their brief conversation she learned that he was still considering her offer. The African-American man with the Harvard MBA was being courted by some of the largest corporations in America. She hoped she'd sweetened the pot just enough in her last proposal and that this was just a ploy to strengthen his bargaining power.

As she replaced the receiver she felt a pang of apprehension. She was so close to realizing all her professional dreams. Rahid's appointment would remain top secret—for now. She'd led each of the five division heads to believe he was being considered for vice president of international operations. She'd use the possibility of becoming second only to her as a means to get them to see things her way. Once she had what she wanted, she'd introduce Rahid.

She pressed the speaker button and began dialing.

CHAPTER SEVEN

"*B*ut I want to wear my hair up. A French twist with curly tendrils in the front, side and back," Ariana whined to Jackie.

"Well, you do what you want. I'm wearing mine down. I thought we wanted our dates not to be able to tell us apart! You're always changing *something*," Alisa yelled.

"Girls, girls. Must you argue about every little thing? And why on earth would you want your dates not to be able to tell you apart?"

"Just so we can play tricks on them. We do it all the time." Alisa fell onto the bed, her chin coming to rest in her hands. "It freaks them out."

"I don't get it." Jackie didn't want to even imagine the things the girls did with each other's dates. "But okay." In her heart she knew it was all Alisa's idea. "Miss Shanky will be here at four sharp."

"Mom, do you really think she'll have us done by five? She's sooooooo slow." Worry creased Ariana's forehead.

"She promised that since she's already permed and washed your hair it would be very quick tomorrow."

"This *is* Miss Shanky." Alisa put her hands on her hips and cocked her head. "Mom, you are so gullible. You've had dreds so long you've forgotten what she's like. She can whip your hair for sure, but it takes days for her to do it. She gets to telling her stories and waving that comb. She can't talk and work at the same time. I think you should call her to see if she can come earlier."

"We need to be really grateful she's making a house call on a Friday." Looking at her watch, Jackie said, "Let me try to reach her now, but I'm not making any promises." As she reached for the phone it rang. "Hello?"

"Hi, Jacqueline. This is Catherine." Trying to muster a nonchalant tone, Catherine asked, "How've you been?"

Jackie's demeanor changed, along with her hue, as she shifted the phone from her left ear to her right. "I'm doing quite well. How are you, and what can I do for you?"

Purposely avoiding her questions Catherine asked, "May I speak with Ariana and Alisa?"

Jackie's immediate reaction was to say of course you can't speak to *my* daughters, but knew she shouldn't. Why was she calling? They hadn't spoken to her in more than three years. What could she possibly want from them? Something wasn't right. Jackie could just feel it. This wasn't an I-was-just-thinking-about-you call.

"Jacqueline, are my daughters available or not?" Catherine's tone was harsher than she'd meant it to be. "I mean Ariana and Alisa. I haven't spoken to them in ages, and Terrance said I could call anytime."

"They're right here." Without another word, Jackie handed Alisa the phone.

With a questioning look, Alisa said, "Hello?"

"Hello, darling, this is your mother," Catherine sang on the other end of the connection. "I hope I wasn't interrupting anything." She gushed on, "But I just thought I'd give you a call to find out what you want for graduation. I know it's coming up soon."

Disdain clouded Alisa's beautifully clear brown eyes. "We're planning our prom night now with *our mother*. We graduate at the end of the month."

Alisa's words and tone nicked Catherine but didn't draw blood. "Sounds like I'm just in time. What is it that I can get you? Your dresses? Car service? You name it and it's yours."

Alisa sighed and rolled her eyes at the same moment. "The prom is tomorrow night and everything is all taken care of. Would you like to speak to Ari?"

"But, darling, you haven't told me what it is you want for a graduation present."

Catherine's benign tone aggravated Alisa. "I'll get back to you after the prom." Without giving Catherine a chance to utter another syllable, Alisa passed the phone to her sister.

"Hi, Catherine," Ariana said with no emotion.

"Hello, Ariana." Catherine tried to hide her disappointment at Alisa's lack of enthusiasm for her offer of a lavish gift. "I know you must be excited about the prom tomorrow. Alisa tells me there's nothing else you need for your big night. Is that true? I can't imagine there isn't *something* I can do."

"No, I can't think of anything else we might need." Without malice or forethought Ariana continued, "Mom and Daddy have done everything. We're really excited. We were just talking about getting our hair done tomorrow."

Silent seconds ticked by loudly. "I see." Another beat. "What festivities do you have planned for prom night?"

With excitement Ariana answered the woman who'd given her life. "Mom and Daddy are letting us have an after party, and we've invited our friends. We can stay up all night!"

There was that phrase again—"*Mom and Daddy.*" "That sounds very exciting. I asked your sister what she wanted from me for graduation, and she said she'd call me back after the prom. What about you? Do you know what you want from me?"

After a long pause Ariana said slowly, "It would be nice if you would come to the ceremony."

Pain shot through Jackie's heart. Alisa and Michelle stared at Ariana in disbelief.

Catherine smiled before speaking. "Ariana, nothing would give me more pleasure. Please be sure to send me the information as soon as possible. Do you need my address? You can also e-mail it."

"I don't know if we have your address. You move all the time. The last address we have is in Colorado."

"No, sweetie, I'm in California now. Is your e-mail still the same?"

"Yes, it hasn't changed."

"I'll e-mail you and then you'll have mine." A slight pang of guilt crept through Catherine.

"Okay." Ariana felt tears burning behind her eyelids.

"Is Terrance around? I'd like to talk to him."

"Daddy took Michael and T.J. to the movies. Do you want me to tell him to call you?"

"That would be great, and I'll give you and Alisa a call on Sunday or Monday to see what your decision is regarding your gifts. And remember your moth— I'm very rich, so no need to worry about the cost of the gifts."

"Okay, Catherine. Good-bye."

Ariana hit the Off button and turned to face her family. All eyes peered at her. "What?"

Alisa gladly spoke up first. "I don't believe you just invited Catherine to our graduation. Why would you do such a thing without asking me if I wanted her there? You should have talked it over with Mom and Daddy, too."

This time the tears formed puddles in Ariana's eyes. "I don't know why I said it. It just came out."

"You should learn to think before you speak. Jackie has been our mother for a long time, and how do you think it will make her feel?"

Speaking over the lump in her throat Jackie managed, "No, no, Alisa. If Ariana wants Catherine at your graduation, I'd have absolutely no problem with it. I think it's good she wants to be involved."

"You're kidding me, right?" Alisa leapt to her feet. "She hasn't been *involved* for eighteen years and now it's okay?"

"I'm sorry!" Ariana bolted from the room.

Michelle ran behind her, calling her name. Jackie sat transfixed. Alisa fell back onto the bed. How was this woman always able to suck the life out of a room? She was thousands of miles away, yet emotional devastation filled the large space.

"It's going to be okay, Alisa." Jackie rubbed Alisa's back. She loved her as much as if she'd given birth to her. "She may or may not come. But if Ariana wants her to be here, then you should consider it for your sister's sake."

"I don't understand. Ariana *always* hated her. Now all of a sudden she wants to see her. What is up with that?"

"Things change, especially when we grow up. I can't explain why she feels the way she does. She may not be able to either. I just know that this is a very special time for you and your sister, and nothing should be raining on your parade. I think you should go check on your sister to make sure she's okay."

Alisa looked at Jackie and hugged her. "You know you're our mom and nothing will ever change that, right?"

"I know, honey," Jackie said, trying to convince herself as much as Alisa.

CHAPTER EIGHT

*J*ackie watched Alisa disappear, waiting a few extra seconds until she was out of earshot before she picked up the phone. She checked the caller ID screen. She pressed Talk.

"Hawkins International. How may I direct your call?" the warm friendly voice answered.

"Hawkins International, as in Catherine Hawkins?" Jackie asked, surprised.

"Ms. Hawkins is our CEO." A little less cheer this time. "How may I direct your call?"

"I'd like to speak with Ms. CEO, please."

"With pleasure," the woman said in her well-rehearsed fashion.

"You have reached the office of Catherine Hawkins, chief executive officer and chairperson of the board of Hawkins International. Our office is currently closed. Please leave a message and we will process your call as soon as we return."

Jackie hit the Off button, laying the phone beside her. "Wow."

"I DON'T KNOW WHY I said it. It just came out." Ariana fought to stay calm. She, in fact, didn't know why the words had tumbled from her lips as easily as ordering a number three combo at Sonic Burger.

"You know you probably hurt Jackie's feelings. I bet she's in her room, crying, right now." Alisa went for the jugular.

"I didn't mean to hurt anyone! Daddy is probably going to be mad at me, too."

"He should be!"

Ariana began to cry in earnest. Michelle ran to her and threw her arms around her. "Don't cry, Ari. Daddy won't be mad at you. I'll explain to him what happened. 'Lisa is just trying to make you sad, that's all."

Alisa stuck her tongue out at Michelle and mouthed the words *I'm gonna get you.* Michelle looked away.

Like the Christmas morning so many years before, with almost no effort Catherine had caused so much pain. Some things never changed.

TERRY RAPIDLY PACED the length of the bedroom. He looked at Jackie, trying to think of the right words to say. There were none. He went to sit on the bed beside her but decided against it.

"You're making me nervous." Jackie patted the bed next to her. "Come sit."

Terry sat on the bed but at the far end next to the footboard. He leaned against it with his head down. "What could she possibly want now? I've always left the door open for her to come visit the girls whenever she wanted, but she never wanted. Now all of a sudden she's inquiring about their graduation?" Terry turned to make eye contact with his wife. "Something's rotten and stinking to high heaven. After eighteen years she is *not* all of a sudden a caring mother."

"I'm thinking the same thing." Jackie slid to the edge of the bed and let her feet graze the thick beige carpet. "There's something else."

Terry grunted, exhaling deeply before he asked, "What else could there possibly be?"

"I don't know what this means, but I used the caller ID to phone Catherine back, and they answered 'Hawkins International.' Of course, I had to ask, 'As in Catherine Hawkins?' The very polite lady told me yes; she's the CEO and chairperson of the board. I don't know, but it sounds like a huge operation. So if this is true, she's even richer than we ever suspected."

"Why do I care about how rich she is?" Terry didn't mean to take his aggravation out on Jackie. "You're Ariana and Alisa's mother."

"I understand that, but this is making me nervous. There's something she wants and you know her. She doesn't care who it hurts, she'll get it."

Terry moved closer to her on the bed and put his arm around her shoulders. "Don't let her get to you. That's what she craves. She's a power addict."

"Ariana wants her to come to the graduation." Jackie let the words linger in the ether.

"What?"

"Ariana asked her if she'd like to come to their graduation." Anxiety held Jackie captive. "Catherine said she would. I don't like this, Terry."

"Honey, you don't have anything to worry about. The girls love *you* as their mother. There's nothing Catherine can waltz in here and do or say that'll change that. I thought we'd long ago gotten past your insecurities."

"What the hell do you mean, my insecurities?" Jackie jerked away from Terry so quickly it made him lose his balance. "I know I've been a good mother to Ariana and Alisa. I know they love and respect me." Jackie stood and turned to look down at Terry as she began speaking very deliberately. "Catherine can't change any of that. What you're failing to see is that this isn't only about Catherine. You seem to have forgotten the havoc she leaves in her wake."

"I just—" Terry tried to speak, but Jackie cut him off.

"You just what?"

"Didn't mean to . . ." Terry gave up.

"You think I'm going to sit by and let her come up in here and disrupt our family? I don't think so!" Jackie breathed fire. "So if you think I'm scared of the hussy, you betta think again."

Terry contemplated his next move and silence seemed the smart way to go. He thought back to the Christmas seven years ago when Catherine descended on their celebration, wielding insults and making threats, transforming a happy day into one filled with pain. It seemed like eternity wrapped up in yesterday. The court battle had been ugly, but he'd held firm to his belief in God's justice and come out the victor. He was sure Jackie was right about there being something Catherine was after. But what? And why now?

"So are you just going to sit there and not say anything?" Jackie snapped.

Terry chuckled inside; *talk about your catch-22!* "Look, baby, we just need to sit back and see what she's up to. I agree that it's probably no good. But let's not project what we *think* she's going to do."

"You know I love you, Terrance Winston Senior," Jackie began in a calmer tone.

Uh-oh, she called me by my whole name.

"But I'm not going to just sit back and wait for Catherine to make a move. If you don't call her back in the morning, I will."

"I'll call her," Terry said flatly.

"Why do you let her intimidate you?" Jackie could feel her temper flaring again. "You're always so nice to her when you talk. She's never done anything but cause us grief!"

"What the hell are you talking about?" This time it was Terry whose temper shifted. "You know I despise that woman."

Terry moved away from Jackie, staring back at her. He hadn't seen this side of her in a very long time. As he thought back, he believed the last time she was this angry, Catherine was the source. What was it about Catherine Hawkins that always brought out the worst in everyone? He'd never let on to Jackie that she was right: Catherine did intimidate him.

As he walked from the bedroom, he could hear Jackie breathing. If he dared to turn around, he was sure he would see smoke escaping from her nose and ears. His thoughts traveled back through forever to the day he'd met Catherine in the student union.

As he'd stared at the bulletin board, looking for a part-time job, Catherine had walked up next to him. He'd felt her presence. Her fragrance had tickled his nose and he'd felt slightly dizzy. As he'd turned slowly to catch a glimpse of the source of his instability, he'd seen her. She had filled the space with an air of sophistication. Her body language had screamed *Don't even think about messing with me*.

He had wanted to speak to her, but fear had gripped his soul. He'd moved a few steps closer under the guise of perusing the bulletin board, but the truth was her scent had intoxicated him to the point that everything else was a blur.

Catherine had startled him when she'd asked, "Hey, you know anyone who tutors statistics?"

Had the scholastic gods shone on him or what? "Statistics?" Terrance had finally managed.

"What are you, an idiot?" she'd barked. "Yes, statistics!"

That should have been his first insight into the personality of the woman who stood inches above him. But he'd been blinded by her headlights. Her beautiful smile, deep chocolate-brown skin and the double D's that fought their way out of her tank top held him spellbound.

As he thought back, he knew how pathetic he must have seemed. He'd taken on the tutoring job, for free, of course. He refused to notice that Catherine had no interest in learning anything. She persuaded him to complete her assignments. With twenty-twenty hindsight he wondered if she'd known all along he was a wiz at everything and she'd manipulated him to get him to do her bidding. "Terrance Winston, are you listening to me?" Jackie's razor-sharp tone pulled him back to the present.

Terry turned to see Jackie standing in the doorway that led to the bedroom suite. "I'm sorry," Terry stumbled. "I was thinking about what it is Catherine could possibly want from us. I'll call her in the morning."

Picking up the phone and passing it to Terry, Jackie said, "She's in California. It's not that late there."

"But you yourself said she didn't answer when you tried to call."

Jackie's aggravation was mounting. "Don't you have her home or cell number?"

Terry knew that was going to be the next question Jackie assaulted him with. Why was Catherine's consistent lack of concern for her children a source of embarrassment for him? Dropping his head, he said softly, "Not since she moved to California."

"Why am I not surprised?" Jackie turned and moved to the walk-in closet, where she began to undress. "All I know is she'd better not be trying no stupid mess. I won't have it. And don't even think she's getting an invitation to the graduation. Not in this lifetime. Those are my daughters. Do I make myself clear?"

Something akin to resentment filled Terry's chest. "Don't let nobody bluff ya. I have the best interest of Ariana and Alisa at heart, and I promise you, I'll let nothing harm them. I agree that Catherine won't be coming to the graduation. You know she has the attention span of an infant."

"You just make sure Catherine and Ariana understand that, then." Jackie slammed the closet door shut with her still inside. Terry surmised that to mean he'd have no one to keep his booty warm tonight.

CHAPTER NINE

*T*he swelling in Catherine's feet and hands woke her before her alarm sounded at five A.M. When was the last time she'd gone to the bathroom? she wondered. She was supposed to record her fluid intake and output daily, but there was no time for such trivial tasks. She had a full staff who responded to her every whimsical call. But who on her staff was supposed to measure her pee?

She rolled out of bed, letting her feet heavily come to rest on the floor. The dim green digits on the clock radio read 4:03. She picked up the half-filled glass of vodka and drank it down. She laughed to herself as she thought perhaps it should have been water she was drinking.

Who would have ever thought her refusing to get treatment for a strep throat would have led to this? She believed she had the flu like everyone else. Besides, she was too busy to be sick. How did the saying go? "Pay me now or pay me later." She reached for the fourteen-karat-gold lighter and matching cigarette case. As she opened the case, she realized she'd smoked the last one just before dropping off to sleep at two.

She picked up the phone and hit the intercom button. Dexter answered immediately. Despite the early hour he sounded fully alert. "Good morning, ma'am," he said, his accent thick.

"Bring me my cigarettes." Catherine hung up without another word.

Within a few short minutes a knock broke through the early morning silence. "Come," Catherine said, agitated.

Careful not to make eye contact with Catherine, Dexter spoke softly, "Ma'am, there are no more in the cabinet in your office. I also checked in the pantry, and there is nothing."

Without looking up, Catherine pointed to the dresser across the room. "Look over there. The last pack is on the dresser."

Dexter scurried in the direction she pointed, retrieving the slender pack, and took it to her. Catherine snatched the cigarettes and brushed Dexter away.

"Will there be anything else, ma'am?" Dexter asked as he backed away.

"Just be gone. I'll call you if I need something else," Catherine snapped.

"May I get ma'am some coffee?"

"No!" Catherine picked up a slipper and threw it in Dexter's direction.

Dexter quickly disappeared through the double doors, closing them. Catherine put the cigarette to her lips, but refused to light it. Dr. Ahmad had warned her to stop smoking and drinking. He'd gone on to tell her that unless she took the high blood pressure medicine regularly her condition would deteriorate quickly.

Seven years earlier, she had failed to receive the promotion she expected to president of La Hacienda's North America operations. It made her mad enough to strike out on her own. Armed with the contacts she'd made she began to build her own empire. Today, she boasted a multibillion-dollar operation with clients and partners on five continents. Hawkins International's annual revenue was in excess of five hundred million dollars.

She moved in powerful circles with friends in high places. She was on the Republican party's A list for the twenty-five-thousand-dollar-a-plate fund-raising dinners. The secretary of state's home number was on her speed dial. She played golf with Hollywood's elite. She slept with senators. Yet at four in the morning as she stared at her swollen body, none of that seemed to matter.

Crushing the imaginary flame in the ashtray, Catherine slid her foot into one slipper and went in search of the other. She then headed to the bathroom in hope of success with the porcelain. Her mind went back to the conversation the night before as she perched herself on the elegantly appointed throne. Jackie's icy tone angered her, Alisa's ambivalence saddened her and Ariana's friendliness astounded her. She wondered if Terry would be curious enough to return her call.

She hadn't spoken to Terry in years. She found him weak and totally inconsequential. She would have no trouble convincing him that the girls should *gladly* donate a kidney to her. Maybe she could get one from each of them so that she'd have *two*. She smiled at the thought. Ah, she was able to go. She quickly measured the output; thirty cc's. Nowhere near enough. She sighed, washed her hands and returned to the large custom-made bed in the center of the massive south wall of the room.

She removed another cigarette from the pack, this time lighting it.

She hit the buzzer again, and Dexter answered immediately, "Yes, ma'am?"

"Bring me a large glass of cranberry juice and water." Without another word she broke the connection. She wondered to herself if Dexter would bring her two glasses or dilute the juice with water. She purposely tested him, and he usually failed. It was the license she used to chastise him. Why had weak men always surrounded her? Was it true that a woman always looks for her father in her men?

Her mother had been an overbearing, Bible-thumping, wasn't-nobody-going-to-Heaven-but-the-Pentecostals woman. With all the God she professed to have, she was never happy. Catherine believed her father had actually willed himself to die when she was nine years old. She knew he loved her, but there was nothing he could do to save her from her mother. She had once seen her mother slap her father with a spatula, and he'd done nothing to provoke her or to protect himself.

She was still angry at her father for leaving her alone with that woman. How much simpler her life would have been if she hadn't let her mother convince her not to have an abortion. But then again . . .

Her mother had told her that one day she'd need her child, and as much as she hated to give in to the truth, her mother had been right. Here she sat, eighteen years later, and the woman's words still haunted her. But what was worse, she'd turned into her mother. There were times she hated herself, but she seemed to have no control over how she treated people. How did the saying go? "An apple tree can't produce acorns."

Dexter's soft knocking startled her slightly. "Come." Her thoughts had caused her body to slump; she sat up straight and cleared her throat.

"Would you like this at your bedside or on the table?"

"Here!" she snapped, pointing to the nightstand.

Dexter had filled a sixteen-ounce crystal tumbler to the brim with cranberry juice and a larger glass with water and ice. Catherine was disappointed.

"Is there anything else I can get for you, ma'am?"

She waved him away. "That'll be all."

She waited until she heard the muffled click of the heavy French doors, before she opened the nightstand drawer. She sighed deeply as she removed her eight prescription bottles one by one. If she was going to live until she got a kidney, perhaps she'd better start to follow doctor's orders.

CHAPTER TEN

$\mathscr{L}$ong before the alarm sounded, Terry lay looking into the darkness. Jackie lay at the edge of the king-size bed, snoring softly. She'd been so angry with him the night before she never said good night, not to mention their traditional kiss— a blatant violation of their never-go-to-bed-angry rule.

What worried him most was that Jackie was right. Catherine still held some mystical power over him. He despised her for her neglect or worse, ambivalence, toward the twins. Since before they were born she never wanted to have anything to do with them. Her greatest gift to them had been life and that had come under protest. Once she found she couldn't use them for her own personal gain, she'd left them, never to look back.

Terry leaned over and kissed Jackie's shoulder. She stirred slightly. The one thing they didn't share was the joy of the early morning. He embraced every morning before sunrise as a gift just waiting to be opened. Jackie, on the other hand, figured there was nothing that couldn't wait until after nine. He decided he needed to clear his head and a run would do him a world of good.

He quickly dressed in the closet. He thought of calling Roland to join him. The friends were almost neighbors, less than a five-minute drive. But this morning he wanted to be alone. He needed to think of how he'd approach Catherine when he called. His hope was that she wanted only to wish the girls well. But in his heart he knew it was nothing that noble.

He tied his running shoes tight and headed out through the garage door. The crisp air was a refreshing change from the typical heavy humidity of May. The quiet, gated community in the Dallas suburb had not yet awakened. As Terry turned off Honeycomb Lane onto Byron Circle he encountered Judge Agnew, his neighbor and friend.

"Good morning, Constance. I haven't seen you in quite a while." Terry jogged in place as he talked. "How've you been?"

"Terrance! It's great to see you. All's well. How is the Winston clan?"

"Everyone is great. It's prom night and I'm a wreck, though."

"Oh, Dad, you'll survive." Constance began a slow trot. "Want to join me?"

Terry fell in step with her, and they ran side by side. "So they tell me. You know it must be fate that I ran into you this morning. The girls heard from Catherine last night for the first time in I can't remember how long and I don't know what to make of it."

"Terry, you worry too much. There's nothing she can do to you anymore. That was settled many years ago. So the most she can do is wish them well as they graduate. You and Jackie are the girls' parents. Case closed."

The two picked up the pace slightly. "I guess you're right. Of course, Jackie's ticked. But I must say Catherine has the worst timing. Ariana invited her to the graduation. I was stunned."

"What are you really worried about, Terry?"

Terry was beginning to get winded. "I don't know, Constance, but the hairs on the back of my neck are standing up and that's not a good sign."

"Humph" was Constance's only response. The two ran in silence as they kicked it up a notch. Judge Agnew had seen hundreds if not thousands of cases since the *Hawkins v. Winston* decision was handed down, but she could see the scene in the courtroom as if it were yesterday.

Catherine had been undone by her own miscalculation of people. She'd been blinded by a sexy detective posing as a personal trainer turned lover when she confided in him that her plan was not to be a mother to Alisa after she gained custody of the one twin but instead to use her as a pawn to get the promotion she felt she deserved. The scene outside the courtroom still made Constance's blood run cold as she thought back to when Catherine stared her children in their eyes and said she had never loved them.

Many parents had appeared before her bench on various charges of neglect and abuse, but Catherine's emotional cruelty ranked up with the best—or perhaps worst is more accurate—of them. In the years since the hearing the Agnews and Winstons had become friends, and she was more than pleased when they purchased a home in her neighborhood. The two families, along with the Carpenters, represented the only *flavor* in the upper-class development.

As Constance and Terry approached the two-mile mark,

they both slowed to a fast trot. Though out of breath Terry began, "Connie, you're certain Catherine can't come up with some off-the-wall mess to disrupt our family?"

Taking in large gulps of air as she spoke, the good judge said, "Legally there's absolutely nothing she can do. On the other hand, I wouldn't underestimate the connivery of a woman like Catherine." With that, Constance darted far ahead of Terrance, leaving him in her dust with his own demons to face.

CHAPTER ELEVEN

"*G*ood morning, Daddy." Ariana startled Terry.

Glancing at the clock as he entered the kitchen from the garage he smiled. "Good morning, princess. What are you doing up so early? I'd think you would have taken advantage of this day off from school."

Her hands wrapped tightly around a glass of milk, Ariana lowered her head. "I couldn't sleep."

Terry joined her at the long table, sitting on the end closest to Ariana. "Oh, this must be serious. Are you nervous about the prom tonight?"

She shook her head.

"It can't be the party." Terry put his finger under her chin so that he could make eye contact with her. "Your mother assures me everything is all set. There's supposed to be quite a turnout. So tell Daddy what's bothering you."

A single tear ran down her beautiful face. "I think I've made a very big mistake."

When any of the women in Terry's life cried, from Michelle to his mother, he was rendered helpless. "Honey, nothing can be that bad. What do you think you've done?"

"Alisa is mad at me for inviting Catherine to our graduation. I'm sure I've hurt Mom's feelings." The tears were now free-flowing. "Catherine never shows up for anything anyway. Why did it just come out of my mouth like that?"

Terry moved to comfort Ariana. "Honey, you just did what was in your heart. You haven't talked anymore about Catherine attending the graduation, so I assumed that subject had died on the vine. But don't think you've hurt your mother's feelings one bit. Catherine makes a lot of empty promises as we both know, and I bet this is just another one. So there's no need to worry. And you know if Alisa wasn't mad at you about this, she'd surely find something else."

Ariana fell into her dad's chest crying. "You're just saying that."

"No"—Terry lifted her chin again—"I'm not. Everything is going to be just fine. Today's your big day. Nothing should be making you cry—least of all Catherine. You know she blows in and out of our lives on a whim."

"Why does she do that? She should just leave us alone." Speaking sporadically, Ariana managed, "Every time she does this, I feel so bad."

Ariana's confession astounded Terry. He felt his body tense and hoped it went unnoticed. Ariana had always been the one who was angry or had no emotion at all about Catherine's numerous disappointments. "Honey, no one understands or even knows why Catherine does the things she does. But I promise you, I won't let her ever hurt you. Ever."

"Daddy?"

"Yes, princess?"

"I love you."

Terry hugged her again. "Only half as much as I love you. Now tell me what your dad can do for you early on this very special day to make you smile."

Ariana wiped her eyes and smiled. "Well, maybe you could start with a shower?"

Terry laughed with her. "Oh, see, that is so cold. You trying to say your dad is on funk?"

"Daddy, you smell like a boys' locker room."

"I don't even want to know how *you* know how a boys' locker room smells," Terry teased. "You put on some coffee while I shower, and I'll make you an omelet when I come back. Deal?"

"Deal." Ariana kissed her dad before he stood. "Is it okay if I make the Blue Mountain?"

"The day of my little girls' prom is about as special as it gets for occasions. You bet you can make the Blue Mountain. Maybe it'll stir your mother."

"You're kidding me, right?"

"Miracles have been known to happen," Terry called back from the stairs, "but I'm sure you're correct in your assumption, my sweet."

Ariana walked slowly to the bathroom off the family room. When she turned on the light she stared into her bloodshot eyes in the mirror. *How could she just walk away from me?* Sadness clouded her vision. She quickly washed her hands and splashed her face with cold water. As she flipped the switch, the darkness in the five-by-eight space didn't begin to compare to her own.

"HI, ARI." MICHELLE STARTLED HER. "Are you going to make some breakfast?"

"What are you doing up so early?" Ariana pretended to poke her younger sister.

"Some of us have to go to school today, remember."

"Oh dang, that's true." Ariana began measuring coffee. "Go get dressed. I'll make some of my famous oatmeal."

"I'll have cold cereal, thank you very much," Michelle teased.

"Whatever, squirt!" Ariana tossed the dish towel as Michelle ducked.

Taking on a serious tone, Michelle asked, "Why are your eyes all red? Have you been crying?"

"No!" Ariana protested just a little too hard. "Why would I be crying? Today is my prom. And we're having da bomb party."

"You don't have to yell at me. Just looks like you've been crying is all." Michelle went to retrieve frosted flakes from the pantry. "Can I help you get dressed tonight?"

Ariana couldn't help the heavy feeling that engulfed her. She tried to lighten her voice. "Sure, squirt. You can help Auntie Veronica with my makeup."

"Word?"

Laughing earnestly, Ariana simply said, "Word."

The sisters went about their duties, preparing breakfast in silence. Ariana was lost in her thoughts. She wanted to see Catherine, her real mother. She didn't understand why. She just knew that she did. She was afraid to share her desires with anyone else. None of them would understand. Alisa had come to truly hate Catherine since she'd abandoned them in court. Her father never mentioned Catherine except when he received a postcard. She wasn't quite sure how Jackie felt about her *real* mother, but she was sure it wasn't good.

None of her friends had these issues and would surely not understand. She felt so alone. Her sadness deepened.

Michael bounced into the kitchen fully dressed with his backpack already in place. "Yo, yo, yo! What's up, my peoples?"

His sister stared at him as if he had two heads.

"Daddy's going to drive us to school today, Shelly," Michael said as he searched the refrigerator. "But you'd better get a move on. You know he's not hardly going to wait for you. What's for breakfast, big sis?"

"Oatmeal!" Michelle volunteered.

"I'll have frosted flakes," Michael said flatly.

"Y'all are going to miss me when I'm gone away to college."

"But not your oatmeal!" Michael said as he grabbed a bowl from the glass-front cabinet.

Just as the debate was about to begin, Terry rejoined his children. "Good morning, baby girl." He kissed Michelle on the forehead. "No takers for your sister's world-famous oatmeal?"

"Famous for poisoning people," Michael said in jest.

"Be nice. This is your sister's big day." Terry poured a cup of coffee. "I'd think Alisa would have come alive by now. What time does the spa thing start?"

Ariana stirred the oatmeal absentmindedly. "At ten. What time is Mom getting up?"

"She's awake, but you know it takes her a few minutes."

"Are you excited?" Michelle asked, wide-eyed.

Before she could answer the phone rang. "Who in the world is calling at this hour?" Terry looked at the caller ID.

"Hello?"

"Good morning, Terrance." After a long pause the female

voice at the other end of the connection continued. "This is Catherine."

"I know."

"Can I at least get a good morning? After all, the sun isn't even up here."

"Good morning, Catherine." His vigor evaporated. "What can I do for you?"

"My goodness, there's no need to be hostile. I just wanted to call back to see if the girls had made a decision about what they wanted me to buy them for graduation."

"Today is their prom and they have a very full schedule. I don't know if they've made up their minds, but perhaps later in the weekend or next week would be better."

Hesitating slightly, Catherine pressed on. "I understand. But I'd really like to come for a visit . . . soon."

"How soon?"

"Tonight?"

Incensed Terry yelled. "Tonight?"

All eyes in the room were on him. He tried desperately to control his emotions. Heat rose in him and he felt as if he'd burst.

"I thought I could come by for a few minutes before the girls left to go to their prom. I'd have a chance to see them and then talk to you."

"What on earth do you have to talk to me about?"

"It's complicated." Catherine came as close as she ever would to being humble. "I'd rather do it in person."

"I don't know . . ." Terry began as his eyes locked with Ariana's. "When would you arrive?"

"I can be there by four or four thirty."

"Today?" Terry was genuinely surprised. "I thought you were calling from Los Angeles."

"I have my own jet."

Caught off guard, Terry simply said, "Oh. I guess we'll see you at four-thirty. The girls are leaving at six sharp."

"I'll be there."

Without a good-bye they each hung up. Catherine smiled with a sense of satisfaction.

Worry lines creased Terry's face as he turned to find three sets of eyes staring at him. "You'd better go get your sister and mother. I don't want to have to repeat this news."

"What's wrong, Pops?" Michael held his spoon in midair. He couldn't remember Catherine. He'd drawn his conclusion about the infamous woman from all he'd heard over the years. He didn't know how he knew, but he did. This was not a good thing brewing. "Is Catherine coming to visit?"

"Just do as I said," Terry snapped. "Your sister and mother need to hear this now."

CHAPTER TWELVE

*C*atherine's next call was to her pilot. Alexander Morehead had been in her employ since she'd purchased the Gulfstream Five at a bargain price from a Texas energy company executive just prior to his taking up residence in new government housing. Alex took care of the G-V like it was his own. The aging former air force fighter jet pilot would as soon lay his life on the line for Catherine as get her a cup of coffee. For his loyalty and service she rewarded him both financially and with a few fringe benefits.

"Good morning, Alex." Catherine was extremely pleasant. "I know it's early, but I need you to file a flight plan for Dallas to arrive before four."

"Good morning, Catherine. You know I rise early. It is no bother at all." Alexander's mood matched his boss's. "I'll file the plan immediately and call you back with our departure time."

"Thank you. I'll be waiting for your call." Catherine hung up first.

Feeling a new burst of energy she moved to her dressing room and quickly changed into workout clothes. Today she was going to get a new kidney. It was only a matter of time before she convinced *her daughters* it was the right thing to do. She was confident Terrance would be the easiest of them all to persuade. In spite of everything she still knew Terrance had a thing for her.

The one who worried her was Jackie. She chuckled when she remembered the day the woman had conned her way into the penthouse she rented in Austin to confront her about her plans to sue for custody. She admired spirit, but even Jackie was no match for Catherine Maric.

As she bent to tie her running shoes she felt dizzy. There was no denying that her body was getting weaker daily. She stood as quickly as she dared and steadied herself against the chest that dominated the middle of the dressing room. She had no time to waste. She had to find a way to break the news at least to Terrance on this trip. She didn't know if she'd stay in town for the weekend in hopes of talking to Ariana and Alisa. She'd have to play it all by ear.

Catherine moved from the dressing room back to her bedroom and out the door, down the winding staircase. She made her way the eighth of a mile to a fully equipped gym. Just getting there had tired her out. But she was determined to beat this thing. On one of her sleepless nights she'd seen the biography of Teddy Roosevelt. She was amazed at how the infirm young boy willed and worked himself into a healthy man who later became president. And there was no way a white boy could do something this descendent of African royalty couldn't.

Catherine began slowly on the elliptical machine as she let her mind wander to the upcoming events. She was fully aware that she had to tread lightly at first. She didn't know how the girls would react to her news. Would they be sad, resentful or, worst of all, just not care? She shook her head, trying to clear it. *Since when did I care what anyone thought of me?*

Her mother's words haunted her again: *"You're going to need those children someday, and when they turn their backs on you, maybe then you'll understand the pain you've caused them."* To drown out her mother's voice, Catherine picked up her pace. The steady hum of the state-of-the-art machine failed to meet her purpose.

Catherine's strength lasted less than thirty minutes. She removed a bottle of water from the refrigerator and drank it down without stopping. Now, if she could only handle at least three more of these before noon, she'd be on target for her daily intake requirement.

As she left the gym she heard the phone ringing in her office. She contemplated the pros and cons of answering it at this hour and remembered she was expecting a call from Alex. Though she ran to the phone she wasn't in time. She fell into the high-backed leather executive chair, exhausted. While gathering her strength and catching her breath the red light illuminated on her desk phone, indicating she had voice mail. Without picking up the receiver she pressed the button and the woman with the famous voice and no face announced she had one new message. As she had suspected, Alex had called to tell her what time to be at the Burbank airport.

"Hi, Catherine. Everything is all set, and we're to take off at eleven seventeen. I just need to know how many will be traveling with you so that I can have the galley readied. Ralph Pazzo is the cocaptain, and Francisco is your cabin steward.

Armundo is in South America on a family emergency. Please call me back as soon as possible. As always, it is my pleasure to serve you."

Catherine smiled as she pressed the Delete button. Discretion being the better part of valor, this man certainly knew how to please her. Alexander Morehead saw to even the minutest of details both in the air and in her bed. She purred slightly as she thought of a night with him in Dallas.

She pressed the Speaker button and dialed his number. He picked up on the first ring. "This is Alex."

"This is Lady Catherine. I'll be flying alone in case that is of special interest to you."

"Always at your service. We'll touch down just after three thirty. Do you need me to arrange for ground transportation?"

"That would be wonderful, since my assistant won't amble in for hours yet. And after my little visit, perhaps you and I can make some intimate plans of our own."

"Nothing would please me more, my lady."

Catherine loved the way he talked to her. She was even more impressed that he never crossed the line. He knew when to be her employee and when to be her lover. Perhaps it was his very comfortable life with his wife and three children that kept him grounded. But whatever the reason, she enjoyed the stolen moments and never questioned it. "I'll see you at eleven. And I know, I know—don't be late."

He laughed and added, "You're as perceptive as you are beautiful. If we lose our takeoff time, it could make you late for your appointment."

"And we can't do that."

"Just one last point before you hang up. I'll order shrimp, cracked crab and lobster for lunch?"

"Hmmmm, sounds yummy. But add some caviar and champagne to the menu. I'm celebrating."

"Why but of course. May I ask what is the occasion?"

"Let's just say this is the most important acquisition of my life and I'm going to close the deal."

CHAPTER THIRTEEN

*T*rudging into the kitchen Jackie groaned. "Good morning."

"Good morning, Mommy," Michelle and Michael said together.

Ariana stared at Jackie for a few minutes before she mumbled, "Good morning, Mom."

"What's so all-fired important that it couldn't wait?" Jackie removed a mug from the dishwasher and poured a cup of coffee, yawning. "You know I don't appreciate this one little bit. And many people could suffer today because of your lack of judgment, Mr. Winston."

"Good morning." Alisa bounced into the kitchen. "Why is everyone up so early?"

Jackie announced, "Your father is about to enlighten us now. And, believe me, it better be good."

"Catherine is coming for a visit," Terry blurted.

"What for?" Alisa said with disdain.

Jackie set her mug down on the counter with a loud thud. "When?"

Terry drew in lots of air and continued. "She'll be here today between four and four thirty. As for why, I can't really answer that. She claims she wants to visit the girls, and see them on prom night and talk to me."

Jackie was fully awake now. "What could she possibly want to talk about with you? We don't care what she's doing or where she's doing it. And what we're doing is none of her concern."

Ariana stared from one parent to the other. She blamed herself. If she hadn't invited Catherine to the graduation, none of this would be happening.

"I agree with you on all counts. But we'll just have to wait and see. But I've known that woman for a lot of years and there's more to this than she's saying." Terry tried to appease his wife.

"How dare you invite her here without consulting me!" Jackie's voice rose a little more with each word.

Trying to defend himself Terry retorted, "I didn't invite her. She just told me she was coming."

"And you couldn't say no?"

The children stood watching the exchange between their parents, each wanting to say something to defuse the pending argument. Michelle decided to speak up. "Mom, what should I wear to school today?"

Turning her attention to Michelle, Jackie said, "What?"

"What should I wear to school today?" she repeated.

"Since when do you consult me on fashion?"

"I just wanted to know what you thought." Michelle smiled.

Terry looked at his baby girl and felt warm. He knew what

she was trying to do. "Jackie, that's her way of saying how ridiculous it is for us to continue to argue about this."

Jackie looked between Terry and Michelle. She wanted to be angry but felt blindsided by the wisdom of a thirteen-year-old. "She's right. Why should we be arguing over something Catherine has done? She's promised to come before and not shown up. I guess we should just face it when the time comes."

"She sounded different this time. She said she wants to talk to me face-to-face."

"We'll just wait and see. And as for you, miss thang, those new jeans you just had to have a month ago, which I haven't seen you in, will work quite nicely. You'd better get a move on. You don't want to be late."

"Why does Catherine always have to mess things up?" Alisa said more to herself.

"We don't know that she's going to mess anything up," Ariana snapped.

Jackie and Terry stared, reading each other's thoughts. *What is this all about?*

"Because that's what she does. Ever since I can remember, she would promise to do this or that, but something else more important always came up. Are you forgetting how she tried to separate us or that she told us she never loved us?" Alisa said.

Tears filled Ariana's eyes. "I remember, but maybe she's changed."

"Sure she has. That's why she's calling after all this time and wanting to drop by. I agree with Daddy. There's something in this for her."

"Girls, you have a day filled with fun plans and this is no way to get it started." Terry now tried to work the magic on the twins that Michelle had worked on him and Jackie. "I say we just pretend we didn't get this early morning call. Michelle, you hurry and dress, I'll get you to school. Ariana and Alisa, you two get ready to be pampered all day. Jackie, you have a cup of coffee and finish waking up."

Terry was amazed at how Catherine could disrupt his family without even being there. Nothing had changed. He'd always protected those he loved and would do so until the day he died. "Has anyone bothered to get T.J. up?"

"Oh, my goodness, I totally forgot about him. Let me run up and get him ready." Jackie said, darting off as she spoke.

"He can have some of my oatmeal," Ariana volunteered.

"No!" Everyone yelled.

CHAPTER FOURTEEN

*C*atherine folded the red lingerie and carefully placed it in the black carry-on bag. She hadn't had a night of romance since the last time she was with Alex. He had a way of making her feel alive.

After taking one last look around the room, Catherine picked up the phone to call her chauffeur, Jonathan. "I'm ready." She didn't mince words.

She passed Jonathan on the stairs. "I'll be waiting in the foyer. It's only the small bag on the luggage stand."

"Yes, ma'am." Jonathan averted his eyes.

Dexter appeared at the bottom of the stairs with a glass of cranberry juice in one hand and Catherine's cashmere sweater in the other. "Will there be anything else before you leave, ma'am?"

"That'll be all."

"Thank you, ma'am." Dexter waited for Catherine to consume the juice and pass him the glass. "Safe travels."

Jonathan met Catherine at the bottom of the stairs, taking her sweater and briefcase. "Are you ready, ma'am?"

Catherine didn't answer but followed Jonathan. The typical June gloom had paid Los Angeles an early visit and the May morning was overcast. She sighed because she wanted to feel the sun on her face. Jonathan opened the back door of the midnight blue Maybach 62, and Catherine slid comfortably inside. After closing the door he went to the trunk, opened it and placed the luggage carefully inside, and within thirty seconds he'd slipped behind the wheel. With his turn of the key the opulent vehicle sprang to life.

Jonathan easily maneuvered his precious cargo down the half-mile driveway and onto the private road. Catherine sat back with her thoughts and relaxed.

Did the girls still look like her? She couldn't believe it had been more than eighteen years since she'd given birth to them. Where had the years gone? Her mother had been wrong. She didn't regret her decision; she'd built an empire to rival the best of them—Donald, Oprah or Bill. She dined with royalty, could have any man—married or single—she wanted, vacationed in some of the most exotic locations this side of heaven and even now she was being chauffeured to her private jet in a car that cost more than some people earned in a lifetime.

She reclined her seat and adjusted the opacity of the car roof to allow more daylight through. Most days she enjoyed the privacy afforded by the tinted windows, but today she craved light.

Now where was she? Ah yes, her wonderful existence. She failed to see the downside to her life. While she had no friends to speak of, she had little need for those trivial relationships. Women either didn't understand her or despised her. Even when she was a child, girlfriends were more a convenience than a necessity. But now she bought her *friends;* that way when she was done with them it was easy to move on.

She adjusted herself in the seat so the soft leather caressed her body. Now how was she going to approach Terry with her *situation?* She'd planned on treating this like any other business deal. She rethought her strategy; Terry had proven to her on more than one occasion that he couldn't be bought. When he'd initially refused the one million dollars she'd sent him after she relinquished her parental rights, even she was stunned. She considered this man with his high moral fiber a fool but one she was forced to deal with. She had to appeal to his human sensibility. She wasn't sure how she was going to make it happen, but without a shadow of a doubt before the landing gear touched the tarmac at Dallas Love Field she'd know what to do.

CHAPTER FIFTEEN

"*H*ey you." Jackie entered the spacious bathroom, waving a white face towel. "Truce?"

Terry averted his eyes from his image in the mirror to Jackie. Though he tried not to, he smiled broadly. "Is this to be construed as an apology?"

Jackie walked over to him and reached up, kissing him on the nose, transferring shaving cream to her lips. "I don't know if I have anything to apologize for, but I do know that none of this is your fault."

"How do we always let Catherine do this to us?" Terry took the white towel from Jackie and wiped her lips before he turned back to the mirror. "It's like Satan himself lives in that woman. She takes us to a place no one else would dare even try."

"You know, you have a point. And good Christian folks we are, the first thing we should have done was prayed. But noooooo, we go at each other." Jackie's eyes met Terry's in the mirror. "I *am* sorry."

"Me, too." Terry's words seemed to ooze into Jackie's pores. "I need to ask you something."

"Not now, baby," Jackie teased. "I have a full day."

Throwing his head back, laughing, Terry pulled Jackie close to him, kissing her full on the lips. "Girl, you betta watch out now." He backed up slightly. "But this is serious."

"What is it?"

"This morning when I came in from running, Ariana was in the kitchen. She was crying."

"Whatever for?" Jackie turned and sat on the counter between the two sinks. "Today should be the happiest day in her young life."

"I agree. But she thinks we're mad at her because she invited Catherine to the graduation. More important, she thinks she's hurt your feelings."

Jackie broke her gaze, looking at her hands.

Terry lifted her chin with his fingers, looking into her eyes. "Jack, talk to me."

"I'm not sure what I feel." Jackie refused to make eye contact with him. "On one hand, Catherine did give them life, and I don't care how many court papers we have, nothing can change that. But on the other hand, I've been their mother for almost eight years. I resent her for coming back now. I don't know if I thought she never would or that the girls would never want to have a relationship with her. I know I won't tolerate her coming to the graduation acting like she's mother of the year.

"You read and hear about this kind of thing all the time. I guess I just never thought it would happen to us. Well, I guess I really mean me."

"You know, there's nothing to stop Michael and Michelle's father from coming back."

"Puh-leeze!" Jackie wondered if this was Terry's poor attempt to make her feel better. "You know that tired Negro ain't hardly going to come looking for them. He was merely a sperm donor. I would have had the same support system if I'd gone for artificial insemination from someone I didn't know. So don't even think this is the same thing."

Terry wiped his hands, moved in front of Jackie and spoke softly. "First of all, we're in this thing together. Second, you know Ariana and Alisa love you. You're the only mother they've ever known. There's nothing that Catherine can do to change *that*. They don't need her now. Alisa and Ariana are grown women! I'll let her know when I talk to her that she's not welcome at the graduation and not to ever think she can just drop in on us again."

Jackie pulled back and looked at Terry. "Did I just hear you say they are women?"

They both laughed. "Yeah, I guess I did." The serious look returned. "But you're missing my point."

"I hear you, Terry, but it doesn't change how I feel. I just want to know what she's up to and what about her timing. Today of all days; like 'Lisa said, the only day a girl looks forward to more is her wedding."

"We won't let her ruin it. I promise you!"

"And how are you going to stop her without getting the police involved?"

Terry laughed halfheartedly. "Shhh, if you don't know, you can't tell."

"A wife can't be made to testify against her husband."

Terry hugged Jackie, this time smearing shaving cream in her hair. "Now that's what I'm talking about. You'd better get ready to have a fantastic day with *your* daughters. Because if I have my way, it'll be a long time before there's a wedding day up in here."

$\mathcal{T}$he valet opened the door for Jackie and Alisa simultaneously, while another opened the front passenger door for Ariana. The young man with the curly red hair and freckles so dense they deepend his complexion flushed red when he smiled.

Jim, according to his name tag, asked, "May I have your last name please?"

"Winston."

"Well, Ms. Winston, we are pleased to have you with us today. Is this a special occasion for you and are these lovely young ladies your sisters?"

Blushing Jackie said, "These are my daughters."

"Surely you jest. And I must be seeing double. Are you twins?"

"Yes," Ariana and Alisa said.

"Then the pleasure is doubled. Is there a special occasion that brings you to us today?"

"It's our prom tonight," Alisa gladly shared.

"Welcome to the House of Beauty where you step into a wonderland of pampering, Ms. Winston times three."

"Thank you." Jackie took the receipt from the very pleasant young man.

"My associate Charles will escort you inside, and again, enjoy your day."

"Thank you very much. If the rest of the staff is as warm and friendly as you, I'm sure today will be one to remember." Jackie made a mental note to tip him very handsomely when she retrieved the car.

Charles offered Alisa and Ariana each an arm, which they took, giggling. Jackie followed close on their heels, relishing their gaiety. As they stepped inside, the decor of the 1887 Victorian took their breath away.

A pleasant woman greeted them as they stepped up to the desk. "Welcome to the House of Beauty. How may we be of service to you today?"

Now this is what I'm talkin' about, Jackie thought but said, "Hi, we're the Winstons. We're here for a day of pampering before my lovely daughters head off to the prom."

"Oh, yes, Ms. Winston. We've been anxiously awaiting your arrival. If you'll sign here we'll get you started. Ariana and Alisa, how old are you?"

"Eighteen," they both answered.

"Great, then I'll need your signatures also."

They both looked to Jackie for guidance. She nodded, acknowledging that it was okay to sign.

"If you'll follow Dianne, she'll get you robes and slippers and give you a tour of the facility."

Jackie started to relax. She hadn't thought of Catherine in at least forty-five seconds. Though she'd intended this to be a special treat for Ariana and Alisa, she was going to thoroughly enjoy the day, too.

With wide-eyed amazement the girls took it all in. The spa was fully equipped with many modern amenities, nestled in old-world charm. When Dianne was done with the tour and explanation of the facilities, she took them to the locker room. She handed them robes and slippers, and Jackie chastised the young woman for providing her with a robe that didn't fit.

Handing Jackie a robe of a slightly different color and texture, Dianne said, "Ms. Winston, I've taken the liberty of supplying one of our deluxe robes for your comfort. I hope it meets with your approval."

Jackie looked at her suspiciously, at which Dianne smiled knowingly. "You can change here or have privacy behind one of these curtains. You each have appointments for facials, manicures, pedicures and massages. The first appointment is in forty minutes. In the meantime you can relax in here or work out."

"Today is about the pampering. Y'all young folks can work out if you want, but I'm going to just enjoy the serenity of the House of Beauty," Jackie quipped.

"Oh, Mom! Don't you want to work up a sweat first?" Ariana asked jokingly.

"I'm going to see how much I can sweat walking over to that bowl of fruit I saw when we came in here."

The Winston women all laughed. It seemed the issues surrounding Catherine's visit were forgotten as they undressed in the locker room. The laughter was abundant as the mother and daughters began to enjoy what was rightfully their time together on a very special day.

CHAPTER SEVENTEEN

"*W*ow, Mom, I see what all the hype is about. That massage was da bizomb! I feel like I have no muscles in my body. I just want to go to sleep," Ariana said as they stood waiting for Jim to bring the car.

"That *was* pretty incredible," Alisa added. "I love the way my face feels so cool and clean. I understand why you do this once a month. I need to make a lot of money because I *will* be doing this all the time."

"I'm glad you enjoyed it. I've gone to other facilities with Auntie Cedes so many times, but I have to tell you, it was really special to come here for the first time with *my* daughters."

There was something about the way Jackie put emphasis on the word "*my*" that made Ariana twitch. "I had a really good time. Thanks again, Mom. I'm starving. Do we have time for lunch?"

"Funny you should ask—we have reservations at the Adolphus for a late lunch." Jackie smiled with satisfaction.

"You've thought of everything, Mom," Alisa said, hugging Jackie.

"Only the best will do for you today and always." Jackie stepped around the Volvo XC90 and handed Jim a twenty-dollar bill.

Jim smiled broadly and held the door for Jackie as she said, "I expect you to share that with Charles."

"Indeed, Ms. Winston." She was pleased he remembered her name.

The happy trio rolled away with Beyoncé singing loudly to them. All seemed right with the universe to mother and daughters. Little did they know . . .

 **CHAPTER EIGHTEEN**

"Miss Shanky, I love it! It's exactly what I wanted. I can't believe you came over to do our hair." Ariana swooned as she checked her coif from all angles.

"It's my pleasure." The aging beautician hugged both the girls. "I'm just stunned at how grown-up you are. Now, I'm going to get out of here so your Auntie Veronica can do your makeup."

"Miss Shanky, I can't thank you enough for doing this. I know how busy it is in the shop on Friday," Jackie said as she began writing a check.

"Chile, I took care of your mama." Miss Shanky's voice yielded slightly to her emotions. "God rest her soul. I took care of you and now it's my honor to take care of your daughters."

Jackie hugged the woman she'd known most of her life and passed her the check, which included a very generous tip. Miss

Shanky quietly gathered her things and left the flurry of activity surrounding Ariana and Alisa.

"Auntie Vee, I think I want purple glitter eye shadow," Alisa said as she peered into the mirror, checking her pores. "It'll match my dress."

Veronica smiled and wondered how to break the news to her brother's oldest that she wasn't going to make her up to look like she should be working at Obsessions Gentleman's Club. "I thought something very subtle to accent your natural beauty would be nice. You don't want anything to take away from those gorgeous baby browns."

Alisa looked in the mirror at her eyes. "You really think so?"

"An auntie knows these things. I'm really surprised you're both wearing the same dress. You told me like two years ago you were individuals."

Jackie returned from her bathroom with an array of makeup in assorted shades, textures and purposes. "They have this plan they don't think I know about to trick their dates."

Raising her eyebrows Veronica smiled wickedly. "You don't say? All I know is you better be careful you're not the one that gets played. I know a whole bunch of fellas in every age group that have special dreams about twins."

"Veronica!" Jackie chastised.

"What?" Veronica pretended not to understand. "All I know is they are two very beautiful young ladies, with bangin' bodies. Can't you see they aren't babies anymore, Jackie? You're almost as bad as your husband. You better learn to speak openly with them like I do. Ain't that right, girls?"

"Oh, Auntie Vee." Ariana blushed.

"But I'm being down. Honey, these teenagers could tell you stuff that would make your nappy kitchen straight. So I just believe in keepin' it real. That way no one is surprised by anything."

"I'm very open with them." Jackie was defensive. "We've discussed the birds and the bees."

Alisa rolled her eyes toward the ceiling and mumbled, "Oh, brotha."

"Last time I checked, there was no statistics on how many birds had sexually transmitted diseases. And the stingers these precious flowers have to worry about ain't hardly on a bee."

Ariana and Alisa both laughed until Jackie gave them the evil *mama* eye. "Auntie Vee, don't worry. We know everything we need to know to be safe. Mom just isn't comfortable talking about sex and Daddy's even worse. All he says is don't do it," Ariana said as she removed her purple pumps from their box.

"I believe in—" The chime of the doorbell interrupted Veronica's rise to the soapbox.

All the air seemed to evaporate from the room. No one moved. Jackie glanced at the clock—4:40. It had to be Catherine. "Terry'll get it," she finally managed.

The mood of the room shifted faster than gas prices during vacation season. The women all looked from one to the other and held their breaths.

TERRY APPROACHED THE FRONT DOOR with weighted feet. His palms began to sweat. The closer he got to the mahogany double doors with the leaded glass panes, the faster his heart beat. He took a minute and peered through the glass before opening the door.

Catherine looked thinner than when he'd seen her last. Her beauty took him aback. He stood staring for a long moment before speaking. "Hi, Catherine."

"I thought you were going to make me stand on the porch forever." Catherine walked toward the entrance, but Terry didn't move. "Well?"

Reluctant but amenable Terry finally stepped aside. "Come in."

"Thank you," Catherine said as she stepped into the foyer. She looked around her and whistled slightly through her teeth. "I see you've moved up in the world since I saw you last. Very quaint but nice."

"Thank you." Terry was cool and unassuming. "We enjoy our home very much."

"Did you hit the lottery or something?" Catherine asked, only half joking. "Or are you spending Ariana and Alisa's money?"

Terry ignored her remark and said, "The girls are upstairs with their mother, getting ready. You can join me and the others in the family room or would you be more comfortable waiting in the living room?"

Terry's dig didn't go unnoticed. "It's really wonderful that Jackie treats Ariana and Alisa as her own."

"Because they are," Terry snapped. "Family or living room?" His temporary moment of awe fled.

"Let's join the rest of the Winstons, shall we? Lead the way." Catherine's arrogance began to sicken Terry.

As they entered the family room, all eyes focused on the archway. Michael and Michelle sat stoically while T.J. bounced around the room like a jumping bean. Terry cleared his throat. "Guys, I think you remember Miss Catherine."

"I don't know her." T.J. slid across the hardwood floor on his knee, stopping just in front of his dad.

"I guess you were too young the last time she came to visit."

"Who are you?" T.J. stood looking up at Catherine curiously.

Michael and Michelle called him at the same time. "T.J.! Don't be rude. Come sit with us."

"Aren't you adorable." Catherine patted him on the head. "I'm a very old friend of your dad's."

"Hi, Miss Catherine," Michelle said as Michael sat with his arms crossed.

"Michael?" Terry chastised.

"Hi."

"It's so nice to see all of you again." Catherine moved to the side chair and sat. "It's really something how much you've grown."

"Can I offer you something to drink?" Terry's patience had already worn thin.

"I'd love some wine. What do you have in the way of a Burgundy?" Catherine toyed with him.

"Imported or domestic?" *Bam!*

"Imported, of course." Catherine sat deeper in the plush seat.

"Red or white?"

Catherine was genuinely surprised. "Red, please."

"Does a 2000 Bonnes Mares meet with your approval?"

Raising her left eyebrow, Catherine smiled and nodded. "Indeed."

"I'll just go down to the wine cellar. Back in a second." Terry disappeared behind the massive staircase.

"So, Michael and Michelle, what grade are you in now?" Catherine turned her attention to the very quiet pair.

"Eighth," Michelle answered. "We're graduating from middle school."

"How nice. So there'll be two graduations here this year. I bet you're excited, Michael."

His eyes narrowed as he said, "I guess."

"And what about you, little man? What grade are you in?"

"I'm in the first grade! I get to go to camp this summer. I was student of the month."

Catherine laughed as she began to feel at home with Terrance's children. "That's pretty terrific. What do you want to be when you grow up?"

"A fireman!" With that T.J. jumped from the couch and began running around the room, making the sound of a fire truck.

"How much longer do you think Ariana and Alisa will be? They knew I'd be here at four-thirty."

"Good luck. You'll be lucky if they're ready by six when the limo arrives." Michael seemed pleased to relay the news.

Catherine began to sigh but caught herself. "Well, the fine art of beauty does take time."

"That it does, kinda like a real fine wine." Terry appeared, offering the dusty bottle for Catherine's approval. "As promised, a very rich Burgundy."

"I'm rather impressed at your acquired sophistication. You're far from the Terrance I knew back in college." Catherine crossed her legs, looking up at Terry.

"We've all changed, Catherine, some for the better, others . . . well, you know what I'm saying. I'll get you a glass." Terry went behind the bar, removed the cork with a distinctive popping sound and retrieved a crystal red wine glass. His first thought was to have some wine, but he decided he needed to have his wits about him.

He poured a thimble full in the glass and took it to Catherine to sample. The sound of footsteps on the staircase caused everyone's attention to shift. Veronica approached.

"This is quite good. It will do nicely." Catherine looked toward Veronica. "Nice to see you again, Veronica. Terry was just pouring me a lovely glass of wine. Will you join me?"

"Catherine." Veronica moved past her and joined Michael and Michelle on the sofa. "I'll pass."

Veronica was seething. Catherine was fully aware she was a recovering alcoholic. Veronica had worked hard for six years five months and seventeen days to retain the adjective "recovering." Veronica looked at Terry and rolled her eyes. He knew it meant *You'd better check her before I do.*

"How much longer before my d— I mean Ariana and Alisa are ready?"

She glanced at the other children to see if they had noticed her slip. Before she could speak Veronica said to Terry, "*My* nieces are almost ready and want you to tape them coming down the stairs. They look so beautiful. Their mother has outdone herself. The three of them have had a lovely day." She looked this time at Catherine.

"I don't know what all the fuss is about." Michael stood and moved to the kitchen. "It's just a stupid dance. Why do girls get all this attention?"

"Son, get used to it." Terry walked over to the refrigerator and retrieved an A&W root beer and handed it to Michael. "I wish I had an explanation, but this is only the beginning. It gets worse from here."

"But if you ask Terrance, Michael, to be honest, he'll tell you we're so worth all the fuss." Catherine sipped the wine as she eyed Terry.

"Michael, my boy, there're some women who are worth all this fuss and more, and then, on the other hand, you'll discover some who aren't." Terry shot a glance at Catherine. "When you're ready, it'll be my job to teach you the difference."

"I'll grab the camera from the office; I'll be right back." Terry disappeared down the hall.

Veronica turned to Catherine with venomous eyes. "So what brings you to Dallas? How long has it been, three—four years?"

"It's been a while, but I couldn't let this special occasion pass without being here. And you're right." Catherine's icy eyes met Veronica's. "I have no excuse. It's been way too long."

There was a rumbled shuffling at the top of the staircase, followed by giggles. One of the twins said, "Daddy, are you ready with the camera?"

"Here I come." With his voice growing louder with each word, Terry continued, "Wait right there. Let me get into place." Terry stood at the foot of the stairs, looking through the lens of the camera to focus it. "I'm ready!"

"Are you sure, Daddy?"

"I'm sure, princess. Strut your stuff."

The two sisters began descending the stairs from opposite ends. They slowly came into the camera's view, and Terry pulled his eye away from the camera to take in the full picture of his daughters' loveliness. There was nothing to prepare him for what he saw. He remembered back to the day of his wedding and the first time he saw Jackie in her bridal gown. But this was different. He saw Alisa and Ariana as women. Their deep purple gowns hugged every curve. The three-inch heels made them well over six feet tall. Pieces of their mother's diamond jewelry adorned their necks. And, oh my god, they had cleavage!

"Daddy, are you taping?" Alisa asked as she met Ariana on

the landing. They looped arms and slowly began the journey to the foot of the stairs.

Michael, Michelle and T.J. ran and stood next to their father. Catherine stood slowly, never taking her eyes off the staircase. She willed her body to move forward but felt transfixed. From where she stood she saw two identical pairs of royal purple shoes, with straps that encircled four identical ankles. Her heartbeat increased slightly. The legs she saw looked so much like her own.

"Wow, you look like Mia Thermopolis!" T.J. exclaimed, referring to the main character in *The Princess Diaries*. "But you're black."

Everyone laughed and Michelle said, "Wow!"

Catherine walked toward the center of the action in awe. As the two girls descended the stairs it was like she was transported back in time. Ariana and Alisa were her mirror image.

"You're going to rue the day you gave your babies away." Her mother really needed to leave her alone. She felt a sudden longing to recapture their childhood.

Terry continued recording the moment for all posterity. Jackie moved slowly down the steps behind them, beaming with pride. Veronica walked over and hugged them, wiping away a tear. Even Michael seemed impressed by the appearance of his sisters.

"Hello, Ariana and Alisa," Catherine said softly. "You look so beautiful."

Ariana fought back tears as she stared at Catherine. "Hi."

"Girl, you better not mess up your makeup as hard as I worked," Veronica quipped.

"I'm not, Auntie Vee." Ariana was embarrassed by Veronica's words. "I don't know what you're talking about."

Alisa planted her feet firmly and folded her arms, refusing to speak. To her shame Catherine didn't know which daughter had spoken to her. She willed someone to call a name and have the twins react. She'd bet her next month's net profit the defiant one was Ariana. She remembered Alisa as being compassionate.

"Aren't you going to speak, Alisa?" Terry removed the camera from his face.

"I was waiting to see if Catherine knows which one of us didn't speak to her." Alisa never broke eye contact with Catherine.

"This is a wonderful evening following a splendid day." Jackie moved around the twins, walking toward the kitchen. "Let's take some still pictures before your dates arrive and then all go into the family room for champagne and sparkling cider."

"Good idea." Veronica added, "I'll help you."

Catherine felt about as welcome as a pork chop at a bar mitzvah. She didn't know what to do and had even less to say. She was second-guessing her decision to join this little party. *You need a kidney. That's why you're here.* "Alisa, I assure you I know who you are," she lied. "I was just giving you a chance to adjust to me being here."

"Yeah, right." Alisa brushed past Catherine and walked to the family room.

Terry caught up to Alisa, whispering, "Okay, that'll be enough! I don't care how you feel about Catherine being here. You won't be disrespectful."

Alisa turned so quickly to confront her father that she startled him. "You have to have respect to be disrespected." She left him fumbling for a retort.

"Terrance, she has every right to feel what she feels. Just leave her alone." Catherine played the sympathy card. "I'm fine."

Ariana interrupted them. "I'm glad you came." She continued without making eye contact, "Would you like to come into the family room?"

"I would like that very much. I wish I'd remembered to bring a camera. You two are just the epitome of elegance. Have you considered modeling?"

"No," Alisa spat from the family room.

Okay, this is going to be harder than I thought. Walking with Ariana to the family room, she wanted to interlock arms, but she dared not. "Whatever you decide to do I know you'll be successful. After all, you come from successful genes."

Jackie shot Catherine a glance as she entered the family room with two champagne buckets. She placed them both on the table with a little more noise than necessary. "They've had a wonderful example to follow in their father."

The vultures were circling. As much as Veronica hated Catherine and wanted to put all of her size nines up her ass, she wouldn't do anything to ruin her nieces' big night. She only had to keep the peace for an hour. "So, Catherine, I hear you have your own company now. That's all right."

Ahhh, finally a comfort zone. "I've been quite lucky. We have offices in Brazil, Paris, Barcelona, Munich, Rome, and I'm looking to expand every day."

"Really?" Veronica was genuinely surprised.

Michael perked up. "Is it true you have your own jet?"

Catherine smiled inside. "I do; a Gulfstream Five. Do you know what that is?"

"I know it's real fast," Michael boasted.

"Very fast. It can fly five hundred and ninety miles per hour. I can fly from Los Angeles to London without stopping."

Ariana and Alisa stared at Catherine for different reasons. Alisa was disgusted by Catherine's flamboyant display of power and money. Ariana felt bewildered because she still wondered why this woman had walked away from her. She loved Jackie, but she had lived inside Catherine.

"Word?" Michael moved to the edge of the sofa.

"Word?" Catherine looked to the other adults in the room for help.

Veronica rolled her eyes, wondering if Catherine was that out of touch with her people or that she wanted everyone to think she was. "It means 'oh, really?' "

"Okay. Can I get you two coming down the steps again? Then we'll go out back in front of the fountain." Terry diverted the room's attention as he directed the photo shoot.

"How about a picture with Alisa sitting in the fan-back chair and Ariana standing behind it?" Jackie added as she set a tray of champagne flutes on the table between the buckets.

"That will be a really nice shot." Catherine hesitated, and then added, "I'd love a picture with the two of you."

"I'm sure we can arrange that." Terry looked at the twins for confirmation. "Right, girls?"

Ariana smiled at Catherine and nodded. Alisa stiffened her back and stared.

Jackie had a faraway look in her eyes as she softly said, "Momma C. would be so proud."

The twins were posed in front of statues, trees and permanent fixtures until they were seeing spots before their eyes. Terry consumed one roll of film and half of another. There were individual, dual and every conceivable combination of family poses. Everyone had been photographed with the twins, except Catherine.

"I think that does it," Terry finally said.

Disappointment crept into Catherine's chest, but she said nothing. Her feelings of intrusion were growing by the second.

"We didn't get a picture with Catherine." Ariana lowered her eyes, not daring to look in Alisa's direction.

"We sure didn't." Terry picked up the camera. "Where'd you like to pose?"

"Nowhere," Alisa whispered, loud enough for everyone to hear.

Jackie came to the rescue. "I think a pose in here would be lovely," she said, pointing to the enormous arrangement of white lilies and gardenias perched on top of the round table in the foyer.

"That's a grand idea. Catherine, you stand in the middle." Terry waved his directions. "Alisa, move in closer."

The lens captured Alisa's tense stance, Ariana's near cuddle and Catherine's genuine smile. With the flash from the camera came the chime of the doorbell.

"I got it." Michelle slid across the marble foyer in her stockinged feet, using her hands to stop her motion when she arrived at the front door. Without looking, she opened the door and was greeted by two tuxedo-clad young men carrying flowers encased in plastic. She giggled before she said, "Your dates are here."

"Silly girl, move out of the way and let them in," Jackie teased as she walked toward the door. She extended her hand. "Hi, Trey and Vincent. We've been waiting for you to take more pictures." Jackie shook hands first with Vincent, then Trey.

"Mooooommmm," Alisa whined, embarrassed.

"Don't Mom me. I'll never have your prom night again." Jackie closed the door behind the boys as they walked farther into the Winston home.

"Mr. Winston," Trey said, extending his hand.

Vincent extended his hand, "Good evening, sir."

Terry took each of their hands without a smile. At least these knuckleheads knew to be polite to big daddy. He sized both of the boys up and tried to plant his thoughts into their heads. *Don't you dare think about touching my babies. I don't even want you slow dancing with them. And if you kiss them, may your jockstraps be filled with the fleas of a thousand camels.*

"Forgive my husband. He's been traumatized by this event, and he seems to have lost his manners." Jackie grabbed Terry's arm and pulled him in her direction. "Say good evening, dear."

Terry groaned and managed, "Good evening, dear."

Everyone laughed except Terry, who failed to see the humor. He'd been an eighteen-year-old young man. He'd also gone to his prom. He remembered his thoughts as though they were yesterday. He involuntarily balled up his fist.

Jackie, seeing the steam coming from Terry's nose, scrambled for a solution, but before she could come up with something clever Trey put his foot square in it.

"Man, you are beautiful. You look so sexy!"

Veronica put her head in her hand, shaking it. Jackie stepped between Trey and Terry. "I don't think you've met the rest of the family, guys. This is the twins' aunt Veronica and this is Catherine. She's . . ." Jackie fished for a believable explanation.

Catherine extended her hand, "I'm an old family friend. I've known Ariana and Alisa since before they were born and just wanted to share this special occasion with them."

"Wow. Ariana looks exactly like you," Vincent said as he put his fist up to his mouth, looking at his date. "You're not related to her? You look like you could be her older sister!"

Alisa grabbed Trey's arm and dragged him toward the backyard. "Come on. I want to take a picture by the fountain with you pinning on the corsage."

"Good idea." Terry followed the two as the rest of the clan went outside.

Catherine remained behind. She sat heavily in the side chair. The emotional drain of the evening was quickly turning into physical fatigue. Watching Terry's reaction to the young suitors made her wonder if she should even ask him to convince the twins to help her.

She rehearsed in her head what she'd say once the twins were gone. Should she talk to Terrance alone? She couldn't quite read Jackie. She believed her to be covering hostility with hospitality. She needed a drink. She went in search of the bottle of wine Terrance had opened for her earlier. She eyed it on the counter next to the refrigerator, its door filled with homework assignments, report cards and preschool artwork. Pictures with magnetic frames held each piece of paper in place.

As she stared at each one carefully she saw a happy family—a family with five children that all belonged together. But she wasn't trying to divide them. Once she got what she needed, she'd be gone. Perhaps she wanted to be friends with Ariana and Alisa, but you can't miss what you never had. Seeing them now confused her. She wasn't sure what she felt. She didn't think she had ever loved anyone or anything except money and power. But there was a twinge of something she didn't understand. She poured a glass of wine and walked back to the chair. She felt light-headed as she sat down.

Through the large windows she could see the family as they congregated around Ariana, Alisa, Trey and Vincent. Terry, the proud father, took picture after picture. Even at this distance Catherine could see him tense up each time one of the boys touched the twins. Suddenly Catherine couldn't breathe. She had to leave. She gulped the wine, gathered her purse and headed for the nearest exit.

$\mathcal{W}$ithout looking through the leaded glass panes Catherine opened the front door. To her astonishment standing before her was Roland Carpenter and a woman whom she presumed was his wife. There was no doubt the tall, handsome young lads were his sons.

"Catherine?" Roland was as shocked as Catherine.

"Roland, nice to see you again. It's been a very long time." The truth was, Roland hadn't seen Catherine since they'd left the courthouse seven years before. All his dealings had been through her lawyer during the adoption process. "How've you been?"

"It *has* been a while." Catherine extended her hand. "This must be Mrs. Carpenter."

"Mercedes." Roland's wife accepted the gesture but neglected to add it was a pleasure. Instead, she wondered why Catherine was here on prom night.

"There's no doubt these are your sons. They're as handsome as their father. My name is Catherine Hawkins. Your father and I go back to our college days."

The taller of the two extended his hand and said, "I'm Marshall and this is my brother, Maxwell."

Catherine smiled suggestively at Roland but spoke to Marshall and his brother. "It's surely my pleasure to meet you."

No, this skank ho is not flirting with my husband and I'm standing right here. And what the hell is wrong with him?

"Were you leaving?" Roland smiled broadly.

Pushing past Roland and Catherine, Mercedes pulled her sons with her. "Excuse us."

Moving to the side, slightly annoyed at Mercedes, Catherine lied, "I was only going out to the car to grab a smoke."

"Nonsense." Roland started to walk in, and this time Catherine stepped to the side. "That's a disgusting habit and someone as lovely as you shouldn't do it."

Roland could see Mercedes in the backyard, and her arms were flailing. This was not a good sign. He needed to get out his platinum American Express to cover the hell there was going to be to pay. His curiosity was getting the better of him as to why Catherine was here. He knew charm worked so much better than confrontation.

Catherine smiled to herself. She'd come closer to loving Roland Carpenter than she had anyone else. She'd seen the potential in him the day they'd met in college. When she stepped into the Sonic with Terry, she knew she'd made a mistake wasting her time with the likes of a science major. Roland had been as ambitious as he was handsome. As he'd passed out flyers for his bid to be student body president, his hand had brushed her slightly. An electrical current had surged through her body.

It had disappointed her that when she presented him with

an offer she thought was impossible to refuse, he'd spouted some nonsense about his loyalty to his friendship with Terry. She'd never forgiven him for that rejection. It was unmistakable; he was flirting with her now. Even his wife saw it. Maybe there were still possibilities.

With a flurry of laughter and energy the group returned to the family room. Catherine followed Roland and reclaimed her seat in hopes no one had noticed she'd planned to make an exit.

"You kids got a nice limo." Roland stretched his long body out on the chaise that matched the sofa and side chair.

"The limo is here already?" Vincent looked at his watch. "We told them six."

"I think the car you're referring to is mine." Catherine crossed her legs and sat back in the chair.

"I see you still roll in style, Ms. Hawkins." Roland toyed with her. "So what are you up to these days?"

Mercedes exhaled loudly and stormed into the kitchen. Jackie followed close on her heels.

"Calm down." Jackie tried to placate her best friend who she'd known since birth. "You know how your husband is and he's harmless."

"Has he forgotten what that bitch did to this family?" Mercedes ranted.

"Gurl, don't let Catherine work your salvation like that. She sho 'nuff ain't worth it. At least one of *your* children isn't looking at her like the prodigal mother has returned."

Mercedes stopped fuming and stared at Jackie. "What?"

"You heard me. Ariana couldn't be happier that Catherine is here. She's trying hard not to hurt my feelings, but the facts are unchanged. She's happy to see her mother."

"Stop it. You're that child's mother and she knows it.

Catherine will blow in here, upset everyone's apple cart and then be gone, leaving you and Terry to make applesauce."

Jackie dropped her head, looking at the counter. "I guess."

Terry yelled from the family room, "If we're going to have a toast before the kids leave, we'd better get started."

Mercedes grabbed her friend's hand and gave it a little squeeze. "Everything is going to be just fine."

"Promise?"

"If not, I'll just have to cut her."

"Come on here, girl. Help me get more champagne and cider."

The women carried two bottles in each hand. Roland rushed to assist them. He took two bottles from Jackie and then from Mercedes as he tried to sneak her a kiss. She pulled away so quickly he lost his balance. She walked around him to the family room.

Terry and Roland each popped the cork on a bottle of champagne as Jackie opened the cider. Halfway through the pouring the doorbell chimed.

"I'll get it!" Michael darted past the adults with T.J. close on his heels.

"Good evening. I'm Theodore. I'll be your driver this evening."

"Yeah, right!" Michael teased. "You want my sisters. Tia and Tamara, it's for you!"

"Daddyyyyyy!" Alisa's face flushed hot. "Do something with him! He's so embarrassing."

"I'll handle this, Mr. Winston." Vincent set his glass of cider on the table and walked to the front door. He reached into his pocket and handed Theodore something that resembled green paper with a dead president on it. When he returned he said, "He'll be waiting by the car until we're ready."

Roland turned to Vincent and said, "Good man. Handle your business."

Though Terry was impressed, he refused to let Vincent know. When everyone's glass was filled, Terry proposed a toast. "All those years ago when I stared through the window of the nursery, I couldn't have imagined an evening like this. You've grown into intelligent, ambitious, beautiful young women. And I just want to say how very proud I am to be your father. To the young men to whom I've entrusted you, don't make me come looking for you with my shotgun."

Jackie slapped his arm. Alisa and Ariana yelled at the same time, "Daddy!"

"What?" Terry couldn't hold in the laughter. "I just want it to be clear. Now it's your mother's turn."

Catherine shifted uneasily in her seat as Jackie raised her glass. "Thank you for allowing me to be your mother. I'm so very proud. Above all else, make memories tonight that'll last a lifetime. And I promise the after party will be, as you say, off the heezy fo' sheezy!"

Alisa stepped to Jackie and kissed her. "We love you, Mom." When she turned she locked eyes with Catherine.

The room grew quiet as everyone partook of their libation of choice. Catherine wondered if Alisa was intentionally trying to get her goat. She smiled inside; Alisa was truly her daughter.

"We'd better get going." Vincent took Alisa's glass and picked up the purple shawl and clutch purse from the stool at the bar. "Is this one yours?"

Alisa smiled at her date. "And which one am I?"

Vincent's confidence wavered. "You're Alisa."

Ariana asked with a smug look. "Is she?"

"You girls be nice." Jackie laughed despite her words. "Don't play with your dates like that."

"Oh, let the games begin." Roland chuckled as he pulled two one-hundred-dollar bills from his breast pocket. "From the looks of things, gentlemen, you've got your hands full tonight. This is in case some unexpected expenses arise."

"Thank you, Mr. Carpenter, but we have this," Vincent said assuredly.

Trey punched his friend. "Fool!"

Amused, Roland continued, "Son, you're young. But believe me when I tell you with beautiful, ambitious and smart women there are always unexpected expenses."

"Dude, listen to the man," Trey pleaded with his friend. "Look at him. He knows these things."

The adults all laughed and Vincent saw the wisdom of the advice. Trey gathered the shawl and purse for his date, whichever one she was, and the four headed for the waiting chariot.

The proud parents, godparents, auntie and siblings all stood on the porch and waved, yelling embarrassingly. Catherine stood among them but wasn't quite sure she fit in. The hardest part of the evening was still ahead of her. Now she had to face Terry.

CHAPTER TWENTY

*A*s the long vehicle pulled away from the curb everyone moved back into the house. Catherine was the last to enter. She was so tired and she wondered if she should broach the subject tonight or schedule a meeting for later into the weekend. Staying in Dallas for the entire weekend would give her time with Alex. But then again, she could send him packing and arrange for a drink with Roland.

Terry interrupted her thoughts. "It was nice of you to come by tonight, Catherine. You've missed so many special times in their lives and you can never get those back, but I guess there's nothing to say you can't move forward from here."

Was he brushing her off? Asking her to leave? "I understand all of that, Terrance. But being here tonight was good for all of us."

The silence grew uncomfortable. Terry really wanted her gone but didn't quite know how to express it. He was sure

Mercedes could do it effortlessly. Instead of showing her out, Terry offered, "Would you like more champagne or wine?"

"Actually, I would." Catherine vacillated. "But I need to talk to you. I'm not so sure this is the right time. I understand from T.J. you're going to be preparing for an after party."

Trepidation increased his blood pressure. *Here it comes. I knew there was more to this little visit.* "What can I do for you? Is this something I should get Jackie for?"

"I'd really rather talk to you alone."

"Does this concern the girls?"

"It does."

Very curtly Terry said, "Then I'll get Jackie."

Veronica was assisting T.J. with his overnight bag. "We're going to get moving. It's going to be a Blockbuster night." Her eyes moistened and her voice softened. "They're absolutely beautiful, Terry. I wish Mom could have been here. You know she thought about flying in to surprise y'all, but decided that she couldn't do prom and graduation."

Only half listening Terry answered, "I know. She called us last night. Excuse me for a minute." Terry went in search of Jackie.

"I can't believe that woman." Terry walked in on Mercedes as she bent Jackie's ear.

"Excuse me, ladies. I hate to interrupt your little *session*, but, Jackie, Catherine wants to talk to us."

Surprised, Jackie stared at Terry. "About what?"

"She hasn't said, but something in my gut tells me this is the real reason she's here."

"Do you want us to leave?" Mercedes asked.

"Absolutely not. Who's going to help us with the party?" Jackie didn't mean to snap. "Besides this isn't going to take long."

Veronica had managed to gather her niece, nephews and the Carpenters' two boys and headed for the door. "I'm taking the Volvo because I need a seven seater, in case you haven't noticed."

Jackie waved Veronica off as she absentmindedly told her to get the keys from the hook by the garage door. She went directly to Catherine and asked, "What could you possibly have to talk to us about?"

Veronica's hand stopped in midair as she reached for the keys. Roland took the champagne glass from his lips. All eyes were on the two women as they squared off.

"I actually wanted to talk to Terrance, but he insisted we include you." The nice, cordial woman had left the building and the Catherine everyone knew and hated had replaced her.

"Does this concern Ariana and Alisa?" Jackie moved a step closer.

Taking a defensive stance, Catherine stood firm. "Yes, you might say that it does."

"Then my husband is correct. I need to be in on any conversation that involves *our* daughters."

Catherine's eyes scanned the room. "Perhaps we can take this somewhere private."

"This is my family. We have no secrets from them."

Catherine appealed to Terry with her eyes. "I'd really rather not discuss this in front of everyone. It's very personal."

"Let's go into the office." Terry gestured for Catherine to walk ahead of him. "We'll be comfortable in there."

Jackie looked at Terry in disbelief. Like she gave a cat's fur ball about Catherine's comfort. "Very well. The office is this way."

Veronica, Mercedes and Roland made eye contact as the

trio disappeared. Veronica surely didn't want to leave. But she also didn't want the children to see any fireworks in case Catherine lit Jackie's fuse. "We'd better get going." She opened the garage door and the five youngsters disappeared. Veronica turned to Mercedes and mouthed the words "call me" before she followed the children.

"What do you think that's all about?" Roland turned to Mercedes.

"You tell me." Mercedes lit into him. "You two were very chummy."

"Come on, Cedes, let it rest." Roland was agitated by his wife's consistent jealousy. "You know, charming people is what I do. I'm a lawyer, for goodness sakes. I figured charm would get me further than conflict. Like everyone else, I want to know what the hell she's doing here."

"Well, you surely poured on the *charm*, and she looked at you like you were a piece of hot Southern fried chicken and she had a bottle of Louisiana hot sauce."

"You know, we could sit here bickering or we could ease down the hallway toward the office to hear what we can hear."

Even though she was angry, she couldn't help but laugh at her silly husband. "I'll race you."

"Wait—we should remove our shoes." Roland bent down, untying his running shoes.

"You act like you've done this before."

"I'm a lawyer. Eavesdropping is in our job description."

The stealthy movement of the pair went unnoticed as they approached the door, which had been left slightly ajar.

Jackie was talking. "Enough of beating around the bush. I'm sorry you've got some health challenges, but what does that have to do with us, most specifically our daughters?"

Roland and Mercedes leaned in closer.

"In case you've forgotten, Jacqueline, I'm the one who gave birth to *your daughters*. But I'm sure every time you look at them, you see that, don't you?

"And you, Terrance, I know you see me in Alisa. She's as defiant as I was at her age. So let's come down off your high and mighty horses. True enough, I signed away my rights. But at the time it seemed the best thing for all concerned. You've done a wonderful job raising them. But your job is done. They're adults."

"I'm still not seeing your point." Terry began pacing.

"Don't think I didn't see the longing in Ariana's eyes. That yearning is for me—her real mother."

"*I am* her real mother!"

"On paper. But the truth is it's my blood that runs through their veins. They share my DNA, not yours. And that, Terrance, brings me to the point of my visit."

"Oh, you mean this wasn't just to see your daughters off to their prom?" Jackie was seething. "I'm stunned."

Just outside the office Mercedes turned and stared at Roland. She whispered, "Dayummmmmmmmm."

Catherine ignored Jackie and continued. "I've told you that I've been under the weather lately. It's a little more serious than that. You see, about a year ago I had the flu or so I thought. I was in Paris and was just going to wait until I got back to Los Angeles to see my doctor. I got sicker and sicker. When I finally went to the doctor I was diagnosed with strep throat."

"And this was the big medical emergency?" Terry stopped pacing. "This is so like you. Everything is all about you, Catherine Marie Hawkins."

"Please let me finish," Catherine said impatiently. "By me not seeking treatment, the strep infection caused severe damage."

"Would you please get to the point?" Jackie was beginning to get nervous. "What kind of damage?"

"It destroyed my kidneys. Unless I have a transplant I'll have to go on dialysis for the rest of my life."

Jackie sat in the executive chair behind the desk. Terry turned to Catherine, looking her in the eyes. "What are you saying?"

Terry looked from Catherine to Jackie and back again. "You want Ariana or Alisa to give you a kidney?"

Catherine looked from Jackie back to Terry. "They're the best chance I have."

"Then you have no chance at all. There's no way I'm going to let them even consider such a thing. They're starting college in the fall."

"I hate to be the one to break this to you, but it's not your decision to make. They're eighteen. Besides, this won't affect them starting college. The recovery time for a donor is about four weeks."

Jackie leapt up from the desk, knocking the clock to the floor. "You need to get out of this house and, more important, out of our lives. I'll see you in hell before I let this happen."

"I only talked to you first as a courtesy. I don't need your permission to go to them. And I *will* be talking to them. So I'd prepare them if I were you." Catherine turned on her heels and headed for the office door. She stopped abruptly, pivoted and stretched out her hand.

Terry jumped involuntarily as a result of her quick move and reached for the small piece of paper in her hand.

"This is my card with all my numbers. I've written my cell phone number on the back." Catherine smiled wickedly. "You have a pleasant evening now, you hear."

Roland and Mercedes were so stunned by what they'd heard they couldn't move. Catherine brushed past them as she made a quick exit.

as the front door slammed, Mercedes and Roland rushed into the office. Jackie sat behind the large cherry banker's desk with her eyes fixed on nothing in particular. Terry stood in the middle of the room, staring at the door but not seeing his friends.

Mercedes rushed to Jackie as she asked, "Gurl, are you okay?"

Jackie didn't answer.

"Man, we heard everything. Is she nuts?"

Bewildered Terry looked at Roland. "Is she right?"

"You mean about not requiring your permission?"

Terry only nodded.

"I'm afraid so, bruh," Roland answered in a defeated tone.

"I won't stand for it. How dare she walk up in my house telling me I have to tell my children something?"

Jackie looked at Terry with a glazed look in her eyes. "Your children?"

"Baby, you know what I mean." Terry realized how this whole evening must have made Jackie feel. "You know you're the only mother the girls know."

"This woman is a piece of work. This reminds me of that Christmas when she came to the house slinging insults." Mercedes rubbed Jackie's back. "And, Terry, I'm surprised at you."

"Damn, woman, cut the man some slack," Roland charged. "We don't need to fight among ourselves."

"The only one trying to fight here is you!" Mercedes walked from around the desk and stood in front of Roland. "I just think Terry should be more aware of how Jackie feels about all this."

"My man didn't mean anything by what he said," Roland retorted.

"Sure—" Mercedes began.

"Look, you two, believe it or not, this isn't about y'all," Jackie interrupted. "I know Terry didn't mean anything by what he said. I'm just feeling real insecure right about now. There's no doubt Ariana is having birth mother separation issues."

Roland realized how immature he and his wife were acting in light of their best friends' plight. "We're sorry. I guess we have a couple issues of our own."

Looking embarrassed, Mercedes added, "Roland's right. I'm sorry for attacking you, Terry. Gurl, please forgive me. What can we do to help?"

"You know what? This is all a bad dream." Jackie stood, moving around the desk. "We have a party to get ready for. I'm not going to let that woman ruin this evening."

"Jackie's right." Mercedes stood behind her friend, gently pushing her toward the door. "Let's get ready for the party and deal with this later."

The friends walked into the long hallway. As they moved away from the office they stopped to hug. Mercedes held Jackie, and she felt her sob silently. She rubbed her between the shoulder blades and slightly rocked back and forth. Mercedes's mind flashed back to the many years and tears they'd shed together.

Momma C. and Margaret, Mercedes's mother, had met in the hospital the day Jackie and Mercedes were born, and there was nothing of consequence they hadn't shared since then. Raised more as cousins than friends, one didn't know what to do without the other. There was never a time when they hadn't been able to comfort each other. They'd had a lifelong die-for-the-other kind of friendship that was rare. They shared one heart that beat in two bodies. They'd weathered hurricane Catherine seven years earlier, and it would be no different this time. Mercedes knew that Jackie couldn't love Ariana and Alisa any more than if she'd given birth to them. Just when you thought life couldn't get any better . . .

Mercedes envied the love and trust Terry and Jackie shared. There was no one the other could even see. A naked woman could lie across the hood of Terry's Yukon and he'd tell her to please move because he couldn't see the road. Her husband, on the other hand, had an eye that wandered the four corners of the earth. She wanted so desperately to trust him, but his lifestyle before they were married always loomed in the shadows of her mind.

Mercedes blinked quickly to remove her selfish thoughts and to focus on her friend. "You going to be okay?"

Jackie stood, snapping her posture straight, almost military style, as she wiped her eyes with both hands. "Yes. Let's go get ready for a party."

The men remained in the office, where Terry paced. "Why

would she come up in here today of all days with this craziness."

"Why not?" Roland said very matter-of-factly. "This is what Catherine does. It's her world and we all just lease space in it."

"I just don't get her. She's had literally no contact with 'Lisa and Ari for three years—and that was a phone call saying she was going to be in town and would like to take them to dinner. Do you think her ass showed up?"

"Why are you always so surprised? Don't you realize she's been this way since you met her? It didn't change when she gave birth to the twins. Why do you see the same behavior and expect a different result? Man, you know I love you, but wake up. Catherine Marie is all about Catherine Marie. And could you please stop pacing? You're making me dizzy."

Terry sighed and turned to Roland. "Can't we get a court order to stop this?" He continued pacing.

"There's no reason to. The twins are of legal age and in good health. Besides, you're forgetting one thing. *They* haven't agreed to do it."

"Oh my God, you're right." Terry slapped his hands together. "Why didn't I think of that? They want nothing to do with her."

Roland smiled but said nothing. Too many times he'd seen a birth mother come back into the picture and tear asunder seemingly rock-solid, loving families.

CHAPTER TWENTY-TWO

*C*atherine guzzled vodka as the car maneuvered through the streets of Dallas en route to the hotel. Her senses were keen, and the sound of the ice rolling around in the glass agitated her. The evening had taken its toll, and exhaustion covered her like a handmade quilt on a cold winter's night.

She wasn't prepared for the twins to look so much like her. Alisa had more of her personality and spunk. Ariana seemed more like Terry—weak and passive. If she had to choose her mark it would be Ariana. She would win her over with no problem at all. She didn't understand why Terrance and Jacqueline would have any objection to one of the girls giving her a kidney—after all she *was* the girls' mother.

Terrance, being the good Christian man he professed to be, would come around and encourage the girls to do the right thing. In the meantime Catherine needed to get her ducks aligned for her leave of absence. Before the surgery there was one major deal she needed to finalize that would require gathering the various Hawkins International presidents from around the globe. She glanced at the exquisite diamond timepiece on her left wrist and decided to call Claire. It was only a little before five in Los Angeles.

Claire answered on the first ring. "Ms. Hawkins's office. This is Claire Holden speaking."

Not bothering with any pleasantries Catherine got right to the point. "I need to set up a meeting with Brazil, Paris, Munich, Barcelona and Rome. Have them fly into Los Angeles for a meeting on Wednesday. Call the staff at my Kauai villa and let them know we'll be there on Wednesday evening. We'll all fly over together on the G-V."

"How long should I tell them to be prepared to stay?"

Catherine felt in control again, "For as long as I tell them."

"Is there anything else, Ms. Hawkins?" Claire's tone was flat at best.

"I'll call you if there is. Please make sure those e-mails go out before you leave today."

"Yes, ma'am."

Catherine hung up without any further words. She turned to look out the window and take in the benign view. She poured another glass of vodka, crossed her legs and relaxed.

CHAPTER TWENTY-THREE

*A*riana and Alisa were so overwhelmed by the joy of the evening that they didn't notice the somber mood of their parents and godparents. Jackie and Mercedes went through the motions of playing the perfect hostesses to twenty-three giggling teenagers.

The caterer had provided a young person's dream menu: pizza, hamburgers, fries and soda. The group had sung karaoke, played board games and finally many of them had fallen asleep watching *Drumline*. Half the guests left between four and six, promising to call when they reached their homes. Those that remained made beds from sleeping bags, exercise mats, quilts and comforters. The exhausted young people littered the floor in the family, living and dining rooms.

Jackie lounged in the overstuffed chair in the family room as she read. Her mind wandered as she thought how pleased she was at how well it had all turned out. The girls were a hit with their friends and everyone was safe. Terry startled her as he kissed her on the neck.

"Good morning, baby," he mumbled as he nuzzled her.

Jackie stretched as she looked up at him, smiling. "Hey, good morning to you."

"Where's your partner in crime?" Terry moved around the chair and sat on the couch adjacent to her.

"She faded at about five thirty." Jackie laid Jacquelin Thomas's latest novel on the end table, placing her glasses on top of it. "We had a good time with the kids, though. They'll probably sleep until noon. You and Roland going to take the day shift?"

"What's to watch?"

Jackie raised her left eyebrow. "Boys and girls sleeping in the same room?"

Terry laughed and then said, "I see your point."

Jackie took on a serious tone. "So how are you?"

"I'm fine." Terry wasn't very convincing.

"I know you're fine." Jackie sat up and moved to the edge of the cushion. "But I'm asking you how you're doing with this bombshell Catherine dropped on us."

Terry let out a huge sigh and stood, looking around to see if everyone was sleeping. He began pacing, but most of the floor space was covered with unconscious high school seniors. He returned to the couch and sank heavily into it. "I don't know what I'm going to do. If what Catherine says is true and she's really sick, how can I not talk to the girls about helping her?"

Jackie stared at him in disbelief. "Why are you trippin'?"

"Keep your voice down," Terry cautioned. "I know she's never done anything but bring us grief. But this is her life we're talking about."

"Her life? What about the life of Ariana and Alisa?" Jackie

struggled to keep her voice to a whisper. "I don't care a thing about her. Let the heifer croak."

"Come on now, Jackie, we're Christians. You can't say something like that."

Jackie stood. "Oh, I'm sorry, Terry. You're right. What I should've said is let the bitch die." She suddenly stormed off, tripping over a young man in a blue sleeping bag.

Terry ran after his wife, catching her on the second step. "Baby, listen to me. I know you don't like Catherine and, truth be told, neither do I, but if her life is in jeopardy we're bound by God's law to help her."

Darts shot from Jackie's eyes into Terry's soul. "God's law? What about God's law about motherhood? There's nothing that makes me happier than being Ari and 'Lisa's mother. But if Catherine had done what she was supposed to, even halfway, I'd feel different. It's easy to walk away from a difficult situation. It takes courage to stay and fight. Those children have meant nothing to her for eighteen years and now you want me to feel sorry for her and encourage them to let someone cut into their body and take a part of them away?"

Terry placed his hand on Jackie's arm as he began to speak. "This thing kept me up all night. Everything you said rolled through my brain a million times, but I always came up with the same question: 'What would Jesus do?' "

Jackie looked down at her arm and back into Terry's eyes. "Jesus didn't have children," she spat, looking down at her arm again.

Terry removed his hand as Jackie's eyes spoke volumes. Without another syllable Jackie ran up the stairs. Terry watched as she turned right at the landing and disappeared down the hall. The slam of the bedroom door reverberated through the neighborhood, rattling the house like a sonic boom.

The sound woke Alisa as she slumbered on the living room floor. "Daddy, what's wrong with Mom? I could hear you in my sleep."

"I'm sorry, princess," Terry said as he walked toward the living room. "We didn't mean to wake you." Terry wanted to change the subject. "I hear y'all brought the house down and the sun up."

"Oh, Daddy, we did!" Alisa crawled out from under the handmade quilt, exposing her pink-footed pajamas. "You and Mom are the best. Everyone had a blast. We're going to be the talk of the school on Monday." She stepped over a still Ariana to get to her father, putting her arms around his neck while planting a kiss on his cheek.

Terry's arms encircled her as he drew her close. He held her for a long moment, thinking how blessed he was to be her father.

As he slowly let her go she looked into his eyes. "What's wrong, Daddy? Are you mad about the mess? We're going to clean it up as soon as everyone wakes up. Is that why Mom slammed the door?"

"No. No, of course not." Terry was fishing for a viable response. "Your mom and I just had a little misunderstanding. We'll work it out. There's nothing for you to be concerned about. Are you going to go back to sleep?"

Alisa stretched as she moved away from Terry. "No, I'm going to wake everyone up so we can clean up before we go to breakfast."

"I thought I was making breakfast."

Alisa yawned again. "We discussed it and everyone wants something different, so we decided we'd go to IHOP instead."

Terry pretended to be crushed, but in fact he was relieved. "Well, I guess that'll be okay. I was just looking forward to showing off my skills to your friends. Maybe I can persuade your uncle to join us."

"Oh, Daddy, that would be cool!" Alisa kissed him again. "I'll get everyone up."

"You're really going to wake everyone up now?" Terry was surprised. "It's still early."

"Yep."

Ariana didn't move as she lay listening to the conversation between her dad and sister. She'd always been a light sleeper and the slightest noise would awaken her from even the deepest slumber. The sound of her dad's voice when he'd first ventured into the family room had brought her out of dreamland. She'd heard the conversation between her mom and dad. The words *"let the bitch die"* played over and over in her head as she wondered what was wrong with Catherine.

CHAPTER TWENTY-FOUR

*J*ackie stared out the kitchen window as she watched the two carloads of teenagers back onto Honeycomb Lane. Terry had orchestrated the cleanup without a word to her. Roland had tried fruitlessly to engage her in conversation. Her feelings of betrayal weighed heavily on her spirit.

Mercedes stole glances as Jackie moved around the kitchen with fast, deliberate motion. She wasn't sure what to say to get her friend to open up. The wrong thing could set her off.

"Why don't you let me do that?" Mercedes took the sponge from Jackie as she washed the punch bowl. "You gonna mess around and break something."

Jackie stared at her, wanting to rebuff, but just handed her the dripping sponge instead. "Here."

"You want to talk about it or should I stand over here and act like Molly maid with my mouth closed?"

"Your mouth being closed works real good for me right now." Jackie began sweeping the floor.

"Gurl, when you slammed that door this morning I sat straight up in bed." Mercedes stared at the apples on the dish towel as she dried the crystal punch bowl.

"I thought you were keeping your mouth closed?"

"You'd feel better if you talked it out."

"You mean *you'd* feel better if you knew why I'm so livid."

Mercedes smiled. "That, too."

Jackie stopped sweeping and leaned on the broom. One lone tear trickled down her left cheek. Mercedes placed the punch bowl and towel on the counter and walked slowly to where Jackie stood. She held her for a long moment as she felt her body convulse. Mercedes wondered what she could do to soothe Jackie's troubled soul.

"I can't believe Terry wants one of the girls to give Catherine a kidney."

Mercedes stepped away, straightening her back. "What?"

"You heard me." Jackie wiped her eyes and cheeks with the backs of her hands. "He says as Christians we need to think about what Jesus would do."

"I don't know if I'm that saved." Mercedes passed her a damp paper towel to wipe her nose. "As far as I'm concerned this is what the evil witch deserves for all the pain she's caused this family."

"Humph, who you telling? The thing I love most about my husband is the same thing that drives me crazy. He's just so forgiving. But I won't back down on this. How dare she come up in *my* house telling me what she's going to do with *my* children?" Jackie began sweeping imaginary trash on the ceramic tile. "I felt like whippin' on her until T.J. got tired. Even sick she's just so damned smug. Like we're all here to do her bidding."

"Roland and I heard most of the conversation. I was

stunned. We talked about it when I went up to bed this morning."

"And on the night of their prom. She's sitting here, pretending she just wanted to see them. All the while knowing the bomb she was about to drop."

Mercedes sat, trying to choose her next words carefully. "Do you think she picked yesterday on purpose?"

"Without a doubt," Jackie spat. "She could have called us anytime and said she wanted to stop by, but she chose last night."

"Well, at least she didn't say anything to them on their special day. I wouldn't put anything past her."

Jackie's blood rushed to her face as she flashed angry red. "So you think she did us a favor?"

"Don't even think you're going to turn your anger on me," Mercedes chastised. "You know good and hell well what I meant."

Jackie lowered her head and whispered, "What do you think we should do?"

"Gurl, I can't even begin to tell you how to handle this. I did ask Roland what could be done legally."

"And?"

Mercedes looked at the floor for a beat, then met her friend's eyes square. "The day the twins turned eighteen they became legally enabled to make all medical decisions. I know this isn't what you want to hear. But it's the fact, Jack."

"In my head I know that's the case. But in my heart I was hoping for something different. These are my babies." Jackie paused, at a loss for words, before asking, "Want some coffee?"

"I thought you'd never ask." Mercedes went to the coffeemaker while Jackie retrieved two mugs from the cupboard.

Mercedes poured the coffee. She went to the counter and pulled out two bar stools, patting one of them. "Come talk to me."

Jackie sat on the stool's thick cushion. She sighed deeply. "Where do I start?"

"The beginning always works."

"I hate Catherine," Jackie blurted, "for a multitude of reasons."

"Hate's a pretty strong word, but I understand." Mercedes stirred sugar and cream into her coffee.

The friends talked on endlessly, teetering between laughter, sadness and anger.

The grandfather clock in the foyer softly gonged eleven times. "This house is too quiet!" Jackie shot from her seat and ran to the table in the family room to retrieve the multi-function remote control. With the push of a single button, the television, surround-sound audio system and cable box awakened. Jackie pushed a few buttons and the channel changed to the smooth jazz music station. The soulful saxophone of Grover Washington seemed to pour from every direction around them. She lowered the volume before she returned to the counter.

"That's better. My own thoughts were screaming too loud in my head."

Looking serious, Mercedes asked softly, "How and when are you going to tell the girls that their mother wants one of them to give her a kidney?"

Tears once again filled Jackie's eyes. "How dare you call that woman *their mother*!"

"I'm sorry, but you know what I mean," Mercedes said, not really apologizing. "But the question still remains. When are you going to tell them?"

"I don't know. And how can I pretend I agree with this? Terry thinks one of them should do it, and I *know* they shouldn't. Suppose something goes wrong?"

"There's always that slim possibility, but the donor usually—"

"Usually? What about the unusually?"

Ignoring the interruption Mercedes continued, "makes a swift and full recovery. Given their age it would take no time at all."

"So you think I'm wrong, too?" Jackie screamed the question. "I thought you were my friend! We've been like sisters our whole lives and you'd betray me like this? You need to get the hell out of my house!"

Mercedes sat, stunned. Her first instinct was to gather her belongings and just leave Jackie to fight her demons alone. But she knew she had to stick this out no matter how much it hurt in the moment. "Of course, there's the very remote chance that something could go wrong. But you can get your teeth cleaned and something could happen."

Jackie looked at her in disbelief. "Let me repeat this so you really understand me." She turned up the volume to scream. "Get out of my house!"

Mercedes sat deeper in the bar stool, digging her butt cheeks into the cushion. No matter what the words were that came from Jackie's mouth, she knew in her heart she wanted Mercedes to stay put. "I'm not going anywhere. I'm going to sit right here until we come up with a plan."

CHAPTER TWENTY-FIVE

*A*lex kissed Catherine gently on her shoulder, awakening her. "Good morning. I didn't mean to wake you." He smiled broadly.

"Then why did you?" Catherine snapped.

"You look so beautiful sleeping, I couldn't resist." Alex kissed her, this time on the lips. "Let's fly down to Mexico for lunch today."

"I don't feel up to it." Catherine turned her back on her lover du jour.

The sensuous touches stopped as concern filled his voice. "Is there something wrong?"

"Nothing that you leaving me alone wouldn't cure." Catherine's words sliced the cool air around them. "Maybe we should return to L.A. today and I'll come back on Monday. Dallas is such a bore."

"I wanted to spend the weekend with you."

Catherine turned and shot him a glance. "Since when does

what you want matter? You should go back to Gloria. I'm sure she misses you."

Alex lay flat on his back, exposing his muscle-rippled hairy chest, staring at the ceiling. "I've been wanting to talk to you about Gloria."

"Why?" The single word dripped sarcasm.

"I want to marry you, Catherine."

The thick, throaty laughter mocked him. "You what?"

"I'm in love with you." Alex's words had less confidence. "I have been since I first came to work for you. I tried to fight it, but it's pointless. We belong together."

"Are you listening to yourself? How pathetic is this? You work for me. As a fringe benefit you get to do me. Everything you have, including that pathetic hard thing between your legs"—she carved through his manhood with every word—"I've given to you. What can you bring to me?"

He rolled over and sat on the side of the bed, his back to her. "I thought you cared for me," he said softly.

Catherine decided she needed to be a little kinder to the man who held her life in his hands every time she boarded her jet. "Alex, you are a wonderful lover and an even better pilot." Pausing for effect, she continued more gently, "but I don't want you to give up your beautiful family for me."

"But I'm in love with you, Catherine." He turned, staring at her with pleading eyes. "I only want to be with you."

Sighing Catherine thought, *Give him some brown sugar and he wants to make gingerbread*, but said. "Look, Alex, I need you right where you are. I've got some serious issues I need to deal with and I can't concentrate on much else. Let me get this handled and then maybe we can talk more about us."

"Promise?"

Catherine ate weak men for lunch. She would begin looking for a new pilot immediately. Smiling she said, "Promise."

Alex smiled broadly, reaching for Catherine. He could take her to places that few other men could, and she felt like going on a journey. She began kissing him and then straddled him. "I need you to file a flight plan for Lihue on Wednesday in the late afternoon. The heads of all of the overseas operations will be joining us."

"My sweet, we can talk about flight plans later." Alex began panting. "Right now all I want to do is relish this moment."

"I decide when we talk about what," she said as she moved from on top of him and fell back onto the bed, leaving his flag flying at full mast.

"Catherine, come on. Don't do this." Alex turned to her pleading. "I'm sorry."

"I've lost the urge. File a flight plan for Maine. I feel like lobster today."

CHAPTER TWENTY-SIX

"*S*ince when do you not clean your plate?" Terry asked Ariana as she made circles in the syrup with her scrambled eggs.

"I'm just not hungry." Ariana refused to look at her father, because he could read her as easily as a *Sports Illustrated* swimsuit edition.

"Too much partying last night?" Terry teased.

"Maybe."

Trying to draw more than a one-word response from Ariana, Terry pressed on. "So what do you want to do after breakfast?"

"Whatever."

Roland raised his left eyebrow. The only person on earth who knew the twins as well as Terry was him. "Okay, so what's up? Not hungry, not talking. Let me take your pulse." Roland grabbed her wrist and pretended to look at his watch. "We'd better call nine-one-one! I don't think she's going to make it."

"Oh, stop, Uncle Roland!"

"Oh, so, you are okay?"

"Yes! I just have a lot on my mind."

"What in the world could have you so concerned? You've already been accepted to the college of your choice, you're an honor student and, based on the crowd at your house last night, you are one of the most popular girls in school."

Staring at the eggs she said softly. "You wouldn't understand. No one would."

Roland eyed Terry, who shrugged, before he continued, "Did some good-for-nothing wannabe thug hurt my princess? Give me his name," Roland only half joked.

Looking up, she shot a glance first to her father and then to Roland. "No, no. It's nothing like that."

Terry spoke up this time. "Honey, what's wrong?"

Ariana looked around the table and then back at him. "Nothing."

Terry would *never* understand the creatures he adored more than anything—females. It was more than obvious there was something bothering her, but she claimed everything was just fine. He sighed, inwardly wondering if he should press for more information or wait until they were alone. He decided on the latter. "Okay, for now."

Relief shone in her eyes as she smiled.

The group finished breakfast and Roland insisted he pick up the tab. Ariana rode with her godfather and Alisa with her father as they dropped each of their friends home before returning to Winston manor.

"You're sorta quiet," Terry said as he drove leisurely through the Saturday-afternoon traffic.

Alisa stretched. "I'm just sleepy."

"Did you have a good time last night?"

Turning to face her father, Alisa enthusiastically said,

"Daddy, it was the *best*! Do you know everyone will be talking about this until graduation? You and Mom are da bomb!"

Smiling, Terry stole a quick glance at her. "You really did have a good time, didn't you?"

"Yep."

"What about your sister?"

"Oh, she had a blast, too. Her and Vincent danced all night."

"Then what do you think is bothering her now?"

"I don't know. She has been in a funky mood since she got up. You know how she can be."

"Yeah, she *can* go there. I'm just surprised, because I'd think the joy from last night would at least spill over into today."

"Don't worry about her. She'll be just fine."

"You're probably right." Terry vacillated between should he or shouldn't he ask the next question. Should won by a landslide. "What did you think of Catherine showing up last night?"

"I didn't care." Alisa's words were too burdened with emotion and spoken too quickly for her to be telling the truth.

As Terry slowed to a stop at the traffic signal, he turned to look at Alisa full on. "I don't think you're being honest with your dear ole dad. You have to feel something about seeing her after all this time."

"I just don't know why she even bothered. Ever since Mom adopted us, she could have been in our lives. But everything else was more important, like it has always been. So now all of a sudden when we're eighteen she wants to come around. I don't think so."

"I see."

"Why does she do that?"

"Do what?"

"Pretend like we matter to her."

"I'm sure you do matter." The left-turn arrow changed to green and Terry proceeded. "Catherine is just who she is. I'm sure she's thought of you often. She has surely provided for your future."

"Daddy, you are kidding me, right?"

"No, I believe Catherine cares for you in her own way. Not being a mother, I wouldn't know these things. But I know for me no matter where you went or what you did, I would *always* worry, wonder, stress over and most of all love you, because you are a part of me."

"We're a part of you because you made us a part of you. You've never left us. Uncle Roland has always told Ari and me what you did for us when you were in college, barely scraping by for yourself, yet you took us and raised us."

"Catherine always paid child support."

"I'm talking about in the beginning." Alisa's voice had a trace of salt, which she knew better than to use with her father, but she couldn't rein in her anger. "Dad, I'm a grown woman. You don't have to keep lying to protect our image of her. I know what I know."

"*I'm a grown woman.*" The words assaulted him. "You ain't that grown."

Alisa looked out of the passenger window as silence filled the car.

"Besides, I'm not trying to protect her image. Catherine's image is so tainted it's beyond shielding."

"Daddy, you always take up for her and make excuses for what she's done or I should say hasn't done." Hurt made her chest constrict. "Do you honestly think we don't know?"

Words abandoned him as his thoughts skidded. "I . . ."

"What, Daddy?" Alisa's resentment rankled with each breath she took. "Even now you're pretending like her showing up last night was okay."

Terry stared through the windshield in silence.

"IT'S JUST YOU AND ME now." Roland pushed the power button on the car stereo and looked at Ariana as they sat in front of the home of the last of her friends he'd dropped off. "Talk to me."

"About what?"

"Don't play with me." Roland pretended to tease. "Remember, I desonexed your behind. I know you better than you know you."

"Uncle Roland!"

"Unless you want me to tell all your friends about how you used to pull your diaper off and crawl around with your cute little butt up in the air . . ."

"You wouldn't. Please tell me you wouldn't!"

"Start talking or I'll start with home skillet we just dropped off."

Sighing, Ariana asked slowly, "What do you want to know?"

"I think you know precisely what I'm talking about. You've been moping around since you got up this morning."

"Why did Catherine really come to see us last night?" Ariana picked imaginary lint from her sweatpants. "She claimed she just wanted to see us, but I heard Mom and Daddy arguing this morning."

Roland didn't want to be the one to break the news to Ariana, and lying wasn't an option. "I didn't hear them, so I can't really say why they were arguing."

"But I'm asking what you know about Catherine."

Well, I guess you're not ten anymore and being elusive isn't going to work. "I know Catherine had a private conversation with your mom and dad last night before she left."

"What did she say to them to make Mom say Catherine should die?"

"What?" Roland was genuinely surprised.

"Mom said, 'Let the b— die.' " Ariana made eye contact with Roland for the first time. "I know Daddy tells you everything, so don't pretend you don't know what I'm talking about."

Roland put the car in drive and pulled away from the curb. He was relieved it was only a short drive back to Honeycomb Lane. "I think we need to continue this conversation when we get back to your house."

Ariana only stared out the window.

CHAPTER TWENTY-SEVEN

*R*oland pulled into the driveway just behind Terry, and the four converged on the front porch at the same time. The mood of each girl was the perfect reflection of the other. Roland stared at Terry with eyes that told him they needed to talk.

"I'm going to take a shower," Alisa said with a trace of agitation in her tone.

"Me, too," Ariana stated flatly as she shot a glance at Roland.

The men watched as the girls disappeared up the stairs in silence. "Want some more coffee?" Terry asked as he headed for the kitchen.

"No, I'm cool. But I'll join you in the kitchen."

"Jackie?" Terry called out.

"Out here," Jackie answered from the patio.

Terry and Roland followed her voice, bypassing the kitchen. Jackie and Mercedes sat on the patio chairs, each with a mug in hand.

"Hey." Terry bent to kiss Jackie.

Refusing to kiss him back, she turned, causing his lips to land on her right cheek. "Hey."

Roland took a seat across from Mercedes before he began. "Ariana heard you two arguing this morning."

Jackie sat up, placing the mug on the tempered-glass table with great emphasis. "What did she hear?"

Terry fell back into the fourth chair. "Damn."

"I don't know how much she heard," Roland continued. "She wanted me to tell her why Catherine *really* stopped by. But she did hear you, Jackie. Apparently, you said you wanted Catherine dead?"

Jackie sank further into her seat. "Oh my God, I never meant for her to hear me. I thought they were all asleep."

"You're going to have to tell them something." Mercedes took a sip of coffee before she continued. "And you don't have a whole lot of time to do it."

"Well, Ari isn't the only one asking questions. 'Lisa asked me, too." Terry sat up straight. "She's pretty ticked off at me because she thinks I should have denied Catherine the visit."

Jackie turned to the side, crossing her legs as she mumbled, "I'm glad I'm not the only one."

As tension mounted, Terry pretended to not hear Jackie. "What else did Ari say?"

"She knew I had information I wasn't sharing, and of course I wouldn't dare lie to her. I simply told her she needed to talk to"—Roland pointed between Jackie and Terry—"the two of you."

"Where are they now?" Mercedes asked.

"Taking showers." Terry began to rub his unshaven chin. "We'd better come up with a plan to tell them what this is all about before they come back down."

"I'm not telling them that Catherine needs an organ

donor," Jackie spat as she stood. "And, oh, by the way, bam, you're it!"

Mercedes grabbed her by the wrist. "Jack, sit down. We need to keep our heads. We know Catherine will be back in the not-too-distant future. If we don't talk to them with love and compassion before she does, there's no telling what she'll say."

"She's right," Roland added. "I hate this as much as you do, but if we don't tell them, Catherine will. And when she does, she won't care how they feel."

Angry tears burned behind Jackie's eyelids as she spoke softly, "I hate that woman."

"Can I get an amen?" Mercedes said, picking up her coffee again. "I think we should start with the truth as we know it."

"I agree." Roland stood. "When is Veronica bringing the kids back?"

"She called this morning to say it would be sometime this evening." Mercedes stared at him questioningly. "Why?"

"Good. That gives us some time to strategize. What we need to do now while they're showering is determine how you'll tell them the truth."

"I don't want them to know the truth." Jackie reasoned, looking from one to the other, "Do you know how much it'll hurt them to know their *mother* only came by on prom night to ask them for a kidney?"

"But they already know something's up," Mercedes said. "You don't want them to find the truth later and be mad at you."

"She's right, baby."

Jackie rolled her eyes at Terry.

Roland navigated the conversation with ease and finesse.

"Look, you two, you can be mad at each other later. But for now we need to concentrate on 'Lisa and Ari."

Mercedes spoke up. "I think you tell them why Catherine came. Don't delay the inevitable."

"You seem to be going deaf. I've said this as many ways as I could for you to understand I'm not telling them sh . . ."

Terry sighed. "Honey, we have to tell them. Catherine *will* be back."

"So let me get this straight." Jackie paused for effect. "I'm supposed to say, oh, by the way, that friendly little visit from Catherine last night wasn't really all that friendly. The real reason she came was to tell you she needs a kidney and she wants—no, expects—one of you to give it to her."

"I understood you the first three times you said it, but now I need you to hear me clearly," Roland said very sternly. "With a different attitude, but, yes, that's exactly what you have to tell them." Roland stared pointedly at Jackie.

"I won't do it."

Terry wasn't sure what he felt at that moment. He wanted to agree with Jackie, but he couldn't. Was it because he felt sorry for Catherine? Or did the girls have a right to know the truth and make their own decision?

"I don't know that we have a choice."

"I don't think you have a choice either." The adults all turned, suddenly staring at Ariana and Alisa in the doorway, not knowing which of them had spoken.

"How long have you been standing there?" Terry managed to find his voice.

"Long enough." Alisa moved toward them as Ariana remained in the doorway.

"I thought you were going to shower?" Roland was buying time for Jackie and Terry.

"We decided to come talk to Mom and Daddy first." Ariana finally moved onto the patio.

"What do you want to talk about, princess?" Terry tried unsuccessfully to make his voice void of tension.

"Daddy, we're not little girls anymore." Ariana moved to sit on the newly built bench between her mother and father. "We want straight talk about Catherine."

"Yes, Daddy." Alisa sat next to her. "The truth."

Roland tried again to stall, giving Terry time to think. "Do you want us to leave?"

Though Mercedes wanted to be smack-dab in the middle of the mix she added, "That may be a good idea. Give you all some privacy."

"Don't be ridiculous! You're as much a part of this family as we are," Jackie quickly asserted. "Besides, we need some objectivity here."

"Very well, we'll stay. But if at anytime you think we should leave, we won't be in the least offended."

Sighing, Terry stood and moved a few feet away from their piercing stares. He felt five pairs of eyes on his back, stabbing at his conscience. He turned, took a deep breath and began. "I don't know how much you've overheard or suspect about Catherine's visit. She's sick."

Ariana shot a glance at Jackie as the words *let the bitch die* played over in her head. "What's wrong with her?"

"More important, why do we care?" Alisa's question stepped on Ariana's sensibilities.

Terry looked from one twin to the other, then to the other three, hoping to draw strength from at least one of them. "As I said, she's sick . . ."—Terry paused again—"and her kidneys are failing."

"Is she dying?" Ariana asked softly.

"There are alternatives with kidney failure, but her best chance is with a kidney transplant."

"You're kidding me, right?" Alisa searched her father's face first and then the others' questioningly.

"What does that have to do with us?" Ariana met her father's eyes squarely.

Terry answered Alisa first. "No, this is all too serious."

As he turned to answer Ariana, Alisa stood. "She expects one of us to give her a kidney, doesn't she?"

"Yes."

"We won't do it." Alisa spoke in a tone that her father would never have accepted under different circumstances. "She has never done a thing for us. She gave us away when we were born and that was the upside."

The pounding in Ariana's chest rushed blood to her fingertips. "If she doesn't get a kidney, will she die?"

Jackie could no longer remain silent. "There's a treatment called dialysis she can have that'll keep her alive until she can find a donor kidney."

"What's a donor kidney?"

Roland answered this time. "That's when the doctors take a kidney from someone living or someone that's been killed in some sort of accident and put it in the sick person."

Alisa sat with her arms folded as Ariana continued asking questions. "How can one living person give another a kidney? Won't that person then die?"

"Oh, no!" Mercedes answered. "God has given us more duplicates than not—our lungs, kidneys, eyes, ears, arms and legs, just to name a few."

"If we don't need two, why do we have them?" Though Alisa tried to pretend she wasn't interested, her curiosity was getting the better of her.

"No one can answer that question. It's just God's perfect plan. Even some of the organs we have only one of we don't use the entire thing."

"Why can't she just get a kidney from a dead person or get that dialysis treatment?" Alisa asked with disgust. "Why is she coming to us?"

"It's a little more complicated than getting an organ from just anyone. Your blood relatives are your best chance, especially a sibling if the two people have the same two parents."

"Did she try to get a kidney from someone else before she came here?"

Jackie tapped the edge of the coffee mug with her fingertip. "We're not sure. She told us after you left last night. She wanted us to talk to you first. She's coming back to talk to you herself."

"We don't have anything to talk to her about." Alisa leapt to her feet. "When she looked at me outside the courtroom and told me she had never loved me, our talking days ended right then and there."

"Doesn't she have a brother?" Ariana asked.

"As far as I know she does. But I haven't heard anything about him in such a long time," Terry replied.

"Do you think she even went to anyone else or did she just come straight to us?"

"I don't know the answer to that question." Terry was beginning to feel weak in the knees. He knew now he should have contacted Catherine before he talked to the twins. He felt so ill prepared.

"None of that even matters. We're not doing it!"

"Why doesn't she want to do dialysis? What is it anyway?"

"Do you know what the kidneys do?" Jackie asked Ariana.

"I think I remember from biology. They filter the blood and make you go pee."

"That's exactly right. Well, when the kidneys fail, they don't do that any longer and you can't urinate. If all the impurities aren't removed from your blood, your body will poison itself. So what the dialysis machine does is take the place of your kidneys."

"Do they put the dialysis machine in your body?"

"No. You have to go into a clinic three times a week and they run your blood through the machine and it takes all the impurities out."

"They take all your blood out of your body and put it back?"

"In theory, yes. But what actually happens is one tube removes your blood while the other one replaces it. So you're never without enough blood to keep you alive. But it's a very difficult process and many people who are on dialysis can't work, because the whole thing makes them so weak and as soon as you get your strength back it's time to do it again," Mercedes explained.

The adults all looked at Mercedes with amazement as she explained. Roland finally asked, "Honey, how do you know all of this?"

"One of the men I work with has been on dialysis for years. He explained it to all of us a long time ago."

Alisa seemed to be bored with the explanation. "That's all very interesting. But as for Ariana and me, Catherine can just get hooked up to the machine three times a week or a day for that matter. Our kidneys will stay right where God put them."

"Stop answering for me!" Ariana's words and attitude assaulted everyone. "I want to hear more."

"What else do you want to know?"

"If she gets a kidney from someone, will she still have to do dialysis?"

"If the operation is a success and her body doesn't reject it, then, no, she won't have to continue on dialysis. She'll live a normal life, just like you and me."

"What does 'reject it' mean?"

"Even though they do all the tests to make sure that the person giving the kidney and the person receiving it are a perfect match, a person's body may still say, *oh, no, I don't like this thing in me.*"

"How many times does it not work?"

"I don't know."

Alisa stood, moving away from her sister. "Why are you asking all of these questions like you're even thinking about doing *anything* for her. I'd give a kidney to our neighbor's cat, Fluffy, before I'd give it to her."

Ariana looked away, remaining silent.

Terry spoke up for the first time since he'd broken the news. "Ariana?"

"Yes?"

"What's wrong?" Terry moved in front of her line of vision. "What are you thinking?"

"I don't know." Tears began to trickle onto her sweatshirt.

Jackie's loathing of Catherine magnified tenfold. Tears always surrounded anything to do with that woman. She moved from her seat, next to Ariana. She slipped her arms around Ariana's shoulders. She felt Ariana stiffen. "What don't you know, sweetie?"

Ariana pulled away from Jackie and turned to her. "I heard you say that Catherine should die. That's a terrible thing to say about anybody."

Shame enveloped Jackie as she recoiled in defense of her feelings. *I meant every word of it.* "You're right. I shouldn't have said that. I'm just very angry about all of this and to show up on your prom night was just too much."

"I agree with Mom." Alisa sat down again next to her sister. She examined the face of each adult before she continued. "Catherine doesn't even have the right to come here and ask if she can use our phone because Freddy Krueger is chasing her."

Roland couldn't suppress his desire to laugh. Terry shot him a disapproving glance. "What?" Roland raised his hands and shrugged. "You have to admit that was funny."

Mercedes playfully swatted her husband. "Behave."

Alisa ignored the adults and turned to Ariana. "I won't let you even think about giving that woman your kidney."

"You can't tell me what to do!" Ariana screamed. "She gave birth to us. She's our real mother."

Ariana's words grabbed something in Jackie's chest and began squeezing until she could no longer breathe.

CHAPTER TWENTY-EIGHT

*J*ackie couldn't force the baked chicken, mashed potatoes and green beans dinner over the lump in her throat. Ariana's words played repeatedly in her head like a favorite song sung off-key. She'd lived in constant fear of those very words since the day she'd signed the adoption papers. She'd always thought they'd come as a result of a fight between her and the girls because she'd refused to let them have their way for one reason or another.

The normal dinner chatter was blatantly absent. Michael, Michelle and T.J. didn't know exactly what was wrong, but they sensed the tension and were on their best behavior. Ariana's request to be excused had been denied. She hadn't uttered a word since she'd sat down. Alisa's dark mood and one-word answers aggravated Jackie, but she said nothing. After all, she wasn't their *real* mother.

"Did you all have fun at Aunt Veronica's last night?" Terry's words came so suddenly it made them all jump.

"It was really kewl," Michael answered. "We watched movies and ate popcorn, pizza, homemade chocolate chip cookies. Da bomb."

"Food always makes you happy, doesn't it, son?" Terry teased.

With a blank expression Michael simply said, "Yeah."

"What movies did you watch?" Jackie needed to snap out of her slump.

"Of course, Michael wanted to see car chases and stuff blowing up. But Auntie Vee said no way. We watched *Shark Tale, Shrek* and *Shrek 2*. I fell asleep before *Shrek 2* was over."

T.J. took a big bite of chicken and said with his mouth full, "Then today she took us to Six Flags."

"Oh really?" Jackie was genuinely surprised. She hadn't asked *her* three children anything about their time away. "That must have been a lot of fun."

"Yeah, it was aiight. She let Michelle and me go off by ourselves and she took T.J., Marshall and Maxwell with her. We caught up with some friends from school."

"Sounds like you had a really good time," Terry added, all the while stealing glances at Jackie.

"So how was your big night?" Michelle stared across the table at Ariana and Alisa. "I want to know everything!"

"We had fun," Alisa answered. "The party was off the chain. We stayed up all night and went to breakfast this morning."

"Now tell the truth," Terry began. "You didn't really stay up all night. When I came downstairs this morning you were both catching slobber."

Ariana laid her fork next to her still-full plate and looked from one parent to the other as she heard the words "*let the bitch die*" play again in her head.

"Well, maybe we did sleep for a little while. But the party

was *all that*. I know everyone that didn't come will be sorry when they hear how great everything turned out." Alisa beamed with pride. "Isn't that right, Ari?"

"Yeah."

"What's up with you?" Michael chided Ariana. "You look like your mama died or something."

Ariana stood so quickly she knocked over her iced tea and T.J.'s milk. "What do you know about anything anyway?" With that she ran from the room, crying.

Michael looked, perplexed, first to Terry and then Jackie. "What'd I do?"

Terry and Jackie mopped up the spills with their napkins as Jackie charged, "Get me some paper towels, quick!"

"You get this up and I'll go talk to her." Terry stroked Jackie's arm gently.

"No, let me. She and I need to get this out in the open anyway." Jackie's eyes betrayed her manufactured smile.

Jackie walked swiftly toward the staircase while she still had the nerve to confront Ariana. She rehearsed in her head ten times what she'd say when she knocked on the door. But nothing seemed right.

Preoccupied with her opening, she didn't realize she'd ascended the stairs until she was standing in front of Ariana's bedroom. She knocked softly.

"Who is it?"

"It's your m—" The word "mother" was trapped deep inside her, refusing to be set free. "It's me, Jackie."

After a long hesitation, Ariana finally said, "Come in."

Jackie slowly opened the door and moved across the room to the bed and took a seat next to Ariana, where she lay facedown. "I think we need to talk."

"There's nothing to talk about."

"Oh, I think there is." Jackie took a deep breath before she continued. "First, I want to say how very sorry I am for what I said."

Ariana rose up on her elbows.

"I had no right to say such a hateful ugly thing about Catherine." Jackie looked down at her red fingernails. "I was very angry at her for coming here and telling us that she was going to demand that you be tested to see if you and your sister are compatible donors."

Ariana turned over and sat up next to Jackie.

"I've loved you for so long that I can't remember when I didn't. In my mind, heart and soul you *are* my daughter. I feel my first responsibility is to protect you from anything or anyone who will cause you any type of pain. I saw Catherine as such a threat and I reacted like any mother protecting her young."

"I'm sorry, too." Though Jackie wasn't looking at Ariana, she knew she was crying. "I don't know why I said that Catherine is our real mother. I didn't really mean it. We love you, too."

"Now that we have that out of the way"—Jackie placed her arm around Ariana's shoulders and used her free hand to wipe the tears from her cheeks—"let's talk about what it is that has you feeling so sad."

"I don't know. From the minute I heard she was coming to visit, I've had this funny feeling in the pit of my stomach. Kinda like when you hit a bump in the road or you're on a roller coaster."

"Do you know what causes you to feel like that?"

Ariana shook her head.

"You're weightless for a split second."

"Really?"

"Yep. I learned that when I did an article on the new commercial space expeditions. So what Catherine has done is pull the ground out from under you, so to speak, and you're just floating around."

"I hate this feeling." Ariana was talking more freely.

Jackie thought her next comment through several times before she spoke. "You know, I want to tell you that I understand what you're feeling about Catherine. But the truth is, my mother was a wonderful woman who would have died rather than see me hurt for even a second. If you're mad at me, I won't say I understand, but I will allow you the freedom to feel what you feel."

Ariana lay her head on Jackie's shoulder. "I'm not mad at you. I'm mad at myself for feeling this way. For thinking these thoughts."

Jackie moved Ariana's head from her shoulder so she could make eye contact with her. "Honey, you shouldn't feel angry for caring for the woman who gave you life. Love is an amazing thing. There's enough to go around for everybody to get a share."

"So you're not mad at me?"

Terribly hurt, but not angry. "Honey, of course not."

Ariana reached up to hug Jackie. "Oh, I'm so glad because I want to give Catherine my kidney."

$\mathcal{J}$ackie's eyelids fluttered as she tried to clear the fog Ariana's words had caused. She knew she needed to respond, but sadness, disappointment and astonishment had formed an alliance to hold her tongue hostage. "What did you say?"

Ariana looked down at her hands as they moved. Her voice was barely above a whisper. "I want to give Catherine one of my kidneys." She turned suddenly to look at Jackie. "Please don't be mad. I don't know why I want to do it, I just know it's what I'm supposed to do."

What do you mean, you're supposed to do? I'd feel less amazed if you wanted to do this for a stranger. "Honey, this is your decision and yours alone. No one can tell you what to do in this situation." Jackie fought back tears. Fear gripped her soul. What if something went wrong? This was too risky—she couldn't allow it. She wouldn't allow it!

"You are the best, Mom." Ariana reached for her and hugged her.

There was that word: "*Mom*." Jackie held Ariana close. Rocking back and forth slightly, she didn't know what to feel, but she knew one thing for certain: this wasn't about her. This was about her *daughter* and the turmoil she must be in making this decision. The only thing left to do was support her.

Jackie pulled back slightly and Ariana sat up. Jackie gently brushed Ariana's hair from her tearstained face, staring into her eyes. Despite her feelings, in her best motherly tone she began, "Well, Miss Ariana Winston, if you're going to be donating a kidney, there's a lot of things we have to do first." With her fingertip Jackie wiped away Ariana's tears. "First we have to have a family meeting and tell the others. Then your dad will call Catherine and tell her your decision." Pretending to go along with this foolishness would buy her the time she needed to convince Ariana this was a very bad idea on so many levels.

"Do you think she'll be happy?"

The ungrateful witch will probably not even say thank you. Jackie chose her words carefully. "Honey, how could she not be appreciative. This is a tremendous sacrifice."

Perplexed Ariana asked, "What do you mean?"

"Well, I don't know a whole lot about the process but it will take several weeks of your summer for you to recover. But before that you'll have to be tested, and once that happens I'm sure you'll have to see a counselor."

Ariana reacted like she had been slapped. "Why would I need to see a counselor?"

"I'm not sure that you will, but something this major normally comes with therapy attached. And you're sure you want to do this?"

"I'm sure."

Chile, chile, chile. Catherine is so undeserving of any love from you. "Then we need to call a meeting."

The heaviness in her heart seemed to weigh down her feet as Jackie left Ariana's room. She tried to rush to where she'd left the rest of her family, but her body betrayed her.

As she entered the kitchen where everyone was pitching in to clean up and put away the leftovers, the group paused as though it were a freeze-frame of her life. She couldn't tell how much time had passed before Terry spoke. "Hey, baby, what happened up there? You were gone awhile."

Trying to force a smile, Jackie looked at each of their inquiring faces and then said, "We need to have a family meeting right away. Ariana is going to wash her face and be down in a minute."

Terry moved closer to Jackie. He lowered his voice and asked, "What's going on?"

Jackie turned and walked toward the formal dining room with Terry in tow. When she was out of earshot of the children, she turned to face Terry. "Ariana wants to do it."

Terry's mind raced as he contemplated what the possibilities of *it* were. With horror, he blurted. "With who?"

Jackie stared at him, trying to comprehend what he meant.

"It's that wormy Vincent, isn't it?" Sweat beads were beginning to form on the bridge of his nose. "I'll kill him."

"What the hell are you talking about? Vincent?"

"You said she wants to do *it*," Terry began, clueless. "She wants to have sex?"

Laughing despite what she was feeling, Jackie stared at her husband. "You know, for someone as intelligent as you are, you can come up with some of the most bizarrely ridiculous statements."

"Please tell me what *you're* trying to say."

"First of all, she's eighteen and she doesn't need anyone's permission to have sex, though I doubt she'd ask for it even if she wasn't. Second, and more to the point, the *it* is donate her kidney."

Somewhere in the recesses of her mind Jackie gathered satisfaction from the bewildered and perplexed look on Terry's face. She now realized her reaction wasn't so far off the mark. "What?" he said.

"You heard me."

"I couldn't have." Terry began pacing. "I know you didn't just say Ariana wants to give Catherine a kidney."

"I did indeed."

"Oh my God." Terry stopped pacing to look at Jackie. "I won't have it."

Relieved by Terry's obvious change of heart on the matter, Jackie pressed on. "What happened to the Christian thing to do?"

"That was when I thought there was no way in hell either one of them would agree to do it."

"Don't you think that's a little hypocritical, especially with the guilt trip you laid on me." Jackie's dander was rising.

"I'm sure that it is. But I was secure in knowing that no matter how much I tried to convince them they needed to entertain the possibility, they'd both say no."

"Well, you were wrong. And it didn't even take any convincing. Ariana made up her mind all on her own with very little information."

"Of the two, I surely wouldn't have guessed that Ari would be the one to volunteer. When the girls were younger, Ariana wouldn't even take Catherine's phone calls. I remember that day after Christmas when Catherine took them shopping and

Ariana bolted from the car when they returned. I just don't know what to make of any of this.

"Oh my God, what'll we do now?" Terry asked more to himself than Jackie.

"What will you do about what?" Ariana startled them both with her question.

Terry's heart caught in his throat as he stared into his daughter's eyes. How much had she heard? "I understand we're going to have a family meeting to discuss the possibility of you donating a kidney to Catherine."

Ariana let her eyes focus on the beautiful floral arrangement in the foyer as she whispered. "It's what I want to do, Daddy."

"That's what your mother tells me." Terry forced Ariana to look at him. "I'm just a little surprised is all."

"To tell the truth"—Ariana looked from Terry to Jackie and then back at her father—"me too."

"I don't understand."

Jackie pulled out a chair from the dining room table and took a seat. "I think we should sit down and talk about this. And get the others in here."

"Family meeting," Terry yelled to the crew in the kitchen.

Not needing a lot of encouragement to abandon the cleanup chores, the four trotted off in the direction of their father's voice.

"I think you should sit at the head of the table, Ariana." Jackie patted the seat between her and Terry. "We've called this meeting to make an announcement."

Jackie and Terry brought the children up to date with what had happened in their meeting with Catherine. Terry explained what it meant for a person to have kidney failure and what it meant to be a living organ donor.

"So Miss Catherine wants to take a kidney out of Ariana and Alisa so she won't be sick anymore?" Michelle asked.

"She only needs one, so it would be one or the other, not both."

Michael showed genuine concern, which was an interesting turn of events, since he only paid attention at family meetings when he was in the hot seat. "So how do you decide which one does it?"

Jackie glanced around the table before she spoke. "Well, that's what we're here to discuss."

"There's nothing to discuss as far as I'm concerned." Alisa was openly hostile. "I say if Catherine waits for me to give her a glass of water she'd die of thirst."

"Don't say that!" Ariana yelled.

"Girls, please. You know the rules: no fighting at a family meeting," Jackie refereed.

Fire burned in Ariana's eyes. "Why does everyone think Catherine should die?"

Terry reached out and started to rub her arm to comfort her. "Honey, no one thinks she should die."

"Then why do they"—Ariana pointed to Alisa and then Jackie—"keep saying it?"

Trying to get things back on track Terry said, "Okay, let's make this clear. It's not our first choice to have Catherine come to us with her problem, but she has, so we're going to deal with it the same as we have always dealt with a problem. We're going to discuss it and then work through it."

"Your father's right. We're here to put all of our feelings and concerns on the table. And, Ariana, we promise to keep an open mind. We only want what's best for you."

"What about what's best for Catherine?"

Jackie opened her mouth to speak but thought it better to

hold her tongue. Terry saw her hesitation and spoke up. "As much as Catherine may need this kidney, she isn't our first priority. If she doesn't get the kidney, she won't die. She'll get a treatment called dialysis and she can lead a reasonably normal life."

"So if she gets this treatment, no one will have to give her a kidney?" Michelle asked.

Alisa crossed her arms and turned her body slightly away from her parents. "Well, that's what she should do."

Silently agreeing but visually ignoring Alisa, Jackie answered Michelle's question. "In a way that's true. However, in order to get dialysis Catherine would have to go to a hospital three times a week for several hours each time and they would hook her up to a machine that would clean her blood."

"But if she has the operation because your sister gives her a kidney, other than taking medicine for the rest of her life and maintaining good habits, she'll be just fine," Terry added.

Alisa turned her body back. Sitting up straight, she asked, "So if she doesn't get a kidney from one of us couldn't she get one anyway? I hear about—"

"Why should she have to go somewhere else when we have four perfectly good ones?" Ariana interrupted.

Alisa rolled her eyes and turned to talk to her father. "People all the time get kidneys from strangers."

"That's a very real possibility, but it would take time. She'd be put on what's called a "donor waiting list." Minorities have a much longer wait."

Michelle looked curiously at her father. "Why?"

"Why what?"

"Do black people have to wait longer?"

"There are a lot of factors in donor-recipient compatibility. We as a race are slow to register with the donor agencies, so there are fewer organs available from us, which translates into a longer wait." Terry rubbed his fingers up and down his arm, indicating African Americans.

"Oh, let me see . . ." Alisa pretended to calculate on her fingers. "We've waited for her for more than eighteen years. Think she'd have to wait that long?"

The group stared at Alisa, at a loss for words.

"I didn't think so."

"Okay, so she wasn't around when we were growing up and nobody was madder about that than me." Ariana was talking to Alisa as though they were the only two in the room. "But now things are different. We're grown-up and she needs *us*."

"Do you hear yourself? When we needed her, she wasn't around, but because she needs us we're supposed to just forgive everything and run to her." Alisa's voice seemed to rise with each syllable. "I don't think so!"

Sensing the meeting was getting out of control, Jackie began to speak softly so Alisa and Ariana would have to pay close attention to hear. "Let's look at this logically. If we can, let's take the emotion out it for a minute."

"And how do you propose we do that, my ole great and wise one?" Terry replaced tension with sarcasm.

"Let's look at the facts. No one will dispute that Catherine was an absentee parent. Now you're eighteen, grown if you will."

Terry cleared his throat and she continued. "She comes back and demands that one of you give her a kidney. She makes no apologies for anything she's done nor does she ask what we, your parents, think about any of this.

"While you don't need our permission, it would be wonderful to have our blessing. It would make all this so much easier on everyone." Jackie took a breath.

"Can we get to the point?" Ariana asked impatiently. "Are you going to let me do this or not?"

"I don't get it," Alisa fumed.

"What is it that you want to do?" Jackie asked.

Ariana looked at the table and then between her parents. She fingered the lace runner that adorned the cherrywood high-gloss table, contemplating her answer. "The truth is, I don't know. Maybe . . ." She began crying and T.J. got up from his seat and ran to hug her.

"Don't cry, Ari. I will give her my kidney," T.J. said, taking all the others by surprise.

Ariana wiped her tears and began laughing as she reached down to hug her baby brother. "Thank you, T.J., but I don't think you can."

"I don't want to see you sad."

Jackie felt the overwhelming urge to pick up T.J. and hold him close. What a wondrous gift was the innocence of a child. "Okay, rather than us *discuss* why we think you shouldn't do this thing, let's talk about what it'll take of and from you."

All eyes were on Jackie as she pretended to be the guruette of organ donation. "The first thing that'll happen is a series of tests to find out if you even qualify as a donor. You're very healthy, so the only issue would be if you are compatible."

"What does that mean?" Michael asked.

"Well, we're all made up a little differently. Who your parents are has everything to do with who you become. Your parents' blood types combine to make your blood type and from that your tissue type."

"Is that why it's easier for Miss Catherine to get a kidney from Ari and 'Lisa because she's their real mother?" Without the slightest malicious intent, Michael had cut his mother to the quick.

Seeing Jackie flinch, Terry answered, "Yes, son, Catherine and I are the two people who make up the blood and tissue in Ariana and Alisa."

Jackie was back on solid ground as she continued. "Now we have no idea if the twins are a blend of their father and mother or if one's blood type is more prevalent than the other. That's why we have to do the testing. So although Catherine is their *birth* mother, that's no guarantee either one of the twins is compatible."

"This all so confusing," Michael said.

Michelle exhaled loudly before she said, "You can say that again."

"So what you're saying is that even if I want to give her a kidney I might not be able to?" Ariana seemed surprised.

"That's right, princess." Terry touched her arm reassuringly.

Ariana turned to Alisa with urgency. "Then you'll have to do it, 'Lisa. You just have to!"

"But you don't understand, Ari. If you're not compatible, neither is Alisa. You're identical twins. You have the same DNA, which means your blood and tissue are exactly the same."

Exasperated Ariana put her head in her hands. Jackie watched her and felt her heart tighten. Seeing *her* daughter wrestle with such a life-altering decision tore her up inside. The biggest decision Ariana should have to make is what to wear on her next date. Incompatibility would make life so much simpler for the Winston family.

CHAPTER THIRTY

*T*he cool evening breeze off the ocean gave Catherine a chill. She was beginning to regret her decision to dine alfresco. She picked at the giant lobster before her as she contemplated how she'd break the news to Ariana and Alisa.

"You seem to be in a place far, far away." Alex stared at her as he sipped club soda.

"I have a lot of plans that need my immediate attention and I was mentally working through a few things. As usual, you've chosen the perfect spot. It's very beautiful here."

"Only the best for you, my queen." Alex stroked her arm.

Catherine only stared.

"I'm glad you decided to come." Alex touched her hand gently. "Last night was wonderful with the sound of the waves crashing just outside our window."

Catherine would have shuddered if she thought it would have gone unnoticed. Though only a little time had passed since Alex had made his fatal confession, Catherine had learned to loathe him.

The ring of her cell phone startled her as she thought of ways to get back to Dallas without him.

"This is Catherine Hawkins speaking."

"Hello, Catherine. This is Terry."

An authentic smile made its way across her face. "Well, I must say I'm pleasantly surprised to hear from you today. I hope you're calling with some good news."

"It's news." Terry's tone was flat. "How about a meeting later this evening, let's say in about an hour."

"Today isn't good." Catherine continued to pick at the lobster. "I've jetted off to Maine and I'm rather enjoying myself."

Exasperated, Terry blew air into the receiver. "I thought this was so urgent."

"Oh, but it is. How's tomorrow morning?"

"It's no good. We'll be at church."

Catherine winked at Alex as she said, "Surely your God will forgive you this one time."

Feeling he was totally out of control with the entire situation, he paused before he emphatically said, "No, Catherine, God won't be mad, but, guess what?" Terry didn't wait for an answer. "I say no. If it's not tonight, then it will have to be tomorrow sometime after we're done with church."

"I really need to be back in L.A. before tomorrow night, Terrance."

"Then I guess we'll see you on your next trip. Perhaps you can call them on the phone to see what they have to say about your *situation*."

"Have you told them why I want to meet with them?"

"Yes, we've told them all that we know to tell."

"And?"

"And what?"

Catherine would have been amused under other circumstances by Terry's display of tenacity. "You know full well what I'm asking, Terrance. Are they interested in helping me or not?"

Momentarily, Terry felt a pang of sympathy for her. She was alone in the world with nothing but her money. She didn't even know the proper way to ask for help. "Catherine, will we see you tomorrow or not?"

"Very well, tomorrow it is."

"Good. We'll see you at five." Terry never said good-bye. The next sound she heard was a click, followed by a hollow silence.

"We need to be back in Dallas tomorrow afternoon for a meeting." Catherine stared at the moon's reflection on the water.

"As you wish." Alex reached for her hand to kiss it. "Does this mean we're going to spend another love-filled night here?"

Catherine remained quiet as the mist-filled breeze off the Atlantic kissed her cheeks. She was lost in her thoughts of what news Terry had for her. The twins must have come to some sort of agreement. But when she'd asked if it was good news Terry hadn't indicated one way or the other. She now regretted leaving Dallas. Alex's lips were moving, but there were no words she could decipher.

THE WINSTON HOUSE WAS SUBDUED. The mood was somber, and there was very little conversation. Jackie rubbed the center of Terry's back to help relieve the tension between his shoulders.

"She never ceases to amaze me," Terry finally said as he sat back on the sofa. "Even when she really needs something she's arrogant."

"I think it was Einstein who said insanity is when you keep doing the same thing, expecting a different result."

"You know, Roland said those very words to me." Terry looked at her, astonished. "I guess you're both right. Why would I think *anything* has changed?"

"Precisely," Veronica added as she walked into the family room with a tray of beverages.

"You know, desperate times call for desperate measures." Mercedes followed her with slices of decadent chocolate cake. "We need to eat."

"A brotha like me could use a drink," Roland said as he returned from the bathroom.

"Man, the bar and wine cellar haven't moved." Terry did his best to make a joke. "Help yourself."

"You know what I thought about as I was slicing cake?" Mercedes began chuckling.

"Taking Catherine out into the desert in large trash bags?" Veronica was blowing on a hot cup of chai tea.

Laughing out loud Mercedes had trouble responding. "Not exactly. Though that thought has merit."

"Yeah it does!" Jackie leaned forward to pick up a mug of coffee.

"Remember that Christmas morning Catherine showed up?"

"Remember?" Jackie shouted. "I wanted to kill her with my bare hands when she insulted Momma C."

"I thought I was going to have to physically restrain Cedes." Roland returned to the sofa, a shot glass filled to the rim with a brown liquid in hand. "She was going to give Catherine the beat down."

"I couldn't believe how she insulted *everyone*," Veronica

said with a faraway look in her eyes. "Those were some pretty dark days for me. My drinking was so out of control."

"Yeah and we didn't know how to help you," Terry said sadly. "Now look at you. Working for CNN, got a good man."

"Speaking of good men, where is Wendell?" Mercedes inquired.

"He's in Austin on a case." There was nothing Veronica could do to stop from smiling.

"When are y'all going to take the plunge?" Jackie teased. "Y'all been serious for more than five years. You got a place that you're never in when he's in town. You're practically living together already."

"We've talked about it. But he sees so much on his job that he's just plain scared." Veronica looked a little disappointed.

"I guess I could see the brotha's point," Roland added. "You've been going out almost since you met him when he worked on this custody case, haven't you?"

"We dated on and off back then, but it got serious when I got my life on track. He's a really good guy, but I make sure he doesn't have any cases that require his services the way Catherine did."

They all laughed. Terry said between laughter, "Yeah, he did work real hard with Catherine."

"Honey, do you remember that first New Years' Eve party Jackie tricked me into?" Mercedes teased. "Your date was so wasted."

"Oh don't remind me!" Roland hid his face behind his hand. "Talk about some dark days. My life was a mess before you came along and straightened me out."

Mercedes smiled warmly. At moments like these she wondered where her insecurities ever came from. Trying to suppress the emotions she felt rising, she joked, "Boy, you were some work, believe me!"

"I wish Momma was here to pray over all of this," Jackie said sadly. "There was nothing she couldn't pray away."

"I know that's right," Roland said. "I sure do miss her in the kitchen."

"If you were talking about anyone else, I'd be insulted, but you're so right. No one could make a pot sing like Miss Clara Rogers."

"You know she'd be mighty disappointed in us sitting around, waiting for her to pray for this Catherine situation," Terry said as he set his mug on the coffee table. "Since all our hearts are already bonded, the only thing left for us to do is join hands and pray ourselves."

"Let me lead." With those words the five formed a circle of family unity against the enemy as Veronica went before God in earnest for guidance on how to weather the latest hurricane Catherine.

CHAPTER THIRTY-ONE

*A*riana sat stoically in the family room, wringing her hands, watching the clock. The digital display on the cable box read 4:48. She hadn't slept all night. She couldn't focus in church. Her friends had been calling all afternoon chattering endlessly about prom night and the after party. She'd had almost nothing to say. She counted the hours and now minutes until Catherine would come to visit again and she could tell her the news that was for sure going to make her realize she'd made a mistake and that she truly did love her children.

"Where's your sister?" Terry startled her. "Oh, baby, I'm sorry." He sat next to her, putting his arm around her shoulders. "You're trembling."

Tears welled, but she refused to yield. "She's in her room. She said she's not coming to the meeting."

"We'll just see about that." Terry moved quickly out of the family room, across the foyer and up the stairs to Alisa's room.

Fighting his instinct to just barge in, he stopped and knocked softly.

"Come in."

Alisa sat at her desk with a textbook open in her lap, her fingers perched on the keyboard. "Hey, Daddy."

"What's this I hear about you not coming down to talk with Catherine?" Terry moved and sat on the bench at the foot of her bed.

"There's no reason for me to be there."

"What about to support your sister?"

Alisa turned quickly, and her textbook fell to the floor. "Daddy, I *don't* support her. She's setting herself up for heartbreak."

"Why do you say that?"

"Catherine is going to get what she needs from Ariana, and then she'll never hear from her again. Ariana is only doing this to get Catherine to love us . . . I mean her."

Terry looked straight ahead so that Alisa couldn't read in his eyes that in his heart he knew the same. "Do you really think that's why Ari is doing this?"

"I know that's the reason."

Terry did a mental search for a reasonable response. Before he could speak, Alisa continued. "See, Daddy, even you can't say anything. Catherine is a mean, selfish woman and I want nothing at all to do with her."

"I understand, princess." He lost his resolve as he watched the turmoil in Alisa's eyes. "I really want you to come down and support your sister."

"I can't do that."

"Can't or won't?"

"Both," she said quietly as tears began a steady stream. "I

can't support her because I don't think she should do it. And if I'm there it would be a lie."

Once again, Terry was amazed at his daughter's maturity. He'd taught them good values and independent thinking. He never realized they'd use it against him. "Honey, I just want you to come down and sit with your sister as she talks to Catherine. You don't have to say a word. Your mother and I will be there, and you can sit on the couch with us. I want you to do this to show your sister that while you might not agree with what she's doing, you do love her."

Suddenly Alisa put the book on the desk and leapt into her dad's arms as she began to wail. Terry held her silently as agony poured from her soul. The sound of the doorbell chime brought the tears to an immediate halt as Terry's firstborn sat up, saying, "I can't let Ariana face Catherine alone." Alisa wiped her eyes as she continued. "Let's go."

What just happened here? Terry was bewildered by the swing of the emotional pendulum, but then he realized—she really *is* a woman. He dutifully followed Alisa out of the room and down the hall, where she stood watching the front door as Jackie opened it.

Catherine stared at Jackie, waiting.

"Catherine, please come in." Jackie moved to the side.

"Good . . ." Catherine's eyes were drawn upward as she felt Alisa's stare. "Good evening." She quickly looked away and back to Jackie. "As you know, I'm here to meet with my— with Ariana and Alisa."

Not bothering with pleasantries, Jackie simply said, "Right this way."

Catherine stole a quick glance at Terry and Alisa again before she followed Jackie to the family room where Ariana waited. Alisa and Terry descended the stairs and caught up with them in the archway leading to the family room. The four entered the family room together in silence.

Alisa joined her sister on the center of the couch, while their parents sat at the ends. Catherine sat in the overstuffed chair. Only the sound of breathing could be heard until the five soft gongs of the grandfather clock pierced the air.

Catherine spoke first. "Well, girls, your father tells me that you've got some news for me."

Does an iceberg sit where her heart should be? No hi, girls, how are you, girls? How was the prom, girls? Not even a kiss my— Terry's voice interrupted Jackie's mental tirade.

"Catherine, the least you could do is say hello."

"Perhaps you're right." Catherine *almost* seemed embarrassed. "As you can well imagine, I'm very nervous about all of this. How is everyone?"

"Hi," Alisa and Ariana said together as they reached out for the other's hand.

"Catherine, Jackie and I have spoken to the girls and told them of *your* problem." Terry hesitated, looking at Ariana and Alisa before he continued. "We've explained what's wrong with you and how they may help. As you know, I can't force them to do anything one way or the other."

Catherine's heart caught in her throat. *Oh my God, these little selfish brats aren't going to do it!* She searched their faces in hope of seeing whom she could convince to give her what she needed.

Alisa stared at her dead-on with daggers for eyes. Ariana's gaze was fixed on her hands. Ariana's mind wasn't made up.

"What are you saying, Terrance?" Catherine sat on the edge of the cushion. "I know you and that wife of yours have talked them out of helping me. You can't let the past be just that."

"Catherine—" Terry tried to interrupt her.

"Don't you see I'm talking?" Catherine stood. "I can't believe you'd be so selfish to listen to the poison your father has fed you against me. I did what I thought was best for you."

Alisa leapt to her feet and stood nose to nose with Catherine. "Look, you self-centered witch, against everyone's better judgment my sister is going to give you her kidney." Alisa was so close to Catherine's face she could smell her breath. "Do you remember that day outside the courtroom?"

Catherine's face began to twitch under her right eye as she looked to Terry for help. Terry and Jackie sat stone-faced.

"Do you?" Alisa yelled this time.

"I don't know what you're talking about."

"Sure you don't." Alisa almost laughed. "Let me remind you of something, Miss Catherine: you said you'd never loved us. Guess what? We don't love you either. In fact, if you were on fire, I'd use gasoline to put you out. Divine restitution is a bitch, isn't it? What goes around—"

"That's enough, Alisa!" Terry stood, inwardly smirking, and pulled Alisa back to the sofa.

Jackie silently cheered. Catherine had trouble finding her footing as she moved back to the chair. For the first time since she'd abandoned Ariana and Alisa at the hospital, she felt the gravity of her actions. Her mother had been right all along.

The tension mounted in the room with every passing second. Terry finally found his voice. "Ariana, do you have anything to say?"

Ariana sat with her head down, while Alisa averted her eyes. Ariana began to speak slowly. "Catherine, you are wrong about our dad. He has never said one word against you to us. What we know about you we've discovered all on our own."

Alisa grabbed her hand.

"But you know what our dad did teach us?" Ariana continued, now making eye contact with Catherine. "That God loves us and we are required to do the same for our brothers and sisters." After a beat she said, "or even you."

Terry had never felt prouder of his daughter than he did at that moment.

"So, yes, I'm going to give you my kidney, but I would do it for anyone I thought I could help. It just happens to be the woman that gave birth to us."

as the car pulled in front of the steps of the plane, Catherine took a deep breath. This meeting had to go smoothly to have her plans on track before she had surgery. With the co-operation of the five heads of her foreign divisions, she knew her directives would be carried out flawlessly. Jonathan opened her door, and she said, "Showtime."

"We're ready when you are, ma'am." Franklin, yet another new flight crew member, extended his hand to assist her from the backseat of the Maybach. Unbeknownst to Her Royal Bitchness, once a crew member served on one of her flights, he or she requested to never be assigned again. "And how are you today?"

Catherine paused to take in all that was Franklin. His strong build made her think of a Mandingo warrior, though he barely stood six feet tall. His hands were strong enough to make her feel secure and gentle enough to make her feel pampered. His rich chocolate skin was as smooth as hot fudge. As she found her voice, Catherine finally responded, "The day seems to be brightening even as it wears on." She smiled suggestively.

If Catherine didn't know better, she would have thought this Olympic godlike creature blushed at her words. "Very good, ma'am." Franklin's perfect diction—a voice as rich in tone as King Tutankhamen was in gold—created a melodic aura around her. "The others are comfortably seated and await your arrival."

Never taking her eyes away from Franklin's, Catherine stepped onto the stairs leading to her jet. "Why have you never been the attendant on one of my flights before?"

Smiling broadly, Franklin simply replied, "Very unlucky, I'd say."

Catherine turned and ascended two steps, stopped and stared straight ahead at the Hawkins International logo before she turned and said, "We must make sure that you are *always* available for me."

"Indeed we must." Franklin flashed a knowing smile.

Catherine continued up the stairs and onto the plane, her steps a little lighter. The meeting with Ariana and Alisa, though rocky, had yielded her the desired result. She would get a kidney. She brushed past Alex as he'd stood, watching the exchange between her and Franklin. As she reached the entrance to her private area she turned, giving Alex a smile he interpreted as genuine.

"We're just about ready, Ms. Hawkins." He glanced down at the handsome timepiece Catherine had given him when he came to work for her. "We've been cleared for takeoff in twenty-two minutes."

Catherine stared through him with eyes so cold she'd shed ice chips for tears. "Then perhaps you should take your position in the cockpit, Captain Morehead." She turned and walked to where the division heads were gathered with Franklin close on her heels.

Catherine stopped in the midst of some of the most powerful businessmen in the world, and they all worked for her. Franklin wordlessly extended his hand for her briefcase. She decided that Franklin needed to see more of her body, and she removed her jacket, passing it to him. The silk blouse clung to her full breasts and was smoothly tucked into a snugly fitted skirt that hit her just above the knee. She smiled at him as their eyes met. "Thank you."

"At your service, madam."

Oh you can bet on that, Franklin. "Very good." Catherine reined in her hormones. There would be plenty of time for games with her prospective new playmate.

The five gentlemen had watched the exchange in silence, not quite sure what to make of it. Catherine turned to the group, smiling broadly. "Good day, gentlemen. It's so good of you to join me. I promise that by the time we reach Lihue you'll be as excited by the news I'm going to share with you as I am."

Jean-Michel Guillaume from the Paris office was the first to speak. "*Bonjour*, Mademoiselle Hawkins. *Le plaisir est en effet le mien.*" (Good day, Miss Hawkins. The pleasure is actually mine.)

Catherine studied his handsome face and asked herself again why this distinguished man had not had the pleasure of tasting her delectables. "Jean-Michel, *vous me flattez toujours.*" (Jean-Michel, you always flatter me.) Catherine extended her hand, which Jean-Michel quickly bent to kiss.

The Brazilian head, Jeyson Aruejo, extended his hand.

"*É sempre bom vê-lo*, senhorita Hawkins. *Eu sou excitado pelo prospeto que esta reunião traz.*" (It is always good to see you, Miss Hawkins. I'm excited by the prospect this meeting brings.)

Catherine shook his hand firmly before she responded, "*Você é sempre para a direita para baixo ao negócio*, Jeyson *e eu posso apreciar aquele.*" (You're always right down to business, Jeyson, and I can appreciate that.)

"*Buon giorno, Signorina* Hawkins. *Deve essere proprio una cosa urgente per essere tutti qui a questo riunione. Siamo tutti po' ansiosi di sapere che cosa ci può essere così importante.*" (Good day, Miss Hawkins. This must be quite urgent to bring us all here for this meeting. We're all a little anxious to know what could be so important.) Anthony Esposito had been difficult to work with since Catherine had won his father's company in a not-so-friendly poker game. He fought her on every hand, which under any other circumstances would have resulted in his immediate dismissal. However, Catherine was biding her time until she fully understood the operation and could find a replacement who was truly her ally.

"*Tutti in tempo giusto*, Tony." (All in good time, Tony.) Catherine infuriated Anthony when she called him Tony, and of course she did just that to spite him at every opportunity.

"*Buenas tardes*, Señorita Hawkins. *Es mi placer satisfacerle con hace frente otra vez para hacer frente. Usted es tan encantador como siempre.*" (Good afternoon, Miss Hawkins. It is my pleasure to meet with you again face-to-face. You are as lovely as ever.) Francisco Gómez extended his hand.

Grasping his hand firmly Catherine replied, "*Es siempre bueno verle, tambien*, Francisco." (It is always good to see you, as well, Francisco.)

Turning lastly to David Kleinhaus, Catherine extended

her hand and spoke first. *"Immer gut, Sie zu sehen, David."* (Always good to see you, David.) As much as Catherine could like and respect anyone, she felt that way about David. The German operation he headed had been the first foreign interest to come under her umbrella a little more than six years before. He was proficient, trustworthy and, most of all, loyal.

"Gleichfalls. Ihre neuen Pläne haben mich heugierig gemacht." (The same is true with me, I'm intrigued by your new plans). David said just as Franklin entered their circle, carrying a tray with six crystal champagne flutes.

Catherine lifted a glass from the tray and into the air. The men followed her lead. "Gentlemen, we have gathered here today to unfold a plan that is surely one that will make us all very rich and perhaps one of you second in command of the entire operation."

The men were frozen by her words, their glasses raised in midair. Which among them would be taking a bite from the carrot Catherine had dangled before them for months? The executive vice president would report directly to her and oversee all the operations of Hawkins International on three continents.

"This is Captain Morehead from the cockpit speaking. We have been cleared for takeoff. I am requesting you take your seats and fasten your seat belts securely. Franklin will give you a brief safety demonstration as we taxi. Our flight plan puts flying time at three hours and fifty-four minutes at an altitude of forty-six thousand feet. If there is anything we can do from the cockpit, please do not hesitate to ask."

Catherine settled comfortably into one of only two baby-soft leather seats and fastened the seat belt while she listened to Franklin as he explained the safety features of the luxury aircraft. She gazed out the window as she went over in her head the strategy for the meeting and following retreat to bring her newest cost-cutting plans into action without opposition.

She drained the champagne glass and set it on the table between the two seats. The swelling in her hands was very pronounced. She had to settle this business so she could focus on her next, very essential acquisition—a kidney.

CHAPTER THIRTY-THREE

*A*s the plane accelerated down Runway Seven Left, it lifted off the ground smoothly and soared toward the overcast skies. Within a matter of minutes, the sleek aircraft had penetrated the cloud cover and the sun shone brightly into the cabin. Catherine reclined her seat as her mind wandered back to Alisa's words. As hard as she tried to shake off the feelings, it was increasingly difficult.

She tried to switch off the voice in her head with thoughts of her empire. Satisfaction with her accomplishments caused her to smile from the inside out. She was anxious to get to the planning retreat. Jonah Staples, who had come with her when she left her employer, had proven to be invaluable. He found great pleasure in doing her bidding. He was trusted with her most *delicate* endeavors.

Jonah had an uncanny way of finding dirt in what appeared to be the most pristine operation. And, of course, Catherine used this information however it best suited her. When Jonah

had promised he could deposit one of France's largest per-
fume companies in her lap, she'd laughed at him. She'd never
believed the reports he'd produced, showing that Jean-Michel
had run the family business into the ground after his father
had had a stroke. The younger Guillaume had spent more
time skiing in the Alps and sunning on the French Riviera
than he did at his desk as the CEO. Catherine had purchased
the company for pennies on the dollar and promised Jean-
Michel that if he behaved she'd allow him to remain as the
company head, never making his father the wiser. In three
short years Jean-Michel had learned the true meaning of work
and become richer than he'd ever imagined possible.

Jeyson's attention had been torn away from the thriving
coffee business when his wife had been severely injured in
a car accident, which subsequently led to her prescription
drug—then street drug—addiction. He had all but given up
the business when Hawkins International made him an offer
that seemed too good to be true. Catherine had bought 51
percent of the business and landed him the exclusive contract
to supply one of Europe's largest chain of coffeehouses. She
had brought his beloved Maria to America to one of the best
drug rehabilitation centers in the world, and the Aruejo's were
living blissfully, ever so grateful to Catherine.

The Barcelona-based company had been the easiest of all
the acquisitions. The top-heavy plastics manufacturer had
grown faster than it could manage. Francisco was a brilliant
design engineer who'd left the running of his company to
those who were much more interested in their own financial
gain than the health of the company. He had welcomed her
offer to become his *partner*. She parlayed her 75 percent own-
ership into a minority female-owned business and became one
of the largest contractors for the VA hospitals.

Just prior to the bankruptcy-court order for the liquidation of the German glass company, Catherine had written checks to all David's creditors and become the owner of the small but potentially very successful manufacturer. David had been eternally grateful for her saving all that he had worked for and was her biggest ally.

She acquired the high-end food-preparation company as the result of a poker win in Monte Carlo. When Anthony's father didn't have the cash to ante for a sure-thing bet, he offered the family business to cover the two-and-half-million-dollar wager. As he laid his four of a kind on the table he smiled and sat back confidently. Catherine, in turn, had the look of defeat, just before she slowly laid down, one by one, the three, four, five, six and seven of diamonds—a girl's best friend. The senior Mr. Esposito quietly left the casino, returned to his hotel room and put one bullet through his temple. When Catherine appeared on the doorstep of the company with Mr. Esposito's marker, Anthony had fought her in court and lost. To say that Anthony hated Catherine from the moment she sashayed into his office and announced she was his new boss three days after his father's funeral would be a major understatement. His hostility had blossomed into downright hatred in the year and a half since that fateful event. After she learned all there was to know about his business she would find a way to be rid of him.

Catherine smiled to herself as she thought how each of the men would adopt her cost-cutting plan, despite what they felt it would do to the morale of their employees, many of whom were family. She'd appeal to their basic human instinct—greed. After she'd pit them one against the other to see who could cut cost the most over the next year, she'd make Jonah believe he would become the first executive vice president of international operations, only to pull the rug from under him and place Rahid in that position.

In the meantime, she'd be forced to trust Jonah to handle things while she recovered from surgery. Satisfaction once again washed over her as she thought how easy it had been to get Ariana to volunteer to give her a kidney. The feeling was short-lived as the scene with Alisa replayed in her mind. "*If you were on fire, I'd use gasoline to put you out*" gave her a chill, and she reached for the blanket on the seat next to her.

What had she done that was so terrible? Children live with their fathers all the time for whatever reason. Maybe she had been neglectful over the years. But where was Alisa's Christian spirit? Catherine shook her head, trying to rid herself of those thoughts. Ariana had come through, and that was all that mattered. Her future looked as bright as the sun that shone on her face as the airplane turned slightly.

The melancholy feelings vanished as the crisp, clear voice filled the cabin. "This is Captain Morehead again. We've just moved through twenty-five thousand feet on our way to our cruising altitude, and we're expecting a nice, smooth ride especially ordered by your hostess, Ms. Hawkins. In about five minutes it will be safe for you to move about the cabin as you wish. We're expecting to touch down on the beautiful island of Kauai at six sixteen local time. So sit back and relax. Be sure to let Franklin know if there is anything we can do from the cockpit to make your experience aboard the *Air Queen* more comfortable."

Catherine listened intently as if this were the first time she'd heard Alex give those very same instructions. What she listened for was the slightest indication in his voice that he suspected his impending fate. How dare that silly little man think she'd fall in love with him? She owned him. Franklin startled her as he quietly cleared his throat to capture her attention. "What can I do for you?" she snapped a little harder than she'd intended.

A momentary flicker of surprise flashed in Franklin's eyes before he smiled, saying, "May I freshen your champagne or is there something else you'd like me to get you?"

Franklin's innuendo wasn't lost on Catherine. She liked his ability to subtly entice her. Catherine let her eyes slowly travel the length of his perfectly toned body. His muscular legs teased the fabric of the expensive navy slacks. His white shirt had been custom tailored to fit every ripple. His perfectly manicured fingers were adorned with one ring, indicating pride in his alma mater. Yes, from his flawless, didn't-look-like-a-razor-ever-touched-it face to his spit-shined-to-a-mirror-finish shoes, this man looked delicious and was just begging to be bitten. "Let's start with some water and keep it coming until I've consumed forty-eight ounces."

"Very good, ma'am."

Franklin turned to fulfill her request just as Catherine asked. "Have you prepared the conference area?"

"Indeed." Franklin flashed a smile. "I was well trained in how to cater to your *every* need even before you know you need it."

Catherine caught herself before she smiled. "Very good."

As Franklin disappeared, Catherine unfastened her seat belt and attempted to get up but felt bound to the seat. Her condition worsened a little more each day. She decided to give it just another couple minutes and used the time to contact the cockpit. "Let me speak to the captain, Pazzo."

With a soft click the next sound Catherine heard was Alex's voice. "Yes, Ms. Hawkins."

Catherine smiled. Alex was putting on a really good show for the copilot. "Who's your queen?"

"Why, of course, Ms. Hawkins, that would be you."

Catherine decided that the dismissal of Alexander Morehead would come with mixed emotions but it had to be a total shock at a time when he had absolutely no access to her aircraft. Whatever oath a pilot takes wasn't worth the air that dissipated the words if he thought his boss no longer wanted to so much as look at him.

"That's what I like to hear. I have something quite hot and delicious for you when we get back to Los Angeles. Would you like that?" Catherine used her most suggestive tone.

"I thought Franklin would be handling that for you, Ms. Hawkins."

No, his ass isn't jealous. Catherine's guttural laugh could be heard throughout the cabin. "Only my Alex can handle certain duties." Catherine could feel Alex's smile through the cockpit door.

"Very good. I'll be sure to handle that as soon as we return to Los Angeles." Alex sounded more relaxed. Exactly how she wanted him to be.

Catherine smiled with satisfaction; men were such easy marks. She shook off the ill feelings, stood, squared her shoulders and moved to the middle area of the aircraft where the gentlemen sat. "Shall we?" Catherine pointed to the partition that separated the seating from the conference area.

As the group gathered around the table, well-appointed with posh and sinfully comfortable seats, Franklin appeared, carrying a tray with a variety of beverages and hors d'oeuvres. Catherine's water sat waiting in a crystal tumbler. He placed a different drink in front of each of the gentlemen, with the food in the middle, before he disappeared into the galley.

"Let's get right down to business. We have a lovely meal planned for our flight and I'd just like to get all of this over with so we can focus our full attention on Chef Pierre's magic."

The group made various sounds, indicating their agreement with their leader.

"As I've made each of you aware individually, I'm looking for ways to trim costs across the company. I've brought each of you here so that we can collectively devise a plan that will make each of your divisions more cost effective."

Jean-Michel opened with the first question. "Madam, how do you propose we do this? The Parisian operation is so—how do you say?—*lean* now. We cannot afford to lose another person."

"Jean-Michel, you sorely disappoint me." Catherine sipped her water as she thought. "You're a part of my think tank. Do you believe I'd pull you in from Paris to hear what we can't do?"

Jean-Michel flushed. He opened his mouth to respond but thought better of it.

"We provide some of the most exclusive restaurants in the world and are billing top euros in the marketplace." Anthony was visibly aggravated. "We have been profitable since before you . . ." Though his eyes bored into Catherine, he let the words linger in the air.

Not moved even slightly by his tone or implication Catherine stared deeply into his eyes as she asked, "Since I what, Mr. Esposito?"

Looking around the table at his colleagues for support, he found he had none. "Since you . . . *acquired* us."

Catherine suppressed her amusement at his attempt to flex his imaginary muscles. "And since I've *acquired you*, have your bonus checks not more than quadrupled?"

"I don't deny this, but we've laid off people who have been

with us for decades and replaced them with cheap labor from foreign lands."

"So you don't enjoy making more money?"

Anthony stole quick glances around the table. No one was looking at him. "Many of those who worked for Cucina del Mama have come to be like family. I have been to their homes, their children's weddings; I have seen their grandbabies christened. *Ora non ce la faccio più a guardarli in faccia*." (Now I can no longer face them.)

"Perhaps you can face them better being as poor as they are?"

Ever so humbled, Anthony remained silent. The tension around the table mounted. "I'm quite surprised to receive so much opposition to my making you very rich men. I've underestimated your desire to succeed. Perhaps I need to reevaluate my corporate structure and replace each of you with those whose thinking is more in line with my own."

"Señorita, I am sure I speak for the rest of us when I say we are very interested in your plans to cut costs and improve the bottom line." Francisco attempted damage control. "I think what Señor Esposito is trying to say is we do not want to further hurt employee morale."

Catherine raised her left eyebrow and turned her attention back to Anthony. "Is that what you're *trying* to say?"

Anthony only stared.

Catherine reached for her briefcase on the floor next to her chair. Pain shot up her left side, causing her to hesitate. She willed herself not to wince and slowly sat up straight.

As she'd turned back to the group her eyes met Anthony's.

CHAPTER THIRTY-FOUR

*C*atherine powered up the laptop positioned just to her right and began with a smile. "Gentlemen, when we touch down in Lihue you will be as excited by my plan as I am."

"You have intrigued us all for many weeks with this new plan and how it will make us all very rich." Francisco grinned.

"Well, your wait is over." Catherine touched a few keys on the laptop, and the projection came to life. "Hawkins International realized a profit in all its divisions last year due in no small part to your hard work. I trust that your bonus checks brought a smile to your faces and a trinket or two. What would you say if I told you that with this new plan your bonuses would double by the end of next year?"

They spoke among themselves, and Catherine could read by their expressions that all of the men were pleased with her news—except Anthony. "And what could we possibly do that would raise our profits enough to afford such generosity?" Anthony asked with no expression.

"I'm so glad you asked, Tony." Catherine sat a little taller in her chair. "Franklin, the lights please."

Catherine went through the presentation while the group sat quietly transfixed. At the end of the fifteen-minute pitch, Franklin turned up the lights and Catherine beamed with pride.

"Señorita Catherine, you cannot be serious." Francisco stared at her. "We have a responsibility to the communities in which we do business. Our government will not stand for this."

"You leave your government to me," Catherine retorted. "I have already started the wheels in motion to make this thing happen."

"Why would we agree to such lunacy? We would be taking food out of the mouths of our own children all to make ourselves richer?" Jean-Michel stood and moved away from the rest of the group.

"Please sit down, Monsieur Guillaume." Catherine moved uneasily in her seat. She had misjudged the men's response to her proposal. "Let me finish."

"I think we've heard enough." Anthony's words accosted her. "This is beyond reprehensible! We've brought in foreigners to work in our plants and now you want to take our customer service to India?"

"We have thirty employees in our customer service center," Jeyson fumed. "Most have been with us since they were children working in our bean fields. I cannot do this thing you ask."

David's eyes searched Catherine's face as he spoke. "Surely, this will not work. Do they even speak our languages?"

"David, do you honestly believe I haven't done my research?"

"Who will train these people?" Jean-Michel leaned over the table as he spoke.

"Jean-Michel, I won't take this insolence from you! Sit down now." Catherine regained her footing as she realigned her thinking. "Gentlemen, if you'll let me explain the implementation of my plan."

Anthony mumbled, *"Non vedo l'ora di sentirlo."* (I can't wait to hear this.)

"One way or another the customer-service operations for all the HI interests will be moved to one central location. My initial thought was to bring it here to the California headquarters. But with all of its taxes and insurance woes, California is not employer friendly.

"Many U.S. companies are outsourcing customer service to foreign entities, particularly India. The Indian government is most cooperative, as you may well imagine. So you see, these employees will be replaced no matter what. But now you will all make a very handsome profit from this brilliant move."

Each of the men stared at Catherine, lost in his own thoughts. "Jean-Michel asked who would train these new people." Jeyson spoke in a defeated tone.

"A team of trainers will converge on each of your operations for a month to learn all there is to know about the needs of your customers."

"Are you saying that the people who will be fired are the ones who will have to train their replacements?" David asked in disbelief.

"That's exactly what I'm saying."

"I can't do that!" Jean-Michel was on his feet again. "That is disrespect!"

"Can't or won't?" Catherine asked pointedly.

"I agree with him," David added.

"Gentlemen, you seem to have forgotten, this is *not* a democracy. I run this company. *I* own the controlling interest in each of your businesses. Which translates to I own *you*."

"*Jean-Michel, que penserait votre femme et vos trois petits s'ils savient que vous servez dans la caisse de la société?*" (Jean-Michel, what would your wife and three little ones think of you dipping your pen in the company inkwell?) Catherine's smug look infuriated Jean-Michel, but he fell into the chair with the force of man twice his weight.

"*E, Jeyson, que sua comunidade pensaria de pouco problema da sua esposa com drogas?*" (And, Jeyson, what would your community think of your wife's little problem with drugs?)

Jeyson retorted, "*Você não ousaria!*" (You wouldn't dare!)

"*Tente-me.*" (Try me.) Catherine smiled wickedly.

As Catherine drew aim and shot each of the men between the eyes, her pleasure increased with every passing word. "*Francisco, con su amante y dos niños exteriores a apoyar, pensaría usted se placería saber que he encontrado nuevas maneras de levantar su paga.*" (Francisco, with your mistress and two outside children to support, I would think you would be happy to know I've found new ways to raise your pay.)

Sheer horror clouded Francisco's jet-black eyes. "*¿Cómo usted sabía?*" (How did you know?)

"*Le hago mi negocio para saber que todos lo que necesito saber.*" (I make it my business to know all I need to know.) Catherine smirked.

"You do not own me!" Anthony challenged. "I will no longer stand by and let you humiliate me. I quit."

"Very well then. I accept your resignation effective immediately," Catherine continued calmly. "As you are no longer in the employ of Hawkins International I request that you gather your things and leave so that I may continue with my meeting."

"I will gladly leave your presence once we arrive on the island." Anthony stared at her coldly. "You sicken me."

"You've misunderstood me. I want you off my plane now!" Catherine yelled.

Looking perplexed, Anthony asked, "What do you mean now? We're over the Pacific somewhere up in the heavens."

"That is not my problem. Now leave!"

Anthony sat, staring from one of the men to the other—none of who would make eye contact with him. He had the sinking feeling he was in the pool alone with this barracuda.

"So now, *Tony*, are you beginning to see things my way?" Catherine sneered.

Anthony only glared.

"I can't hear you," Catherine taunted. "I didn't hear you say that you're sorry and you'd like to withdraw your resignation."

The others shuffled papers and otherwise moved nervously in their seats. Perspiration began to form on David's top lip. Jeyson's palms were damp.

With the conviction of a prisoner on death row at the eleventh hour Anthony spoke in a barely audible tone. "I was mistaken. I do not wish to resign."

With the intent of stripping Anthony of all dignity Catherine taunted, "I didn't hear an apology in there anywhere. And please speak up so that we can all hear you."

"I'm sorry that I was hasty in my decision. I do not wish to resign."

"Good. Now let's get back down to business."

CHAPTER THIRTY-FIVE

"*A*riana Winston," The nurse with the pleasant smile and warm eyes called into the doctor's waiting room.

"Here," Ariana answered nervously as she stood.

"Right this way. My name is Krystal and I'm Dr. Forsythe's nurse."

"Can my family come, too?"

"Of course."

The Winston clan followed Nurse Krystal into the inner sanctum of the medical facility dedicated to the treatment of renal diseases. Jackie held Terry's hand tightly as they followed their daughters.

Please have a seat in here." Krystal pointed to a long oak conference table with eight plush chairs. "Doctor will be right in to speak with you."

Before the door was completely closed Ariana began, "I'm scared, Daddy."

Terry moved to her with open arms and embraced her.

"Baby, we can turn around right this second and leave. There's no explanation necessary. You just don't want to do it."

"But I gave my word."

"Just call Catherine and say, '*Oh my bad, I changed my mind.*' " Alisa was openly hostile. "Unlike her at least you'd have the decency to call."

"No!" Ariana snapped. "I want to do it, but I'm just scared of everything they're going to be doing to me."

"Honey, there's nothing to be afraid of." Jackie tried to comfort her. "I'm certain the doctor will explain everything in as much detail as you need."

"I'm sure of that, too," Terry added. "And if we don't like this guy, we'll have Catherine find someone else."

"She isn't worth all this," Alisa said quietly.

I know that's correct! Jackie thought as she reached out for Alisa's hand. Alisa hugged her instead, and Jackie held her silently as she felt the gentle tremors. Dr. Forsythe startled the group as he entered.

"Good afternoon. I'm Bryan Forsythe." The short, aging man extended his hand first to Terry, then to Jackie and finally to the twins. "It looks like I'm seeing double in my old age."

Ariana tried to smile. Alisa teetered between indifference and defiance. Terry spoke. "I'm Terry Winston, the girls' father. This is Ariana"—he touched Ariana's shoulder—"and Alisa."

"It is indeed a pleasure to meet each of you, but most especially you, Miss Ariana. This is a very great and generous thing you're doing for Ms. Hawkins."

"What do I have to do now?" Ariana blurted.

Dr. Forsythe chuckled before he said, "You're very direct. I like that."

"Forgive my daughter. She's a little nervous." Jackie forced a smile.

"Understandably so. I'll get right down to brass tacks. The first thing we have to do is run some tests for compatibility. Once we get those results, we'll know if we should proceed with the donor workup or keep looking."

"But I'm her daughter. I have to be compatible, right?"

Taken aback momentarily, Dr. Forsythe looked from Terry to Jackie. "I'm sorry. I didn't know you were her daughter. I knew you were a relative, but there was no indication . . ."

"She simply gave birth to us. She"—Alisa pointed to Jackie—"is our mother."

"Well, this is even better. To answer your question Ariana, yes, your chances of compatibility are very good but not assured. What other questions may I answer for you?"

"If the blood test shows she's compatible, what happens next?" Jackie inquired.

"We will then start the tedious process of getting Ariana ready to be a donor. She'll be assigned a social worker and psychiatrist. We'll order X-rays and ultrasounds. Once all the testing is done, we'll schedule the surgery."

"My daughter will be starting college in late August." Concern furrowed Terry's brow. "Will all this be done and Ariana recovered in time?"

"The testing process is very quick for the recipient's sake. The new laparoscopic procedure for harvesting the kidney from a donor is much better than previous methods, which required major surgery. The donor is back to normal, daily activities in approximately two weeks."

"Will there be a big scar?" Ariana asked quietly.

"Oh, no. No more than two inches, and in time it won't even be noticeable."

"How long will I be in the hospital?"

"No more than two days. If there are no complications."

Terry straightened his posture. "What kind of complications?"

"Complications are rare for the donor. But I must tell you there is a very low possibility of infection. But we will test Miss Winston's ability to fight infection as a part of the workup."

The family sat, mulling over all the doctor had shared with them. Following a short silence the doctor finally said, "If there are no further questions and not to hold you up any longer, Krystal will give you the lab slips and you'll hear from us in two days."

Terry extended his hand. "Thank you, doctor."

Taking Terry's hand firmly in his, Dr. Forsythe smiled and said, "We're so happy to be working with your family, Mr. Winston."

The four of them stood and followed the doctor to the area where Krystal sat writing in a folder. "Krystal will get you everything you need." Dr. Forsythe gently touched Ariana on her shoulder. "There's no need to worry. You're a healthy young lady and Ms. Hawkins doesn't know how lucky she is to have you."

CHAPTER THIRTY-SIX

The warm, moist air caressed Catherine as she stood on the balcony overlooking the Pacific. Exhaustion would have been a boost of energy compared to how she was feeling. She didn't know how she was going to host the dinner in twenty minutes.

She wasn't prepared for the opposition she'd received to her cost-cutting proposal. Though she'd never capitulated, the exchange had drained her emotionally and physically. A soft knock at her door brought her back to the picturesque balcony. "Come."

A young Samoan man approached her cautiously. "Ma'am?"

"What can I do for you, Gabriel?"

"I am to inform you that all your guests are settled in their rooms and are preparing for dinner."

"Very good." Catherine never looked at the young servant the entire time he spoke.

"Will there be anything else, ma'am?"

"Please have Mr. Staples join me in my suite."

"Right away." With those words Gabriel disappeared into the room.

Catherine adjusted her long body and sank onto the cushion of the chaise longue. If she had the strength, she would take a long hot bath in the Jacuzzi. But as it was she decided to reserve what little vigor she had for dinner. She closed her eyes and let her mind wander. Suddenly she was in the hospital room and her mother was begging her not to give the twins up for adoption.

"Cathy, don't do this thing. Those precious little girls are flesh of your flesh and bone of your bone," her mother had insisted.

"Mama, can't you understand. I'm in college. I have big plans for my future. I'm going to be very rich and powerful. I won't end up like you—two children with no husband, no education and always depending on a God who seems to have a deaf ear to your constant pleas for a financial blessing."

"Chile, don't you blaspheme God with me sitting right here. Have you ever been naked or hungry?"

"But I want to do more than get by. I want to fly first class and have people call me Ms. Hawkins."

"Honey, you can fly first class all you want, but you betta mind you're not on the wrong plane."

Catherine welcomed the knock at the door that made the image of her mother disappear. "Come."

Jonah Staples floated into the room on the wings of contentment, his thousand-dollar Italian shoes barely touching the hardwood floor. "Catherine, my great, how're you this evening?"

"Jonah, it's always so refreshing to be in your presence."

Catherine forced herself to sit up, swinging her feet to the floor. "I wanted to brief you on the meeting on the trip over. Things got a little *turbulent*."

"Oh, I'm sorry to hear that. I know that flying isn't one of your favorite things. It's just a means to an end."

"Indeed not, but the turbulence I speak of was from within the cabin."

"I don't understand."

Catherine filled Jonah in on all the details of the briefing and the subsequent fallout. Jonah was transfixed by what he heard and couldn't fathom anyone challenging Catherine. Period.

"So how do you propose we handle Esposito?" Jonah walked to the bar. "Surely, you don't think this is over?"

"I know it's far from over." The sound of ice clinking into the glass set Catherine's nerves on edge. "He's not to be trusted."

"May I fix you a drink?" Jonah held the ice tongs in midair.

"Vodka on the rocks."

Jonah busied himself with the task as he thought of the repercussions of losing the head of the food-service division. "Then we need to make a move sooner rather than later."

"Strike him before he strikes us?"

"Precisely."

Jonah rejoined Catherine on the balcony, set the drink on the small table next to her and pulled a chair from the round table with the umbrella. Its festive Hawaiian pattern always made him smile.

"What's funny?" Catherine snapped. "I need the division chiefs behind this plan if it's ever to work."

"I wasn't laughing." Jonah's expression changed instantly.

"I agree that we need the cooperation of all those involved. Do you think he'll be able to sway the others?"

"When it's all said and done, the others will see things my way. With the money I've promised them, and the potential to head up international operations, they would be fools to listen to Tony."

Jonah's left eye twitched just a smidgen. She was dangling *his* job before the hungry horses. "What's your strategy?"

"We proceed as planned. You've done a very thorough job getting the tabloid headline on each of them. So if they want to play hardball, you've got the bat and I've got the catcher's mitt."

"I like the way you put things." The last traces of the setting sun mesmerized Jonah as he sipped the expensive cognac. *Should I be worried about my spot on the food chain? A woman like Catherine has the loyalty of a cobra.*

"Shall we?" Catherine drained the tumbler and stood. "We don't want to keep our guests waiting."

"After you, madam." Jonah stepped aside to allow Catherine to pass him. As he watched her walk he noticed her stride lacked its normal confidence.

The two descended the circular stairs and moved to the dining room. The table was dressed with the finest linen, china, crystal and silver. The beautiful bird-of-paradise centerpiece added a splash of color to the all-white settings.

Jean-Michel and David stood as Catherine entered. She moved quickly to the head of the table, where Jonah held her chair. Catherine gestured for them all to be seated. Jonah moved to the other end of the table, where he sat opposite Catherine.

"I trust your accommodations meet with your approval." Catherine looked from Jean-Michel to David.

Jean-Michel said lightly, "Everything is quite lovely. *La vue hors de ma fenêtre est stupéfiante.*" (The view out my window is breathtaking.)

"I, too, am very comfortable," David added.

"Good." Catherine smiled, pleased with her retreat choice. "I want you to enjoy the island in addition to all the work we have to do. The staff is here to make sure all your needs are met."

She glanced down at her watch, then at Jonah. "I'll have Gabriel check on Jeyson, Anthony and Francisco." Jonah shot from the armchair as though it were on fire. As he reached the foot of the stairs, Jonah saw Anthony, Jeyson and Francisco approaching.

"We're holding dinner for you," Jonah chastised. "Ms. Hawkins doesn't like to be kept waiting."

Anthony reached the bottom step, first glancing at his watch. "We were told dinner would be served at seven-thirty."

"And it's now seven thirty-one," Jonah stated flatly.

Anthony stared at Jonah, preparing a retort, when suddenly he realized he knew this man. His face, his voice, everything struck a familiar chord in him.

Jonah was so caught up in his perceived power trip that he wasn't conscious Anthony was staring at him. "Right this way, please."

The four entered the dining room. "How nice of you to join us," Catherine said, her voice laced with sarcasm.

As if by magic, as soon as Jeyson, Anthony and Francisco were seated, the staff went to work. They filled wine and water glasses as efficiently as the wait staff at the best five-star restaurant.

Wine flowed freely as various scrumptious courses were placed before them. The conversations were light as the high-powered executives shared stories of skiing, golfing and impending family vacations. As some staff members cleared the dishes, others poured coffee and served dessert.

Anthony had engaged in little conversation as his gaze always wandered back to Jonah. His curiosity was getting the better of him, which didn't go unnoticed by Catherine.

Gently tapping a spoon against a water glass, Catherine attracted everyone's attention. "I trust the meal has met with your approval."

With slight nods the team unanimously agreed that the evening's feast was indeed a delight.

"Good." Catherine glowed with satisfaction. "This is only the beginning. We have menus fit for kings planned for your stay.

"This evening is a chance for us to relax, to prepare for the meetings over the next several days. I trust we've got all of that nasty opposition out of our systems and we can move ahead with our implementation plan."

Catherine turned her attention to Jonah. "Now that you've all met Jonah, you need to understand that anything he asks for is on my behalf. Any directives are to be treated as if they came from me."

The focus of the room moved from Catherine to the grinning, well-paid flunky seated at the opposite end of the table. Waiting a beat for emphasis before continuing, Catherine leaned back in her chair and smiled smugly as her gaze came to rest squarely on Anthony. "I know that I can count on each of you to cooperate fully."

The members mumbled their agreement, with the exception of Anthony, who met Catherine's stare straight on. "Tony, I didn't hear you."

Seething, Anthony looked into the faces of his comrades

for support but again found none. He slowly began nodding, indicating she could count on his cooperation. His eyes shot to Jonah again as the memory wheels turned. *Per ora* (for now), Anthony thought as he picked up his wineglass and drained it.

CHAPTER THIRTY-SEVEN

*A*riana frowned as the technician removed the latex tourniquet and tightened it again. "I hope I'm not hurting you," the Asian woman said as she focused on the bend of Ariana's right arm.

"It's okay." Ariana winced. "I'm used to it. But if you check right here"—she pointed to a spot slightly off center—"I think you'll find it."

The technician took the advice of her young subject and smiled as she said, "So, you're right." She rubbed the area with an alcohol swab. "You'll feel a slight prick."

Ariana squeezed her eyes shut tight and turned her head.

"You're all done." The pleasant technician beamed. "Now that wasn't so bad, was it?"

"I honestly didn't feel a thing." Ariana gathered her purse and gladly sprang from the chair. "Thank you."

"I wish all my patients were as easy as you. Have a nice day."

Ariana walked into the reception area, where Jackie and Terry sat shoulder to shoulder, making goo-goo eyes at each other. They didn't see her enter.

"Are you okay?" Terry asked Jackie gently.

"I don't know."

Terry looked questioningly into her eyes. "What do you mean, you don't know?"

"Just what I said," Jackie snapped, then quickly added, "I'm sorry, baby. I'm just scared. What if something goes wrong?"

Ariana held her breath as she stood overhearing, yet again, her parents' private concerns. Maybe she had been too hasty in deciding to do this.

"Everything that we've heard and read says that the donor part is a piece of cake."

"Yeah, fruitcake."

"Fruitcake?"

"Very complex and no one you ask ever likes it."

Terry couldn't help but laugh. Even in the face of trying times his wife could always find the comedy in any situation.

"This isn't funny."

"I know." Terry concentrated on the tops of his shoes. "But we have to have a strong front for Ariana. She has to be terrified, yet she is determined to see this thing through. If it were for anyone other than Catherine, I'd probably feel proud of her very adult decision."

"You're right." Jackie held Terry's hand a little tighter and began swinging it back and forth. "Have I told you lately that I love you?"

"Not since this morning. And you're slipping."

Unable to take the embarrassment of her parents' public displays of affection any longer, Ariana cleared her throat.

Terry and Jackie jumped involuntarily as they shot each

other a quick glance. Terry stood as Ariana walked toward them. "How was it?"

"Painless."

Terry shuddered at the very thought of a needle slipping into his daughter's arm. "I can't imagine it being *painless*."

"It really wasn't a big deal. Can we go? This place gives me the creeps." Ariana began moving toward the exit.

Terry grabbed Jackie's hand as she stood. She was trying to will herself to speak some words of encouragement, or should that be words of comfort? But her lips refused to obey her head's commands. Her body didn't seem to want to surrender either.

They walked from the lab hand in hand, catching up with Ariana at the elevator. They kissed each other on the lips, this time taking comfort in the love they knew they shared.

Rolling her eyes, Ariana said, "You two are so embarrassing!" With that the elevator arrived and the three of them entered. Ariana felt as though half of her was missing. Alisa had refused to come, citing she had a headache. The truth made Ariana sad—her sister refused to support her in this decision. The elevator ride seemed endless as the three rode to the lobby in silence.

CHAPTER THIRTY-EIGHT

*C*atherine stood on the balcony outside her bedroom suite as she greeted the early spring morning. Taking all the fortitude she could muster to breathe, she knew she needed to get back to Los Angeles and to Dr. Ahmad as soon as possible. With great effort she returned to the bedroom to shower and dress for the first in a series of planning meetings. If she wasn't able to gather more strength, and soon, she wasn't going to make it.

She stared at her thinning body in the mirror. She laughed as she thought of the many times she would have sold her soul to be this thin. *"Be careful what you wish for."* Why wouldn't her mother shut the hell up?

She stared at her clothes on the vanity chair and took a deep breath. She willed her energy to return, and she quickly showered and dressed. She wanted to be at the breakfast table before the others. She applied a little blush to add color to her cheeks, then lip gloss. "This is as good as it gets, fellas."

Catherine was sipping cranberry juice while reading *The Wall Street Journal* as Jean-Michel and Jonah arrived. "Good morning, Catherine." Jonah beamed.

"Morning." Catherine never put down the paper.

Jean-Michel sat, putting the napkin in his lap. "We're quite anxious about all of this. I'm glad to see we're getting an early start."

Nothing.

Jonah looked nervously at Catherine, still hidden behind her newspaper, and then Jean-Michel. "I assure you when we're done with our implementation presentation you'll be quite surprised at how well you'll do personally."

"We shall see." Jean-Michel's attention shifted as the others entered the dining room. *"Bonjour."* He added a little cheer to his voice.

The round-robin of good mornings abounded as everyone took a seat. The staff appeared, bearing silver coffeepots and crystal juice pitchers. Minutes ticked by as Catherine waited before she finally folded the paper and laid it next to her place setting. "Gentlemen, I trust everyone rested well?"

"We did indeed," Jonah answered for all of them.

Ignoring that none of the others had answered, Catherine straightened her back and smiled. "Today, I will lay out a plan that is going to make you all very rich." She hesitated for emphasis. "You will see that the implementation of this blueprint will make each of your divisions the envy of every corporation in the world. I will guarantee you no less than a fifty-percent increase in your net profits."

The five leaders looked from one to the other but said nothing. Catherine continued. "I understand this may cause some community dissension at first, but, as with all changes, in time no one will even remember what it was like before."

The uncomfortable silence began to choke the vitality out of the morning. While Catherine used it as a power play, Jonah began to fidget. Anthony stared at Jonah as small beads of perspiration began to form on Jonah's upper lip. Why couldn't he remember how he knew Jonah?

Jonah was rescued by the breakfast service. The staff, equipped with silver trays heavy laden with all of the delights of the early morning, began to pile breakfast onto the large china platters. Catherine had only yogurt and toast.

The light conversation over the meal was sparse and labored. Catherine used the time to think over her presentation. She was no stranger to opposition. Each one of the divisions that was represented at this table had come to her through some fancy footwork and insider information. All these men had fought her in the beginning, but now they were richer than they'd ever imagined possible. She knew with her latest plan they would surely come around one by one.

As the dishes were cleared away, Catherine intently watched each man's face. All looked content with the exception of Anthony. She noticed he hadn't finished his meal. She frowned slightly as she saw Anthony staring at Jonah. He studied the man as though he held the formula for world peace.

"Let's adjourn to the conference area." Catherine rose and floated from the room.

The others followed. Jonah caught up to her and smiled with satisfaction. "Showtime! We'll have them eating out of our hands when we're done."

Fighting her annoyance with Jonah's near giddiness, Catherine stopped and turned to face him. Her dark eyes seemed to penetrate his very soul. "Just remember, this is *my* show."

Fumbling for words, Jonah half smiled, then managed, "Of course. I-I . . ." he stammered. "I just meant that as your second in command . . ."

"Nothing has been decided," Catherine whispered. She looked down at the door handle, then back at Jonah.

He quickly took the hint and opened the door leading into the family room turned think tank. The well-appointed room beckoned with plush chairs and cherrywood. The bright morning sunlight filtered through the drapes, casting warmth around the room.

The chairs had been arranged in a semicircle with one chair at the head. Catherine comfortably positioned herself in that chair. She quickly reviewed what she'd shared with them the evening before at dinner as the six watched her stone-faced.

"How many jobs are we talking about?" Jean-Michel finally asked.

"Eventually, the worldwide operation will be moved to India. But, initially, we will cut approximately two hundred and fifty jobs," Catherine said as Jonah distributed a notebook with multicolored pages.

"Tell us again who will train these people," Jeyson asked, not bothering to hide his frustration.

Jonah beamed as Catherine nodded for him to answer. "That's the beauty of this plan. We'll bring the management staff into each of the customer service centers to learn the operation. The current employees will be none the wiser. They'll think, as they have in the past, that we're just growing and adding staff. Once the people we've brought in have learned the ropes, they'll go back to the new center we've set up in India. We'll begin by redirecting about twenty-five percent of the calls to the new center without the current operations' knowledge. We'll be able to see their effectiveness before we make the switch."

"And we'll deceive our current workers?" Anthony stood and began to move about the room. "I know this is legal, but on the ethics scale, this has to be pretty low."

"I assure you, Tony, there's nothing unethical about any of this. Many of the major American companies have already moved their operations."

Anthony threw his head back and laughed. "You want to compare your ethics to those of companies that have stolen the pensions of their employees to buy houses, boats and planes?"

Catherine wasn't amused. "I assure you, this plan will make you all very rich men."

Francisco tapped the notebook lightly with his pen. "We have always shared our company's good fortune with the people that made it happen."

"That is no longer the case," Jonah spoke up.

Catherine shot him a glance. "What Jonah means is our focus has changed."

"You mean *your* focus has changed, don't you?" Anthony stopped pacing. "I don't see how we'll be able to pull this off."

"I think we should listen to what else Catherine has to say," David spoke evenly. "Surely, with this plan we'll be able to move some of these people to other areas within the company."

With a raised eyebrow, Catherine smiled. "There is proposed growth as well and, yes, a fraction, a small fraction, of the people will be moved into other areas. We may have some of the current managers go into the world customer service center to work for a short while to make sure the new management is able to handle it."

"Are you saying that once we've closed the operations in the plant you'll ask the people we're firing to go to India to make sure their replacements are doing a good job?" Jeyson sat on the edge of his cushion.

"And what would be wrong with that?" Jonah was trying to find Catherine's voice. "As Catherine said, we've studied the models from some of the largest corporations in the United States and this is precisely how they did it."

David turned his attention back to Catherine. "Is this true?"

"Absolutely. This is the trend. We'll be behind the times if we don't act now."

None of the men looked at Jonah, which infuriated him. He had to garner their respect. He cleared his throat. "As I was saying—"

A soft knock at the door interrupted them, and Catherine turned agitated and said, "Come in!"

The small woman dressed in a gray and white uniform entered with her head down. "Madam."

"I told you," Catherine snapped. "I didn't want to be disturbed!"

"I know, ma'am, but there's an urgent call for you."

"Who is it?" Catherine's tone was still terse.

The woman looked up for the first time as eyes darted from one person to the next before they came to rest on Catherine.

"Well?" Catherine asked impatiently.

"Ariana Winston." The woman paused for a beat. "She says she's your daughter."

CHAPTER THIRTY-NINE

"*A*riana?" Catherine asked breathlessly as she sat heavily on the bed. "Is something wrong?"

"Hi, Catherine," Ariana said in a cheerful, free-from-stress voice. "Nothing's wrong."

"Then why are you calling me here?" Catherine's frustration indicator was in the red zone. "I'm very busy. And how did you even know to call me here?"

"The very nice lady at your office told me how to reach you. I called your cell phone first, but you didn't answer."

"I'll deal with Claire later," Catherine mumbled. "As I told you, I'm very busy."

Catherine's manner offended Ariana. Ariana imagined *her mother* would have been happy to hear from her. "I'm sorry to bother you."

Catherine realized how she must sound to Ariana and tried to counteract her distasteful tone. "No, no. It's okay. What can I do for you?"

"Are you busy?"

Catherine counted to three in her head before she answered. She'd already told this child she was not busy, but *very* busy. "I'm having meetings with my top executives. But of course I have time to talk to you," she lied.

"Oh good." Ariana recovered quickly, grasping at even the faintest hint of kindness. "I just wanted you to know that I took all the blood tests today."

"And?"

"That's it." Catherine could feel the smile on Ariana's face as she beamed with pride. "I should have the results in a couple days."

Then why in the hell are you calling me now? Call me when you know something. Catherine tried to come up with an apposite response. "That's great. I'm sure Dr. Ahmad will be in touch with both of us as soon as the results are in."

"That's what the lab technician told me." Ariana chattered on. "I just wanted you to know that I was doing what I promised I'd do."

How much of this am I going to have to tolerate in order to get what I need? Silence hung in the airwaves between Dallas and Kauai. Catherine finally responded. "That's nice, dear. But I must get back to my meeting."

Doing her best to hide her disappointment, Ariana simply said a quiet "Okay."

Without another word Catherine clicked the Off button and left Ariana listening to silence, staring into space.

CHAPTER FORTY

*C*atherine stared out at the night sky as the plane moved through the heavens. The meetings had drained what little physical strength she had, and she'd made the decision to fly back to Los Angeles an evening earlier than she'd planned.

Her departure had been swift and quiet; as the men had gathered in the viewing room to enjoy a movie, she made her way to the jet. She was due to arrive in the middle of the night, but that was of no concern to her. A driver would be waiting to whisk her away to her estate. Dr. Ahmad had made the arrangements for her to see a social worker first thing in the morning so that her dialysis could begin.

She lay her head back and closed her eyes. She was too worn out to even play games with Franklin. She sensed his presence as he placed a glass of water and cranberry juice on the table next to where she sat, but she never opened her eyes.

"Ms. Hawkins?" Franklin gently shook her as he called her name. "We're in Los Angeles. Your car is waiting."

Catherine couldn't remember the last time she'd slept through an entire flight. She felt disoriented and unsure of her surroundings. She glanced up at Franklin, then out of the cabin window and into the night. She was beginning to remember. "What time is it, Franklin?"

"Almost two." Franklin offered Catherine his arm. "May I help you up?"

"No! I'm fine." Catherine's manner shocked both of them. "I can manage. Just be sure my luggage is placed in the car." She knew she should apologize, but it just wasn't in her to do so.

"Very good." Franklin seemed no worse for wear, though a little guarded. "Are you okay, Ms. Hawkins? You were very restless in your sleep."

"I told you I'm fine, just tired." Catherine unhooked her seat belt and made an effort to stand. "Now just get me off this thing."

Once again, Franklin offered her assistance. This time she took it in silence. She was glad to have him to lean on. She moved toward the door and measured the stairs before she attempted to descend to the waiting car. Sensing her hesitation, Franklin assisted her. Jonathan quickly moved around to open the door. Catherine entered the car in silence. She never said thank you or good night to Franklin.

The ride from the airport to the hills above Hollywood was one she'd taken many times before, yet everything looked different and new to her. Perhaps it was the way the full moon shone upon every surface, making it glow. Or was it being in touch with her mortality that made everything seem clearer?

Who was Catherine Marie Hawkins? For as long as she could remember she'd been trying to answer that question and prove she was worthy of whatever she had. No matter how hard she'd work, it was never good enough. When she won the state spelling bee but failed to make it to the nationals, her mother never even acknowledged the accomplishment but ragged on her, telling her how disappointed she was and how was she going to be able to face her friends at church after her daughter'd missed such a simple word?

Having high honors in high school and college never seemed to please her mother either. She only ever focused on what Catherine *hadn't* done, instead of the great things she had. Was she still trying to prove to her mother that she was the best, even though the woman had been dead for more than ten years?

As the car pulled into the horseshoe driveway, Catherine breathed a sigh of relief. Home at last, the one place where nothing and no one could touch her. The front door opened immediately and Dexter ran to the car to retrieve her luggage. Had he been sleeping in the foyer, awaiting her arrival?

"Welcome home, ma'am." Dexter smiled.

"Bring those up to my room." Catherine emerged from the car and pushed past Dexter. "I have to be in Century City at nine." The words lingered in the air behind her, though Jonathan knew they were meant for him.

Catherine disappeared into the house and up the stairs into her sanctum. *Free at last!*

"CATHERINE HAWKINS?" A SHORT, SLENDER woman with warm brown skin and dimples stepped into the elegantly decorated waiting room as she called Catherine's name.

Catherine stood without responding, gathering her purse and briefcase.

"Are you Catherine?"

"Who else would I be, since that's the name you called?" Catherine's words dripped with condescension.

The woman raised an eyebrow and looked Catherine up and down. *Oh, so it's going to be like that.* She shifted the folder from her right hand to her left and offered her hand to Catherine. "My name is Maybelline Carter-Storm. But my friends call me May."

Catherine reluctantly took her hand and shook it without conviction. "Hello, Maybelline," Catherine said. "I guess you know my name."

"Right this way." May bit the inside of her lip to refrain from speaking her mind.

Catherine's feet sank deeply into the carpet as she followed May down a long corridor to a doorway about halfway down. "This is my office." May faked a smile. "Please come in and have a seat."

Catherine followed her into the ten-by-ten space cluttered with files, presumed to be patient charts. *Do these all represent people with failed kidneys?* Catherine looked around before she took a seat in one of the two chairs in front of May's desk.

"Why am I here?" Catherine's tone was unchanged from her first encounter with May in the waiting room.

May sat back in her chair, placed her fingertips together and smiled. She'd seen many like Catherine in the fifteen years she'd worked at the Century City facility. The rich believe they are exempt from the trials of the common man. She waited.

"Are you deaf or just stupid?"

May leaned forward in the junior executive chair, placing her arms on a pile of folders. "Let me explain something to you, Catherine Marie."

Catherine flinched at her familiarity.

"Once you walk through the doors of this facility the playing field is level. I don't care how much money you have. It doesn't change a thing. You'll have to come in here two or three times a week and be hooked up to a machine sitting right next to someone who may be receiving government assistance." May sat back. "I'm here to help you get through all of this, answer your questions, even dry your tears, but I won't tolerate you speaking to me like I'm your servant or worse."

Catherine only stared.

"Do I make myself clear?"

"Crystal."

"Good." The smile returned to May's face, this time genuine. "Now that we're on the same page, let's get down to business."

CHAPTER FORTY-ONE

*C*atherine lay on the operating table, staring up at the surgical lamp overhead. The anesthesiologist had given her an injection to calm her. She felt a little drowsy, otherwise all else seemed normal. She thought back to the admitting nurse's question: "*Do you have someone to drive you home when you're all done?*" She had answered yes, but little did the nurse know that it was her chauffeur. "*Do you have anyone that you want the doctor to speak to when he's done with the procedure?*" No.

What a miserable life she was leading. May had been correct when she said that her money didn't mean a thing here. She had waited in a room full of other patients having *day surgery*. Nurses milled about, handling their various duties, none of whom were the slightest bit impressed by who she was or what she had.

Dr. Ahmad interrupted her thoughts, though she hardly recognized him behind the surgical mask. "How's one of my favorite, if not most stubborn, patients?"

Catherine tried to smile, but her face wouldn't cooperate. "I'm okay. Can I tell you a secret?"

"Anything. You know that," Dr Ahmad teased. "It's just twelve of my closest friends listening."

"I'm not sure I want to do this," Catherine said just above a whisper.

"There's nothing to fear. You'll be asleep in just a moment and when you awaken, you'll be in the recovery room."

"The truth is." Catherine struggled to stay awake. "I'm just plain scared."

Dr. Ahmad squeezed her hand and said, "I know. But everything is going to be just fine."

"Ms. Hawkins?" A strange voice called her name. "Ms. Hawkins, time to wake up."

Catherine struggled to open her eyes, but she felt something on her face. "My throat hurts," she managed through the oxygen mask.

"Let me get this thing off you." The woman's face came into focus. "They put a tube down your throat while you were sleeping. The pain will go away shortly. Other than that, how do you feel? Does your arm hurt?"

Catherine waited a beat and realized the surgery was over. Only a second before, she was talking to Dr. Ahmad. Pain found its home in her left arm as she tried to move it but couldn't. "Yes, my arm hurts. A lot!"

"Well, let me just put some medicine into your I.V. and it will take the edge off. You did great and you're in the recovery room. My name is Beatrice and I'm your recovery room nurse. If you need anything at all, just press this button."

She handed Catherine a long cord with a button on the top of it.

Before she could respond Catherine was asleep again. Dr. Ahmad awakened her this time. "Catherine?"

As her eyes fluttered open she recognized Dr. Ahmad's face immediately. "Hi, Doc." A humbled and vulnerable one had replaced the gruff Catherine.

"You did just fine. The shunt is in place and you will begin dialysis tomorrow. The site is going to be sore for a few days, but you should be just fine in a week. I'll leave a prescription for pain medication in case you need it."

"When can I get back to work?"

"I'd really like for you to take it easy for at least a week. You've been pushing yourself really hard. The dialysis is going to take a lot of your strength in the beginning."

A little foggy but fully awake now, Catherine locked eyes with him and said, "We'll see."

"Catherine, I have a question for you," Dr. Ahmad began. "I got a call from the nephrology center in Dallas." He hesitated for a beat. "Who's this young woman who's being tested?"

Catherine looked away. She knew it was only a matter of time before he asked, but in her mind she thought she'd have longer before she would have to explain. "Her name is Ariana Winston."

"That much I know. But according to the center, this is your biological daughter."

Catherine couldn't bring herself to look at him. "Yes. I was very young."

"There's no need to explain anything to me. I just wish you had told me. This brings you a lot of hope."

"I just didn't know if they would do it."

"They?" Dr. Ahmad looked perplexed.

"They're twins. Ariana and Alisa Winston."

Though the good doctor did his best to try to hide his surprise, he couldn't. "You have twin daughters?"

Barely audibly Catherine answered, "Yes."

Catherine couldn't tell how much time passed before Dr. Ahmad spoke again. She wasn't even sure if she'd remained awake. Suddenly she realized she cared what this man thought of her as a mother. What did she think of herself as a mother?

"So, Catherine, are the twins identical?"

"Yes."

"This is very good. If one is compatible, then they both are." Dr. Ahmad seemed so pleased at this latest news. "But when I spoke with the center, they only told me of one person being tested."

Catherine slowly turned to watch Dr. Ahmad's reaction at her next revelation. "That's because only one of them has agreed to save my life, Dr. Ahmad."

CHAPTER FORTY-TWO

"*Per quanto riguarda* Jonah Staples *che cosa mi sa dire?*" (What can you tell me about Jonah Staples?) Anthony spoke quietly into the receiver.

The voice on the other end of the phone explained, "*È quello che ha tradito suo padre. Lo sistemò con la* Hawkins, *quella donna che vinse la compagnia a poker.*" (He's the man who sold out your father. He set him up with that Hawkins woman who won the company in the poker game.)

The words of Anthony's informant became muffled after the disclosure. That is why Jonah had looked so familiar. He'd worked for his father as a consultant, gaining his trust when Jonah betrayed his partner of many years so that Anthony's father could undercut his bids until Jonah's partner was forced to sell. Then this same worm turned on his father, selling him out to the demonic Catherine Hawkins. He'd not been so involved in the company's operation back in those days and had very few dealings with Jonah. Obviously, Jonah didn't remember him.

He thanked the man on the other end of the phone and hung up abruptly. Anthony had to devise a plan. He'd avenge his father's death and bring Catherine down in the same swift movement of the sword. But first he must befriend the Machiavellian Jonah.

CHAPTER FORTY-THREE

"*A*riana, phone," Alisa yelled from the family room.

Ariana picked up the phone in the library and said, "Hello."

"Ariana Winston?" the very serious voice on the other end of the phone asked.

"Speaking."

"This is Dr. Chandler's office at the nephrology center calling. Dr. Forsythe referred you to Dr. Chandler. We have the results from your preliminary tests," the woman went on to say. "Dr. Chandler also understands that you're an identical twin. Is that correct?"

Ariana's heart began to race. This woman was scaring her. "Yes."

"Dr. Chandler would like to see you both as soon as possible. Can you come in now?"

Ariana wished her dad was nearby. "Well, I'm studying."

"This is quite urgent."

"What's wrong?"

"The doctor just needs to see both of you in his office as soon as you can get here.

"My dad isn't home yet."

"Can you call him?"

"I guess I can. You're scaring me." Ariana gripped the phone tighter. "Is there something wrong with me?"

"The doctor will go into all of the details when you get here. Unfortunately, we're unable to give out any information over the telephone in case we're not speaking to the patient."

"Okay, I'll call my dad and we'll be there as soon as we can."

Ariana hung up the phone and ran to the family room, where Alisa was watching reruns of *A Different World.* "We have to go down to the kidney center."

"*We* don't have to go anywhere." Alisa never took her eyes off the television.

"The doctor wants to see both of us," Ariana blurted. "The woman on the phone has me really scared. She said she got my test results and she asked if I had an identical twin, and when I said yes, she said the doctor wants to see both of us." Ariana's hands began to tremble.

Alisa saw her sister's fear and immediately turned off the television. She stood, grabbed Ariana by the hand and headed for the home office where Jackie worked. She didn't bother knocking. She rushed into the room, startling Jackie, with Ariana in tow. "We need to get in touch with Dad right away."

Jackie removed her glasses and turned away from the computer monitor. "Why? What's wrong?"

Alisa relayed what Ariana had told her as her sister stood silently by, transfixed. Jackie moved from around the desk and hugged Ariana. "Let's go. We can call your dad and have him meet us there. I'll also call Auntie Veronica so she can pick up Michelle, Michael and T.J."

Within minutes the three of them were in the car on the way to the nephrology center. Jackie reached Terry, and he promised to meet them there. He was only a few minutes from the center.

They rode in silence, each lost in her thoughts. What could possibly be so urgent that the doctor would want to see Ariana right away and Alisa as well? Jackie's overactive imagination caused fear to grip her heart so tightly she began to have chest pains.

Terry approached the car as Jackie pulled in to a parking space a few feet from his. As she pressed the button to lower the driver's-side window Terry began rapidly firing questions. "What's this all about? I don't understand. What could possibly be wrong?"

"Let me park and we'll go inside," Jackie answered impatiently. "All I know is what Ariana told me. This whole patient confidentiality thing is driving me nuts. These are our children. I don't care how old they are!"

Terry backed away from the SUV. Within seconds the three women were out of the car and heading toward him. Worry drew lines on his face and caused his heart to race.

Ariana and Alisa walked hand in hand in front of their parents into the state-of-the-art facility. Silently the four approached the elevator just as the doors opened, and they stepped inside. Ariana pressed five.

The elevator opened into a reception area decorated with granite, marble and polished steel. The receptionist smiled broadly and greeted them. "Good afternoon. How may I help you?"

"I'm Ariana Winston." Her nerves caused her voice to tremble. "This is my sister Alisa. We're here to see Dr. Chandler."

"Oh, yes." The pleasant woman checked a piece of paper in front of her. "Emily, the doctor's assistant, will be out to get you both in just a moment."

"Thank you," Terry answered as they turned to find seats in the expansive waiting room.

Terry picked up a golf magazine. Jackie stared off into space, while Ariana and Alisa sat holding each other's hand. As Terry thumbed through the magazine, neither the words nor pictures were holding his attention. As he placed the magazine on the granite tabletop, Emily emerged from behind a smoked-glass wall and called Ariana's name.

The four rose in unison and moved toward her. She first looked at the twins and smiled. "You must be Ariana and Alisa."

"Yes, ma'am," Alisa answered. "And these are our parents."

"Very nice to meet you all. I'm Emily Halston and I'll be working with you along with Dr. Chandler." She turned to Jackie and Terry. "Please don't get upset at this next question, but since your daughters are eighteen I must ask this."

Terry shot Jackie a glance and then turned back to Emily.

"Ariana and Alisa, do you mind if your parents come back with you?"

"Of course we don't mind," Ariana snapped. "We don't want to do this alone!"

"Very good. Right this way."

Emily led them down the hallway and made a sharp right turn into a large, smartly decorated office with a view of downtown Dallas. "Have a seat in here. Dr. Chandler and I will be with you in just a moment."

There were four chairs in perfect alignment in front of the desk presumed to belong to Dr. Chandler, as though all of them were anticipated. Ariana and Alisa took the middle seats, with Jackie and Terry on each end.

As Emily closed the door behind her, Jackie breathed deeply as she took Alisa's hand. "Honey, everything is going to be just fine. I'm sure of it. I prayed all the way down here."

Alisa said nothing, but she returned Jackie's squeeze with one of her own. Before they could have time to marinate in their anxiety, Dr. Chandler and Emily entered the room.

"Good afternoon. I'm Dr. Chandler." The medium-built, strikingly handsome black man with chiseled features extended his hand first to Terry, then to the ladies one by one. "Thank you for getting here so quickly. I hope our lack of information didn't cause you too much concern."

"Oh no," Terry lied for all of them.

"Good."

Jackie squirmed in her seat as she waited for this trivial conversation to give way to the real reason for the urgent office visit. Eagerness won. "Dr. Chandler, we understand that there may be some problems with Ariana's preliminary test."

"You must be Mrs. Winston," Dr. Chandler said calmly.

Well, of course I am, you idiot. "Yes, Jacqueline Rogers-Winston. And this is my husband and the twins' father." Jackie pointed toward Terry. "Terrance Winston."

"Then I must presume that these lovely young ladies are Ariana and Alisa. Which is which?"

"I'm Ariana." She pointed to her sister. "This is Alisa."

Jackie could no longer stand the waiting. "Dr. Chandler, why are we here?"

With a slight chuckle, Dr. Chandler said, "I'm sorry. In an effort to help you all relax, I guess I'm making it worse."

Terry cleared his throat and nodded.

The doctor opened a folder and briefly perused the page. "Well, there's good news and then there's some interesting news."

Terry sat up straight. "What do you mean, interesting news?"

"Let's talk about the good news first." Dr. Chandler leaned forward. "In the preliminary testing, Ariana is a perfect match for Catherine Hawkins. They are both AB negative. There are a few more tissue tests we'll need to run, but I'm reasonably certain there will be a match there, as well."

AB negative? Jackie looked from the doctor to Terry as her thoughts ran rampant, but neither noticed the concerned look on her face. *How is that possible? Terry is O.*

"What about the interesting news?" Terry pressed.

"Well, when we did the X-rays, there appears to be some abnormality in Ariana's left kidney. From the radiology report it shows that the kidney is quite small."

Jackie sat on the edge of her chair. "What? How could that be?"

"We're not sure without more pictures. We don't want to do any invasive procedures, but I have ordered more tests. We're going to do an ultrasound, CAT scan and MRI." Dr. Chandler began speaking directly to Ariana. "With these tests we should have conclusive findings as to the state of your left kidney."

"But she's been perfectly healthy." Terry's throat was constricting. "Other than an appendectomy when she was six, she's never had a problem. Wouldn't we have known if something was wrong with her kidney before now?"

"Mother nature is phenomenal. Ariana has two kidneys. If one isn't doing the job, the other will take over and do the work of two. Which makes us none the wiser of any issues until something like this happens."

"Why am I here?" Alisa finally spoke up. "Do you think there is something wrong with one of my kidneys, too?"

"No, no. Actually, we're hoping just the opposite. Since the two of you are identical, everything about you is the same, including your DNA. If Ariana is a compatible donor, then so are you."

Alisa shot from the chair. "I don't care if I'm a compatible donor or not. I won't give Catherine one of my kidneys. Besides, if there *is* something wrong with Ariana, then she may need my kidney."

The doctor looked perplexed. He glanced at Terry for help, but Alisa's tirade continued. "She has never done anything but hurt us. Now she wants us to disrupt our lives for her. I won't, I swear to you. I won't." Tears began to form in the corners of Alisa's eyes.

"Dr. Chandler, I don't know how much you know about this case," Terry began slowly. "Catherine Hawkins is the twins' birth mother. They've lived with me since they were born. She really has had very little to do with their lives. Alisa is resentful, which is quite understandable."

Dr. Chandler glanced at Emily, who shrugged. The doctor turned to Alisa and smiled. "I can understand why you might not want to do this. But I would still encourage you to be tested and, yes, we do want to do the X-rays to make sure your kidneys are both normal. You never know. You may change your mind about becoming a donor."

"You're quite mistaken, Dr. Chandler," Alisa said flatly. "But I do want to be tested in case my sister needs me."

"Well, that's a great place to start. Emily will make sure you get the proper forms and show you where to go. Do any of you have questions so far?" Dr. Chandler smiled reassuringly.

Jackie toyed with the idea of questioning the doctor about the blood type, but thought she'd do more research first. She remembered from her days as a reporter doing an article on blood type possibilities. And if her memory served her right, it wasn't possible for the twins to be AB negative.

Instead she asked, "When will we have the results of the test?"

"It's a little too late today to get Ariana in for all the tests she needs, but I believe we'll be able to get them done tomorrow. And the radiologist will read them and have a report to me within forty-eight hours after that."

"So what you're saying is all we can do now is wait?" Terry asked.

"Mr. Winston, I wish I had a different answer for you, but, yes, now we wait." Dr. Chandler stood and extended his hand to Terry, who took it. "I promise you I won't make you wait a moment longer than necessary. We'll schedule an appointment for three days from now. I'm sure we'll have all the results in by then."

Jackie looked at Ariana and Alisa as she asked, "Do you have any questions for the doctor?"

"Will the test hurt?" Alisa asked.

"Have you had a blood test before?" Emily spoke for the first time since she returned with the doctor.

"Yes."

"That's the extent of the pain. The other tests are painless. The CAT scan and MRI don't hurt, but if you're claustrophobic, you may experience a little discomfort."

"I'm not."

"Good, then there won't be any problems at all," Dr. Chandler answered. Emily will take care of you from here. I have another patient waiting. We'll see you on Thursday."

The doctor left the Winston family numb and bewildered—each for a different reason.

CHAPTER FORTY-FOUR

*A*nthony walked among the tourists as he contemplated his next move. He chose the site of the Roman Colosseum as a reminder that *Anche i grandi cadono.* (Even the greatest among them shall fall.) He checked his watch—he was early.

"Signor Esposito." Anthony turned to see Jonah approaching him. "I hope I haven't kept you waiting."

Anthony stared at Jonah with such disdain, he was afraid the weasel would be able to read his thoughts. "No, not at all. You're actually early."

"Trying to catch that worm." Jonah beamed.

How appropriate. "Shall we have a seat?" Anthony pointed to a bench.

"Indeed." Jonah was almost giddy with anticipation. Anthony's phone call had whetted his appetite for a chance to pull off a coup. Anthony had explained that a house divided could never stand. And with Jonah's help they could take over Hawkins International and, of course, Jonah would be the world leader. Anthony had dealt with the Jonahs of the world since he was a boy. He understood why greed was one of the seven deadly sins.

"How did you explain to Catherine the reason for your visit?" Anthony pulled a cigarette from his breast pocket and offered it to Jonah.

"No need." Jonah raised his hand to refuse. "She's having some kind of surgery today."

"Oh?" Anthony was genuinely surprised. He knew she looked thin and weak, but he attributed it to her evil dealings taking their toll.

"Yeah. She's been really closemouthed about it. But you know nothing gets past Jonah Staples."

Oh really? "What is this surgery for?"

"She has some problems with her kidneys and they had to put a shunt in her arm so they can begin dialysis."

Anthony pondered this newfound information. "Are you sure?"

Looking disappointed that his new confidant doubted him, Jonah retorted, "As sure as the Romans killed Jesus."

Anthony threw back his head and laughed heartily. This was going to make his plan even easier than he ever imagined. With this weakness in Catherine, Jonah would believe he did have a chance of taking over the operation with Anthony's help.

"Look, Jonah, I'm going to shoot straight from the hip with you." Anthony's eyes seemed to burn holes into Jonah's soul. "I want to bring Catherine down. She has destroyed my family and now she wants to try to destroy our very community. I can't let that happen. I need your help to get out from under her. And for this you will be greatly rewarded."

Jonah leaned in closer. "Are you out of your mind? What

can you possibly offer me? I'm her right hand. I'm slated to be second in command."

"Do you really believe that?" Anthony chided. "If she was going to do it, why hasn't she done it already? What else do you have to do to show her that you're worthy?"

"Catherine has . . ." Jonah's resolve wavered slightly. "She knows . . . she's said."

"Just as I suspected," Anthony continued. "Did you know she has taunted each of us with that same potential job?"

Stunned Jonah stood and moved away from Anthony. He walked ten steps and turned back to Anthony. He opened his mouth, said nothing, then came back.

"I don't believe you."

"Have it your way. I have no reason to lie."

"Of course you do. You want me to betray her for *you*!"

Anthony stared at Jonah, giving him time to contemplate the probability of the truth of what he spoke. "Originally I just wanted a way to get away from this evil woman, but now I think with her being ill we can work on taking over the company. Move in while she's down. Make sweeping changes. Get out from under this contract with the Indian government.

"How in heaven's name did she get the Indian officials to agree to such a plan?"

Jonah was reluctant to divulge what he knew to be the truth. But in his heart he knew what Anthony had said was possibly true. *Why hadn't Catherine made me second in command?* "Why shouldn't I just go back and tell Catherine about this conversation?"

"Because, my friend, you are as oppressed by her as the rest of us."

Jonah sat heavily next to Anthony. "I'm listening."

"I think it's time for you to start talking."

Jonah stared at the ground as he began slowly. "It wasn't a matter of convincing the Indian government. They are more than happy to have all of the business from the United States. This is bringing more and more money into a country over-run with poverty. Where the rub comes in, is the company *may* have to make some *contributions* to even be considered."

"What are you saying?"

"Come now, Anthony, you're an intelligent man."

Anthony began to smile on the inside. With every passing second this was getting better and better. "She paid them to be allowed to do business in India? Are you positive about this?"

Jonah only stared.

CHAPTER FORTY-FIVE

"Mommy, why is everyone looking so sad?" Michelle asked as she spread peanut butter on a slice of bread.

Jackie stopped seasoning the pork chops she had thawed for dinner. "What do you mean, honey?"

"Everyone just looks so sad. Ariana and Alisa don't come out of their rooms. Daddy doesn't even hear me talking to him."

"Michelle, I'm so sorry." Jackie rinsed her hands and dried them before she went to where her daughter stood. "There are just some things going on with Ariana's health."

"Does it have anything to do with her kidneys being sick?" Michelle never looked up from the jelly she was generously spreading on top of the peanut butter.

Stunned, Jackie fumbled for the right answer. She decided the truth would work best. "How do you know about Ariana's kidney being deformed?"

Michelle looked up, locking eyes with Jackie. "Mom, we're not babies anymore. We hear y'all talking about it."

"I guess you're right. You have grown up on me." Jackie relaxed a little. "The truth is, Catherine needs a kidney transplant and she has asked Ariana and Alisa to donate one of theirs."

"I know."

Jackie pretended not to be shocked again.

"I was at the family meeting, remember?"

Jackie acknowledged her and continued. "Well, in order to do that, Ariana had to have some lab tests. When they did those tests, they found something a little out of the ordinary with one of her kidneys, so she had to have some more tests and we're waiting for those results. I guess we're just a little anxious, so that's why we've been quiet."

"Oh, okay." Michelle poured a glass of milk, took her sandwich to the table and sat down with the latest edition of *Vibe* magazine.

Jackie stared at her and shook her head. Michelle was totally content with the simple explanation. Jackie glanced at her watch. She had an appointment with a real estate developer and then she was meeting Mercedes after dinner at Starbucks.

So much of her energy was being spent on Catherine's problems, she was losing sight of her own goals. The developer had been the subject of an article she did three years before on the booming Texas, most especially Dallas, real estate market. Her article had brought him a great deal of attention and subsequent business, and he promised her if there was anything he could ever do for her, she need only ask. Tonight she'd planned to ask him to take on Terry as his apprentice.

She grew more apprehensive by the second. She was assured that the meeting with the developer would go well, but what had her nervous was the latest revelation about Michelle's intuition. She was glad she had chosen a location outside the house for the meeting.

Ariana and Alisa strolled into the family room, casually chatting about one of their friends and her dating woes. They had been inseparable since they had left Dr. Chandler's office. It wouldn't have been Jackie's method of choice to get them back on good terms, but it sure was nice to see.

"Mom, what's for dinner?" Alisa called from the family room as she picked up the remote control.

"Pork chops, rice and green beans," Jackie said casually. "You hungry?"

"We're starving," Ariana answered for both of them.

Jackie smiled. The chime from the door leading from the garage into the kitchen announced Terry's arrival. She turned and greeted him with a grin so big it sparked something deep inside him.

"Hey, baby." Terry walked across the kitchen and kissed her. "How's everything?" he asked as he peeped over her shoulder to see what she was cooking.

Jackie kissed him back. "Things are as normal as they can be under the circumstances."

"Thank God for little miracles." Terry turned to Michelle and asked, "Girl, don't you know your mama is making pork chops for dinner and you're eating a PB and J sandwich?"

"Oh, Daddy, I'll still eat dinner. I had soccer practice today and I was starving." Michelle took the last bite of her sandwich before she drained the glass. She got up from the table with an empty plate and glass as she walked toward the dishwasher.

Terry reached over and pulled her close, to give her a hug and kiss. "Okay. I'm going to just have to see this for myself."

"Oh, Daddy!" Michelle laughed. "I'm going to start my homework."

"Sounds like a good plan to me." Jackie admonished, "Tell your brother he should be doing the same."

Michelle bounced from the kitchen and out of sight as Terry returned to the counter where Jackie worked. He sauntered up close behind her and slipped his arm around her waist. "Hmm, you feel good to a worn-out soul."

"You feel pretty good for a worn-out soul." They both laughed. Then Jackie casually added. "I have a meeting with Charles Givens, the developer, after dinner and then I'm meeting Mercedes for coffee after that." She'd hoped there was nothing in her voice to indicate anything was out of the ordinary about the announcement.

"At Starbucks?" Terry stood looking into the refrigerator, finally deciding to grab a beer.

"Yes, we just need some girlfriend time." Jackie waited for the why question.

"You probably should pick up some coffee while you're there." Terry twisted off the top. "We're getting low."

Jackie breathed a sigh of relief. "Oh, good idea." She never looked up from the green beans she was snapping.

"You know what I thought as I drove home?" Terry leaned against the center island as he watched Jackie.

"What's that?"

"We might have never known there was anything wrong with Ariana if Catherine hadn't come back on the scene."

Because Jackie's back was to Terry, he didn't see her roll her eyes. "Are you saying she did us a favor?"

"Don't get your thong twisted. All I'm saying is that God

can always take something ugly and turn it into a beautiful thing."

"Yeah, I guess you're right about that. But I don't hardly want to give Catherine credit for anything."

"I'm just thankful we found out sooner rather than later. It could be nothing, but if it is something I want to know."

Jackie turned to face Terry. "This is all going to work out."

"Promise?"

"No," Jackie shook her head and pointed upward. "He promised."

CHAPTER FORTY-SIX

"*H*eyyyyyyyy," Mercedes sang in her trademark high-pitched voice. "What's shakin'? You had me kinda concerned when you called this morning."

Jackie hugged her friend as they moved toward the counter to order. She ordered two iced venti mocha coconut frappuccinos and paid for them before they found comfortable seats in the corner.

"Gurl, now I *am* scared," Mercedes teased. "You ordered big fraps and didn't even ask me for the money to pay for mine."

"Stop it. You know I don't hardly ask you to pay when I invite you out."

"The only time when you *invite* me out, as you say, is when you've got heavy stuff on your mind. So dish the dirt—what's up?"

Jackie drew in enough air to increase her cup size by two full letters. "Where do I start?"

Mercedes sat up. She now knew this was serious. Just as she was about to ask her what was really going on, the perky blonde with multiple piercings called Jackie's name. "Wait here. I'll get them."

Jackie watched Mercedes dart to the counter and back as though she were weightless. Mercedes removed the straws from their protective packaging and passed one of the icy cold treats to Jackie before she sat down. "Now as I was about to say before Brittney over there interrupted me, what's going on? Is there trouble in paradise? Lemme guess. Catherine!"

Jackie took a long swig from the straw before she answered. "You're partly right. When you think about it—everything comes down to Catherine."

"You want me to beat her down?" Mercedes was only half joking. " 'Cuz you know I've been looking to stomp a mud hole in her behind since prom night."

"Truth be told, you've been looking to do that since that Christmas seven or eight years ago, but this is serious." Jackie played with the condensation on the clear plastic container.

"Okay. Go on. But don't think I'm joking."

Jackie tried to smile, but there was nothing to draw from. She finally sighed and forged ahead. "I told you that Ariana had the blood test to see if she was a match for Catherine. It turns out she is."

"Oh, man! I was hoping she wouldn't be. But go on."

Jackie explained all the concerns brought on by the X-rays and the pending tissue test results. When she'd gotten to that point, she took a deep breath and paused.

"Wow." Mercedes took a drink. "That's deep."

"It gets deeper."

Mercedes frowned but said nothing.

"When Dr. Chandler was explaining how Ariana was a perfect match, he said her blood type is AB negative, just like Catherine. Terry's blood type is O."

Mercedes stared at her with a blank look. She finally said, "And?"

"Don't you understand? If what Dr. Chandler says is true, it's almost impossible for Terry to be the twins' father!"

Mercedes jerked back so fast and hard she knocked over both drinks. She scrambled to set them upright before the thick mixture began to ooze out of the top. "What the hell are you talking about, Jacqueline Rogers-Winston? And how can you be sure?"

"I did some research a while ago. And I know basically what adds up and what doesn't. There are more conclusive tests, of course, like paternity. But believe me, something isn't right."

"Jack, come on, sistahgurlfriend. You know I love you, but you're the queen of overreaction. I just don't see how that can be possible."

"Terry took her word for it that the twins were his." Jackie turned to stare out of the window before she continued slowly. "How can I say anything to Terry about my suspicions?"

"Whoa, hold the Ferrari!" Mercedes leaned in. "You can't say anything to Terry about this. Especially if you're not 250 percent sure."

"Cedes, how can I not say anything?"

"What would be gained by this?"

Jackie searched Mercedes's face as though it held the answers she sought. "I don't know," was all she could manage after several tense moments.

"Look, I can't even pretend to be able to tell you what to do, but please promise you'll pray on this. You could upset a whole bunch of lives with this information and what if you're wrong?"

"But in my heart I know I'm not."

"*A*re you okay?" Jonah asked Catherine for the third time since the meeting had started fifteen minutes before.

"Don't ask me that again," Catherine snapped weakly. The truth was, she was exhausted. She'd had her first dialysis treatment the day before. She'd been unable to get out of bed that morning.

Her mind went back to the minute she walked into the dialysis center. There were seventeen other people hooked up to machines. The steady hum and antiseptic smells made her head spin. She believed she would have collapsed if May hadn't held her arm. The pain in her arm from the shunt was almost unbearable. She'd taken a narcotic just to be able to get through this meeting. If Jonah had a clue what was going on, she'd have to get rid of him today. But for now she was stuck with this brownnosing wannabe.

Jonah eyed her suspiciously. She was sicker than even he thought. How much longer did she think she could keep up this charade? This was the time for him to press her to make his position official. "You know, Catherine, we haven't talked about my appointment to EVP for a while."

"And?"

"Well, I'm just anxious to make it official. I can then take over some of your duties and maybe you can take a vacation for a few weeks, get some rest."

The laser stare should have burned a hole in Jonah's face. "Do I care about your anxiety? I need you right where you are at the moment. The announcement will be made all in good time." Catherine softened her tone as she continued. "Besides why do you think I need a vacation?"

"I didn't say that you needed a vacation, but you certainly have earned one." Jonah began to fidget. "I just—"

"Let me tell you what you just. You just pissed me off. I should fire you instead of promote you. You think there's something wrong with me and that in my moment of weakness I would make a snap judgment?"

"Of course not." Jonah realized with that statement that he was no closer to being the second in command of Hawkins International than Winnie-the-Pooh. "I'm sorry if you took my suggestion in any spirit other than the one I intended."

"You'll be the first to know when my decision is final." Catherine lit a cigarette and took a long drag. "Now for the business at hand."

Jonah had trouble focusing. His mind slipped back to his visit to Rome. Anthony had been right. Catherine was only using him. It would serve her right if he joined forces with Anthony.

"Jonah, are you listening to me?" Catherine asked, agitated.

"I'm sorry. I was just lost in my thoughts about the final phase of this deal."

"You get lost on your own time. Now I've heard from my contact in India. They're waiting for the final payment so that we can start the operation."

"What exactly are we paying for?" Jonah needed to get as much information as he could for Anthony. "I mean, are we paying contractors, the government, who?"

"You need only do as you're told." Catherine eyed him with contempt. "Everything is on a need-to-know basis."

Jonah's rose-colored glasses suddenly shattered.

Catherine slid a piece of paper across the table. "We need to wire two and a half million dollars from this Swiss account,"—Catherine pointed at numbers on the paper—"to this one. In no way must they be able to trace this money back to HI or me personally. Are you clear on how this is to be handled?"

Feeling insulted by the question, Jonah simply nodded.

"And what does that mean?" Catherine taunted. "I don't understand nonverbal communication."

Jonah was beginning to see that she had treated him with the same disrespect and disdain as everyone else, but he'd been too blinded by the light of ambition to see it. *What makes you think that you're so special that you wouldn't be next?* How had his mother put it? *"When someone shows you who she is—believe her the first time."*

"Jonah!" Catherine yelled, startling him. "What in the hell is wrong with you? I'm talking to you and you're ignoring me. Do I need to get someone else to do this?"

"No, no. I'm sorry," Jonah lied. "I guess I'm just concerned about you. I'll handle this right away."

Catherine reached over and touched Jonah's hand. "Thank you for your concern. The truth is, I'm a little under the weather, but I'll be fine in a couple days, I promise you."

"I just want to be sure that if there's anything I can do for you, I'm doing it."

"I appreciate that." Catherine smiled almost wickedly. "And, Jonah, don't worry. You'll get everything that's due you and more. Your loyalty will be justly rewarded."

CHAPTER FORTY-EIGHT

"*A*riana, I'm sorry, but the tests are conclusive." Dr. Chandler looked stoic as he delivered the news. "Your left kidney never developed. This happened—or should I say didn't happen—before you were born."

Jackie gasped. "What do you mean?"

Terry sat transfixed.

Ariana and Alisa held each other's hand so tightly the blood flow was interrupted.

"Let me explain," the doctor continued. "As bad as it may sound, you'll lead a perfectly normal life unless you develop kidney disease in the future. Mother nature is so kind to us and gives us duplicates of many of our vital organs. Your right kidney is doing all the work and it's doing it quite well. All of your levels are perfectly within normal range."

"Because her one kidney is doing all the work, will it wear out faster?" Terry asked.

"Studies have shown that not to be the case. Ariana will live a long and healthy life."

"Will this in any way affect her ability to have children?" Jackie asked, still stunned. "You know, I've been doing a little research on my own. I read that if a woman donates a kidney it could hamper her ability to have children. Is this true?"

"Of course, I can't speak expertly from a gynecological standpoint, but pregnancy does tax the kidneys and in some very rare cases there could be complications. Of course we have no way of knowing one way or the other at this juncture."

"What about Alisa?" Terry blurted. "What did her test show?"

"Miss Alisa is just fine. Two perfectly normal kidneys functioning well."

Both parents gave a sigh of relief. The sisters looked at each other and smiled.

"And that brings me to my next point: the reason you came to me in the first place." Dr. Chandler paused. "Given these new facts, of course it's impossible for Ariana to donate a kidney to Ms. Hawkins."

Ariana's heart sank.

"Alisa, however, is a perfect candidate."

Alisa stood unexpectedly, startling them all as she moved to the other side of the vast office. "A perfect candidate for what? Surely you don't think I'm going to even consider for a minute giving Catherine a kidney bean, never mind my kidney."

Ariana stood and joined her sister near the window. " 'Lisa if you don't do this Catherine may die."

"And the problem with that would be?"

"Please, at least get the other test. Then we'll know for sure."

Alisa turned to her mirror image and spoke slowly. "Ari, there's no point. We both know from our research on the Net if you're compatible, then I am, too. But I'm not going to do it. No way. No how."

Ariana turned to her parents, pleading, "Daddy, please talk to her. Make her see she has to do this."

Terry stood and joined his daughters. "This is not something you can force someone to do. She has to want to do it."

"Ari, what if you need a kidney sometime in the future. Then where would you go?" Alisa tried to reason with her.

"You heard Dr. Chandler. Nothing will happen to me. I'm fine."

"That's not what he said." Alisa tried to make her understand. "He said that it is rare that there are complications, but he didn't use the word 'never.' "

"But I know everything will be fine. I just know it!"

"Daddy, tell her I can't take that chance. Once my kidney is gone there's no getting it back."

Terry felt lost and bewildered. "She's right, Ariana."

Ariana turned to Jackie, who sat staring at the exchanges, her eyes pleading for help. Conflict clouded Jackie's ability to reason. She felt so strongly that Catherine should just leave her family alone, but seeing Ariana's torment broke her heart. "Mom, please."

After a long moment Jackie finally said, "I think we should handle this the way we approach all problems: we need to go to God."

"Your mother's right," Terry quickly added. "Let's pray about this. Alisa, you need to seek God about what you should do. And we'll all pray that we understand and accept your decision."

"Daddy, I mean no disrespect, but I don't need to pray

about anything except forgiveness for the hate I hold for Catherine."

Dr. Chandler cleared his throat, causing them to look at him. "There are obviously some things you need to work out. I agree with you, Mr. Winston. This is not something we can force you to do, Alisa. You have to want to do it for psychological as well as physiological reasons."

Terry moved back to his seat, inviting the twins to do the same with his eyes. He stared down at his hands before he began to speak. "Dr. Chandler, we need some time to talk this over some more."

"That much I've gathered."

"We're sorry."

Alisa sighed hard and interjected. "Daddy, stop it! Nothing will change. I'm not doing it. I'm more convinced now than ever."

Terry continued. "As you can see, Alisa feels very strongly that she wants *nothing* to do with Catherine, even if she can save her life. Obviously, Ariana feels different. With this new development about Ariana's health we have a lot to discuss and pray about as a family."

"I understand." Dr. Chandler added empathetically, "You need some time to digest all that you've learned today." He turned to speak only to Alisa. "Alisa, this is something that you must want to do. No one can begin to force you. Just be aware that strangers have done what you are refusing to do for the woman who gave you life."

Jackie saw crimson. "Dr. Chandler, that's enough. We'll get back to you in a few days." With that Jackie rose and moved toward the door. Her family followed in silence. Ariana turned and looked helplessly at Dr. Chandler.

CHAPTER FORTY-NINE

*T*he ride home was painful at best. No one uttered a word. Terry pulled into the garage, and the twins ran from the car as if someone had announced there was a bomb inside. Jackie and Terry met at the door leading to the kitchen. After a long moment of staring into the other's eyes, they embraced. They each drew strength from the closeness. Terry pulled back and kissed Jackie on the forehead.

As they entered the kitchen in silence, Jackie decided she needed a drink but she made coffee instead. Terry disappeared up the back stairs that led to their bedroom. The eerie silence made Jackie shudder as the sound of the coffeemaker filled the air. As Jackie kicked off her shoes, she fell back on the sofa in the family room and tears began to flow.

She didn't know how long she sat crying when she felt Terry sit next to her. He put one arm around her and pulled her close. His lack of words spoke volumes as he began to rock her back and forth. "It's going to be okay, baby," he finally said.

"You keep saying that, but then something else happens."

Terry chuckled. "Yeah, I guess you're right."

"When are you going to call Catherine and break the news to her?"

"I guess there's no time like the present." Terry rose to retrieve the cordless phone from the charger as he realized he hadn't committed her number to memory. "I'll get the number and be right back."

Jackie felt totally drained but managed to drag herself off the couch and into the kitchen to pour the coffee. Just as she stirred the sugar into the second cup, Terry returned.

"Come sit next to me while I call her. I need you."

Jackie smiled weakly and joined her husband, carrying two coffee mugs. Her heart stopped as she watched him dial. Why was she afraid?

The sound of Terry's voice snapped her back. "Catherine, this is Terry."

"Hi, Terrance." Catherine sounded weak and slightly annoyed. "What can I do for you?"

Terry took a deep breath and began counting to prevent himself from saying something he'd later regret. "We just came from the doctor's office with Ariana."

"And?" Catherine's tone changed.

"It doesn't look good."

Terry heard her expel air. "She's not compatible?"

"Actually, she is." Terry continued, "She's a perfect match."

"Then what's the problem?"

"She only has one good kidney."

"What's wrong with the other one?"

"According to the doctor, it never developed." Terry continued to relay all the news the doctor had given them.

Catherine never asked one question about Ariana's health or potential health issues but instead asked, "Well, if she's compatible, then doesn't that make Alisa compatible, too?"

"You know, Catherine, you're a piece of work. I tell you that the person you gave birth to may have some serious health challenges and you don't even ask how she is."

Jackie stood and started to pace about the room. *Ariana is AB negative. Should I tell him? This witch has used him for more than eighteen years. How can I tell him without proof? It will destroy him.*

"Terrance, you've always been so dramatic," Catherine mocked him. "All I want to know is if Alisa is compatible. Or does she have only one kidney, too?"

"Alisa is just perfect—two working kidneys—and, yes, she too is a perfect match." The next sentence gave him so much pleasure. "But she wants nothing to do with you. She doesn't want to take a chance that her sister may need a kidney in the future and she would have given one to you." *Bam!*

"Well, we'll just see about that."

"What's that supposed to mean?"

"I'll have my pilot file a flight plan right away. I'm coming to Dallas so we can discuss our options."

"Are you not hearing me?"

"I've heard you, Terrance, but the difference between you and me is, 'no' means we're done to you. 'No' just means I have to find another way to get it done to me."

"I've never seen anyone as self-centered and selfish in my life as you. You don't give a cat's fur ball about Ariana and Alisa, do you?"

Silence.

"Amazing," Terry hissed. "You know, before now I was going to talk to Alisa, try to convince her that maybe, just maybe, she should reconsider. But now—"

Catherine expelled a spine-tingling laugh. "You think I need you to speak for me? I'm coming to Dallas and when I leave, Alisa will have agreed to give me a kidney."

"If I were a betting man I'd take some odds on that one." Terry's anger made his hands tremble. "I'd rather see you in—"

Catherine hung up before Terry could finish, an action that proved to push him over the edge. He groaned loudly and threw the phone across the room, shattering it into little pieces.

$\mathcal{A}$riana and Alisa sat on the love seat opposite Catherine, while Jackie and Terry paced. "You see, Alisa, without you, I'll be on dialysis for the rest of my life." Catherine pleaded her case.

Alisa sat stone-faced. Ariana reached over and took her hand, but Alisa pulled away.

"Alisa, honey." Catherine continued after glancing at Terry, "What can I do to convince you this is the right thing to do?"

Alisa suddenly sat forward. "Do you think you can buy me or, better yet, my kidney? Neither is for sale. You come in here after all this time and expect us to just bow down to you because you say so?"

"Alisa, that's enough," Terry interrupted.

Jackie could stand no more. "Let her speak. She has every right to feel the way she feels."

"What are you saying?" Terry was livid.

"You take it any way you please." Jackie moved toward

Terry. "This woman has never brought us anything but grief, yet you are always so politically correct with her. Alisa's right. She thinks she can buy whatever she needs or wants."

"I won't stand by and let you—"

"Mom, Daddy, stop it!" Ariana leapt to her feet and moved between them. "It's not supposed to be like this."

Embarrassed Jackie backed away. Catherine had once again taken her to a place she never allowed anyone else to. She was attacking her husband's manhood and for what? "I want you to leave my house, Catherine. Ariana's right, it's not supposed to be like this. You've brought as much pain to this family as I'm going to stand for."

"This is between me and *my* daughters." Catherine stood and moved toward Jackie. "You heard me. No matter what a piece of paper says, it is my blood that flows through their veins."

From somewhere south of the equator Jackie's hand began an upward circular motion until it was cleared for landing on Catherine's right cheek. Jackie had no idea what she'd done, but the feeling of euphoria that followed was indescribable.

"Mother!" Ariana moved toward the two women and neither knew to whom she referred. She turned to Jackie with fire-filled eyes and asked, "What's wrong with you?"

Catherine held her cheek to quiet the sting. Inside she smiled as she acknowledged Jackie's gumption. "You'll rue the day you did this, Jacqueline." Catherine turned to Terry. "You'll all regret this. I promise you!"

"Catherine, please wait." Ariana placed her hand on Catherine's arm. "Don't go. We need to talk about this more."

Catherine looked down at the hand that looked so much like her own and then into a mirror image of her eyes. "There is nothing more to discuss here. Your *mother* has made a very grave mistake."

"She didn't mean it." Ariana began crying as she turned to Jackie. "Tell her you didn't mean it, Mom. Please tell her!"

Tears welled in the corners of Jackie's eyes as she moved toward Ariana. Her eyes locked with Catherine's as she spoke. "Ariana, I'm sorry that this is so hard for you. I truly am, but I meant every word I said."

Ariana began to cry in earnest.

Jackie reached out for her, never taking her eyes off Catherine. Ariana fell into her arms. "You think I'm scared of your threats? Just what is it that you think you can do to us that's worse than what you've already done?"

Catherine, surprised that Jackie was calling her bluff, only stared.

"That's what I thought." Jackie forged on. "You see, this time we have what you need. And the only person willing to give it to you, can't. Momma C. was right. Just wait on God, because He'll handle it. And, Catherine, you've been handled. Now I'd appreciate it if you'd leave my home and *my family*."

Catherine picked up her purse, then turned to look at Terry, who met her eyes with a cold stare. She looked to Alisa once again, grasping for a glimmer of hope. Nothing. She turned on her heels, heading for the door. As she reached for the knob she hesitated but didn't turn. She opened the door and walked through it slowly. The only sound that could be heard was the soft muffle of the latch engaging.

CHAPTER FIFTY-ONE

A knock on the door leading into her office stole Catherine's attention from the computer screen. "Come."

Claire entered, carrying a stack of binders. "These just arrived." She moved closer to the desk as Catherine waited impatiently. "All of the reports are here except Italy."

Catherine had waited for days for the details of the customer-service implementations. Her illness had made her even less patient, if that were possible. She checked her watch. "Get Italy on the phone."

"Yes, ma'am," Claire said as she turned to leave. "Will there be anything more?"

Catherine hesitated, and then dismissed her. "That will be all. I don't want to be disturbed except when you get Tony on the phone."

"I understand," Claire said as she closed the door behind her.

Catherine looked at the binders and pulled the one from Germany from the stack first. With confidence, she knew David would comply in hopes she'd choose him as the new executive vice president.

As she thumbed through the report she was very pleased with the results. He'd followed her directions to the letter. Germany's customer service was now well into phase one of the transition to India. She smiled with satisfaction as she thought of how uncomplicated her business dealings were, thanks to Jonah. She wondered if she was wise to carry out her plan to oust him for Rahid, but shrugged off her misgivings almost instantly.

She moved to the next binder to find Jeyson was well on his way to completing phase one. After reviewing the other binders she was equally pleased. How dare Anthony miss the deadline? He was living dangerously close to the insubordination borderline.

The phone buzzed and Catherine picked it up quickly. "Yes."

With one word Claire conveyed the reason for the interruption. "Italy."

Without another word Catherine switched to the flashing line. "Tony, where is your report on the first-phase implementation?"

"No hi, Tony, how are you doing, Tony?" Anthony toyed with her.

"Where is my report?"

"There is nothing to report."

"What do you mean?"

"I think I was clear. I don't have anything to tell you because I haven't begun the implementation."

Waiting a beat while filling her lungs with the cool air that filled the room, Catherine then began speaking slowly. "And why is that, Tony?"

"I just haven't had the time. We're very busy here, handling our current workload."

"Is that so?" Catherine seethed. "Are you deliberately trying to piss me off?"

"Would I do that, madam president?" Anthony mocked.

"Anthony, I've had as much of this as I'm going to take. I'll close your operation down and then where will you be?"

"You are too money hungry to do that, and we both know this," Anthony replied calmly. "I'm not afraid of your threats. I'm the most profitable division of HI. So let's not play these silly mind games."

Exasperated, Catherine sighed. "When can I expect your phase-one report?"

"When I get it to you."

Catherine could feel the smug contempt Anthony displayed on the other end of the connection. If she weren't so weak from the dialysis she'd be in Italy before breakfast tomorrow morning. She quickly dismissed the notion of sending Jonah. Anthony would quickly become the whale and Jonah his appetizer. Catherine knew now what she had to do. It was time for plan B.

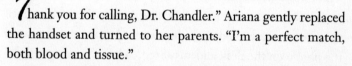

CHAPTER FIFTY-TWO

"*T*hank you for calling, Dr. Chandler." Ariana gently replaced the handset and turned to her parents. "I'm a perfect match, both blood and tissue."

Terry looked at Jackie as her face began to lose color. "But, honey, none of that matters because you can't donate."

Ariana fell heavily into the chair next to the small desk in the kitchen. "I know."

Jackie's heart went out to her child as she struggled with her inability to do what she desired for such an undeserving soul. "Did Dr. Chandler say anything about the results of the other test?"

"He just repeated everything we already knew."

"So it's for sure that you're okay?"

Ariana nodded.

"Oh, thank you, Jesus!" Terry exclaimed. "That's the best news I've had since all of this started."

"But what about the news for Catherine?" Ariana's pain-filled eyes met Terry's. "What will she do if Alisa doesn't give her a kidney?"

"Honey, as much as I know you want to do this, it's not your problem." Jackie moved toward her and began stroking her hair.

"Then whose problem is it?" Ariana jerked away.

Not wanting to say what she felt, Jackie slowly walked away. Terry tried to find an answer to comfort Ariana. "Catherine can live a full life on dialysis. So it's no one's problem."

"But isn't it better to have a kidney?"

Jackie felt compelled to answer. "Of course, it's better, but dialysis *is* a viable alternative."

Ariana leapt from her seat and darted toward the stairs. "I have to convince Alisa to do this. Dr. Chandler says I'm fine with one kidney. I'm not going to need Alisa's."

The parents stood in the kitchen, devoid of emotions until the phone interrupted their desolation. Jackie moved toward the phone on the desk and answered. "Hello."

"Hey, gurl. Wendell and I are on our way over," Veronica announced. "Do you want us to bring anything?"

Jackie stood perplexed as to why her sister-in-law and Veronica's one true love were descending on the house of gloom.

"You there?" Veronica asked.

"I'm here," Jackie managed. "I'm just trying to remember what it is I'm forgetting."

"Gurl, this is family and friends night and it's your turn to host. How in the world could you forget? You look forward to this night of the month more than any of the rest of us."

Jackie slapped herself on the forehead as she said, "Oh my God. I totally forgot. With everything going on with Ariana and this whole Catherine mess."

"Any word from the doctors yet?" Veronica's tone turned serious.

Jackie filled her in on all the details as she knew them, then quickly said, "I can tell you more when you get here. Bring wine. I think I have enough of everything else in the pantry."

After a few quick exchanges Jackie and Veronica hung up. As she turned to Terry she saw the faraway look in her husband's eyes. He finally said, "What time are they coming?"

"Seven."

"Are you up to this?"

"I guess it's a good thing." Jackie forced a smile. "I'll call to make sure the Carpenters are coming."

"Movie or games?" Terry asked as he put his arm around Jackie's shoulders.

"I don't think I could concentrate on a movie, so let's play a game."

"I'll set everything up while you find some snacks." Terry kissed her gently on the forehead. "Let me know if you need me to run to the store."

"Shouldn't we go talk to Ariana and Alisa?" Jackie's eyes were fixed on the pattern in the tile on the kitchen floor. "Ari is up there, pleading her case, and she could convince Alisa to do this thing."

"I think we should just leave them alone. Concentrate on having a good evening with our loved ones and face the dark cloud of Catherine tomorrow."

In silence Jackie set about the task of preparing for a pleasant evening filled with love. She readied snacks while Terry set up two card tables. The time went quickly and just as Jackie pulled the nachos from the oven the doorbell rang.

Roland and Mercedes arrived with the little Carpenters. Veronica and Wendell pulled into the half-circular drive right behind the Carpenters' Range Rover. Just the sight of her family gave Jackie an immediate sense of peace.

With lots of hugs and kisses the families blended into an evening of fun and laughter. The children migrated to the basement to take advantage of the latest PlayStation games and air hockey. Ariana and Alisa had joined the adults shortly after they heard the bell chime. All of the darkness from the earlier part of the evening seemed to have disappeared.

"Auntie Vee, when are you and Mr. Wendell getting married?" Alisa asked nonchalantly as Jackie and Mercedes went to the kitchen to replenish the snacks.

"Sounds like a good question to me!" Jackie yelled behind her as she went to the pantry.

"Yes, Auntie Vee. When *are* we getting married?" Wendell teased.

Veronica blushed as she thought back over the seven years they'd been dating. Her heart filled with joy at the very mention of Wendell's name. As handsome as he was it paled in comparison to the kind and gentle spirit locked inside the massive, muscle-rippling body.

The attraction between the two of them had been instant when they met while he worked on the investigation during the child custody hearings. Veronica had been so worried that she'd wanted him for all the wrong reasons as in days gone by. She had her hands full with her newfound life of sobriety. Her sponsor had warned her about complicating her life in any way.

She viewed Wendell as a major complication. As time went on, and with his refusal to give up on her, he slowly won her heart. Now all these years later she wanted to ask him the same question.

"Auntie Veeeeee?" Ariana's teasing snapped Veronica out of her flashback.

"I've been waiting on you to get over your fears." Veronica stared at Wendell.

"Why on earth would I be afraid with you?"

"But you always said with everything you see in your work, it's hard for you to trust anyone."

"But you're not just anyone, Veronica." He smiled warmly and took her hand. "You're the *only* one."

Veronica looked at her niece and winked. "You know what, Ari?" Veronica turned back to her beloved. "If Wendell will have me, there is nothing that would make me happier than to be his wife."

"Oh, my goodness!" Ariana and Alisa squealed at the same time.

"What did you just say?" Wendell stood suddenly. "Please tell me I wasn't hearing things."

Veronica stood and moved closer to Wendell. "Wendell, there is no reason—"

"Jackie, you and Cedes get in here," Roland interrupted. "You're missing a moment!"

Jackie and Mercedes were way ahead of Roland. They had abandoned the task in the kitchen and were in the family room before Roland finished.

Veronica had stopped talking and had turned to look at her family. Wendell gently turned her to face him again and encouraged her to continue. "Don't stop now. I've waited so long to hear what you're about to say."

Veronica smiled and continued. "As I was saying before I

was so rudely interrupted"—she stole a quick, teasing glance at Roland—"there's no reason for us not to be married. We've talked about this for years now, and nothing is a certainty. But I am sure of one thing and that is I love you."

Wendell lifted her six inches off the floor and kissed her. "Only half as much as I love you."

They kissed again, this time as though there was no one else in the world, not to mention the room, except them.

The other adults in the room began to cheer and clap as Wendell gently let Veronica slip back to her feet. They turned to look at the others, both beaming.

"I don't know what came over me," Veronica finally managed, "but I know this is the right thing at the right time." She stared up at Wendell as he leaned over to kiss her again.

"You can thank me!" Alisa boasted. "I did it!"

Roland leapt to his feet and announced, "This calls for champagne."

"Indeed." Terry walked over to his sister and hugged her tightly as he whispered, "I'm so happy for you. This is the kind of love you've always deserved."

Veronica could only hold on to Terry as the fullness in her heart choked the words from her.

The women filled the remainder of the evening with talk of wedding dates and colors while the men moved to the pool table, where congratulatory talk abounded. Wendell and Veronica bid them all good night shortly after midnight. Mercedes and Jackie cleaned the family room and kitchen as Roland and Terry put away the long-abandoned games.

"What a wonderful turn of events," Mercedes said as she washed champagne flutes.

"Who would have ever thought this day would have ended

on such a pleasant note?" Jackie spooned dip into a plastic container.

"You okay, Jack?" Mercedes stopped washing the glasses and moved closer to her friend. "I know you're happy for Wendell and Veronica, but there's something wrong."

Jackie smiled weakly and said, "You know me too well."

"Out with it," Mercedes encouraged.

"This has absolutely nothing to do with what happened here tonight. In fact, it saved the day for me. It gave me something else to think about instead of wallowing in self-pity."

"Catherine?"

"Who else?" Jackie stopped spooning and turned to Mercedes. "I have to tell Terry."

Puzzled, Mercedes cocked her head to the left and innocently asked, "Tell him what?"

Jackie looked around the room to make sure no one was in earshot. "That Ariana and Alisa are not his children."

CHAPTER FIFTY-THREE

*J*ackie stared at her reflection in the mirror as she held the electric toothbrush in her hand. She'd rehearsed in her head at least one thousand times in the past hour how she would break the news to Terry. Nothing seemed right. Why *did* she feel the burning urge to share what she suspected with him? What would it do to him? What could it do to them?

Terry startled her when he knocked on the bathroom door before he entered. "You aiight in here? You're going to wear the batteries down in that thing."

"Uh, yeah." Jackie struggled. "I'm, uh, fine."

"I know I said it before, but it bears repeating. Isn't it wonderful about Veronica and Wendell?"

Jackie let out a breath, opened the door and stepped into the bedroom. "It is just marvelous. You know we pretty much planned the wedding tonight."

Terry kissed her on the cheek, spanked her playfully on the behind and said, "Why am I not surprised? Hurry up and come to bed, girl. A brotha got a little sumin sumin for ya."

When Jackie didn't respond, Terry turned back to look at her. She still stood staring at her reflection in the mirror above the triple dresser. She didn't see him approach her until he was right next to her.

"What's wrong, baby?" he asked as he slipped his arms around her waist from behind. As her eyes met his, tears flooded forth. He pulled her into his arms and stroked her back. "Everything is going to work out, baby. If I remember, you're the one who told *me* that."

Between sobs Jackie managed, "You don't understand."

"I understand better than anyone can, baby."

"No." Jackie jerked away from Terry and stared at him. "There's something I have to tell you. Something that is so horrific that it may destroy our family as we know it."

Mass confusion painted lines on Terry's face as he backed away. "What are you talking about? Nothing can destroy us. We have God and love—it doesn't get any better than that."

"This is big, really big."

"You're scaring me, Jackie." Terry opened and clenched his fist involuntarily.

"Let's go into the retreat and sit." Jackie took his hand and led him to the sofa overlooking the fountain.

As Jackie sat, she looked out the window, wondering one last time if she was doing the right thing.

"What is this all about?" Terry's voice began to crack as fear gripped his soul.

Jackie took a deep breath before she began. "Remember when we were in Dr. Chandler's office the first time and he told us that Ariana's blood type matched Catherine's perfectly? He said Ariana and Catherine are type AB negative."

"Yeah, I remember. So?"

"You're type O."

"Okay?"

Jackie stared down at her hands. Once the poop was out of the horse, there was no way to put it back.

"Jackie, what are you trying to tell me?"

"A few years ago I did research on blood types for an article. From all of my research I believe that it's impossible for Ariana . . ."

"For Ariana to what?" Terry's pulse began to race.

"If one parent is blood type AB and the other is O, then the child won't be AB. The only way for Ariana to be AB negative is if her father is blood type AB, B or A."

"But you just said I'm type O."

Jackie only stared at Terry to give him a moment to hear his own statement. After a few seconds, which felt like a year, he shot up from the couch.

"What the hell are you trying to tell me, Jackie?" Terry began moving away from her. When she didn't answer quickly enough, he yelled at her. "What are you saying?"

"Ever since I heard the blood type, I've been examining the girls. I've looked for any of your features in them." Jackie stood and moved closer to him. "Other than your gentle spirit, they're Catherine's spitting image."

"So what? Michelle is *your* spitting image." Terry's racing heart made his head pound. "That doesn't mean anything."

"I pray to God I'm wrong." Jackie lowered her voice to barely above a whisper. "The only way to be sure is with a paternity test."

"You're out of your flippin' mind." Terry's anger made the veins in his forehead bulge. "Those are my children in there. I brought them home from the hospital!"

"Keep your voice down. They'll hear you."

Terry moved to within two inches of Jackie's nose as he spoke through clenched teeth. "I don't know what's gotten into you. But your jealousy is out of control. First you accuse me of taking Catherine's side and now you come in here telling me that they aren't my children."

"Terry, listen to me," Jackie pleaded. "I've tormented myself over whether to tell you what I suspected. I didn't want to hurt you, but you deserve to know the truth."

"You know what truth is, Jackie?" Terry spat. "For the past eighteen years I have loved those two girls with every fiber of my being. From the moment I saw them through the nursery window screaming I've known they were a part of me. For nearly a dozen of those years I've loved you, despite your insecurities. But if this is your way of trying to separate me from my daughters, you've lost your mind."

"Nothing is further from the truth." Jackie began to cry. "I only thought you should know. I don't expect you to do anything about it!" Jackie's words came in spurts.

"Then why would you ever tell me such a thing, especially if you aren't certain. You're no expert. You could have the facts wrong, and you and I both know there are always exceptions to the rules of biology."

"You're right," Jackie conceded. "I thought as your wife I should . . ."

"You should what?" Terry startled Jackie with his harsh tone. "Do whatever you can to rip my heart from my body?"

Jackie collapsed in a heap on the couch, wailing.

Terry's anger clouded his vision and thinking. "I need to get out of here before I say or do something that I'll never be able to fix." Terry ran from the room before Jackie was able to stop him.

She felt totally spent. Mercedes had been right. She never should have told him what she suspected. What had she done? The hum of the garage door broke into her despair. Where was he going at this hour?

The sound of peeling rubber left her with her own thoughts and fears as her husband disappeared into the night.

CHAPTER FIFTY-FOUR

"*M*eet me at Denny's," Terry blurted when Roland picked up on the second ring.

For more than twenty years the two friends had been able to read the need of the other. Roland never questioned the reason, he simply said, "I'll be there in fifteen minutes."

"Make it ten." Terry flipped the phone closed without another word.

The short drive to the neighborhood icon was a blur. "*I believe that it's impossible for Ariana . . .*" Jackie's words echoed throughout the car. He turned on the CD player and cranked it, but it couldn't drown out her voice. "*I believe that it's impossible for Ariana . . .*" As he made the right turn into the parking lot he caught sight of Roland in the left turn lane.

They parked side by side and exited their cars at the same time. "Hey, man, what's up?" Roland asked with concern in his voice.

"Sorry to drag you out of the house in the middle of the night." Terry gave him a brotha-to-brotha hug.

"You call, I come. You know we got it like that."

The two walked in silence to the front door of the eating establishment. Despite the lateness of the hour the restaurant was almost full. Fortunately for Terry's nerves, they didn't have to wait to be seated.

The friendly host placed the menus in front of them and told them the server would be with them shortly. They both moved the menus to the side and stared at each other. Terry knew that was his cue.

"So what's up, my brotha?" Roland asked. "And we couldn't have had this conversation two hours ago when I was at your house?"

"Two hours ago, my life hadn't been turned upside down." Terry wouldn't make eye contact with Roland.

"Well, you betta get to talkin', because Cedes was about to break a brotha off more than proper. All that wedding talk got her teakettle whistlin'."

Terry tried to laugh but couldn't find it in his soul. "Jackie told me she doesn't think the twins are mine," he blurted.

A confused look replaced Roland's smile. "What in the hell are you talking about?" He sat up straight. "Why would she say something like that?"

"Because she's jealous and self-centered."

"Jacqueline Rogers-Winston? Come on now."

"She's always been so insecure about everything. But this is going too far."

"Okay, let's back this train up."

The waitress interrupted Roland. Terry ordered two coffees and Roland added a piece of pie. The waitress disappeared as quickly as she'd arrived. Roland continued. "As I was saying, you need to stop and think about who you're talking about. Now, I don't live with the woman, but the one thing I know is she'd walk on broken glass for you."

"But after all this time she is still insecure. Not absolutely sure that I love her. It drives me nuts."

"Okay, with that being said, how did she come to this conclusion about Ari and 'Lisa?"

Terry took a deep breath as the waitress set the coffee before him. He barely heard her when she asked if there was anything else she could get for them at the moment. They declined.

Terry continued. "She was spouting some nonsense about blood types. Saying that it's impossible for them to have the blood type they have if I'm their father."

Roland put down his fork. "What blood type are the twins?"

"AB negative."

"And you?"

"O."

"And Catherine?"

"AB negative."

Roland pushed the pie back. "Are you sure about this?"

Terry stared questioningly at Roland before he answered. "Jackie told me I'm O, and I remember hearing that somewhere, so I'm reasonably sure." Terry's eyes narrowed. "What are you asking me?"

"First things first, you need to change your thinking about Jackie. No matter what her idiosyncrasies, that woman loves the crust in your eyes after a winter sleep." Roland took a sip of coffee. "And I don't know what I would have done if I was the one who had stumbled onto this information, but Jackie is right. Though possible, it is highly improbable that an AB and O mix is going to produce an AB negative."

"That's crazy, Roland." Terry was visibly angry. "You've been there with me since the beginning. There's no way Ariana and Alisa are not my children."

"Look, my brotha, we could be wrong. Maybe you aren't type O, but if you are, the only way to conclusively prove you're their father is a paternity test."

"Why are you trippin'? Now *you* sound like Jackie. I'm not taking any test to prove they are my children. There *is* no test that can tell me I'm not their father!"

"I understand. But—"

Terry shot up from the table and startled Roland. "There is no *but!*" Terry pulled a ten-dollar bill from his pocket and tossed it onto the table and left the restaurant without another word.

Roland started to follow him, but decided he needed to leave him alone, at least for now. He decided to eat the pie and think of what to say to his friend when he called him again.

Terry slid behind the wheel and slammed the door. He wanted to punch Roland for even giving this nonsense consideration. It was a conspiracy between his wife and best friend to . . . to do what? Why would either of them do anything to hurt him?

Was it possible what they said was the truth? Had Catherine deceived him from the beginning? His thoughts were vying for position. He needed time to think. He slipped the key in the ignition, turned it slightly to the right and the car sprang to life. As he backed out of the parking space he didn't know where he was headed, he just knew he needed to get away from here. He didn't remember getting onto the Interstate or when he transitioned to I-20. He didn't have a clue how long he had been driving until he saw the sign welcoming him to Louisiana.

The time had allowed him to think about what to do about the possibility that Ariana and Alisa were not his children—not a damn thing. There was no test or testimony that could change the way he felt about the stars of his life. He needed to talk to Jackie. He needed to hold her. She was more than three hours away; a phone call would have to do.

Despite the clock reading 3:47 on his dash, Jackie picked up on the first ring. "Baby, I'm sorry," Jackie blurted. "I—"

Terry interrupted her. "You've done nothing wrong. It's me that's sorry. I said some ugly things to you and I had no right."

"Where are you?"

"Almost in Shreveport."

"Shreveport?" Jackie exclaimed. "What the hell are you doing in Shreveport?"

"I just started driving and this is where I ended up." Terry sighed. "I'm too far away from you, baby. I need you here with me."

"You should just get a hotel room and come back after you get some rest."

"I don't want to stay away from you all night."

"I got news for you. If you made a U-turn right this minute it would be morning before you got here," Jackie half teased. "I'm just so glad to hear from you."

"Baby, please forgive me for attacking you," Terry pressed on. "I met Roland when I first left and he told me if you have all the facts straight, there is a possibility that I . . ." Terry let the incomplete sentence hang in the car.

"We don't need to make any decisions one way or another tonight. You just need to get off the road and find a safe place to rest. When you get home in the morning, everything will seem a little clearer. Call me when you get into a room."

"Baby?"

"Yes?"

"Do you forgive me?"

"There's nothing to forgive. But if there were, you know I can't be mad at you."

Terry's heart smiled. "I love you."

"I love you, too."

With those words the two hung up. Terry's next instinct was to call Roland, but even a best friend knows when to wait until daybreak.

$\mathcal{C}$atherine ran her hand along the beautiful cherrywood table as she waited for the teleconference to begin. Jonah squirmed in his seat as he wondered why he hadn't been made privy to the purpose of this meeting. And who was this stranger seated next to Catherine? The pair appeared rather chummy as they reviewed the contents of a green folder.

The screen came to life as the conference conductor announced all who were in attendance. The large screen instantly divided into six smaller sections. The leaders from the five divisions of Hawkins International were brought into one room by the state-of-the-art technology.

"Gentlemen, I'm sure you are busy with the implementation of phase two of our plan, so this will be very brief and to the point." Catherine cleared her throat. "As you all know, I've been looking to appoint an executive vice president of the international operation for a while now.

"We've grown and I expect to double the size of the company in the next five years. It's a foolish captain who believes she alone can run a ship. To that end I would like to introduce to you the latest addition to the HI team and my second in command, Rahid MacDonald. Rahid comes to us with a Harvard MBA with emphasis in international commerce. I'm sure you each will welcome him and offer Mr. MacDonald your full cooperation. He will visit each of your facilities within the next two weeks. He will assist you with the implementation of the outsourcing and much more."

Catherine finally took a breath and turned first to Jonah, who sat stunned. Jonah's complexion had turned so sickeningly pale that she thought he might have had some sort of attack. She then turned her attention to the screen as she studied each of the others' expressions.

Jean-Michel seemed the least affected by the news. David looked as devastated as Jonah. She had dangled the carrot before him for so long she almost wanted to apologize—almost. Anthony peered into the camera lens, expressionless. Jeyson seemed nervous and ill at ease. Francisco seemed relieved. Jonah rose and stormed from the room just as Catherine was about to ask if there were any questions. Rahid shot her a glance that asked if he should go after him. Catherine nixed the idea with her eyes. "Gentlemen, do any of you have questions of either me or Mr. MacDonald?"

Jean-Michel spoke up first. "Will I deal only with Rahid or both of you?"

"Starting almost immediately I will be taking some time off to deal with some health issues," Catherine stated very matter-of-factly. "While I will be in constant contact with Mr. MacDonald, you each will be in contact with only him. But I assure you, gentlemen, that the words and requests from him are as though I am speaking. There will be no changes in our plans or timelines."

"Why this change now, one so massive when we are all experiencing the discomfort of this outsourcing?" David's German accent was so thick it made him difficult to understand—a sure sign he was upset.

"I have spread myself too thin for too long. This is the perfect opportunity for Rahid to come on board with the direction HI is taking."

There were questions on the faces of all of them, but no one expressed his concerns. Catherine waited a beat before she addressed Anthony. "Rahid's first stop will be Italy, as Anthony is having problems with phase one of the plan. He will arrive day after tomorrow."

Anthony mumbled something in Italian that couldn't be clearly heard. Catherine ignored him. "If there is nothing else, we will be in conference with each of you in the next few days. Once we have things settled in Tony's plant, Rahid will move on to your facility, David, but there will be more about that later."

The teleconference ended and Catherine smiled with satisfaction. She instructed Rahid to find Jonah and for both of them to meet her in her office in thirty minutes. She knew Jonah's days would be numbered because he'd refuse to cooperate with his new boss.

JONAH WAS IN HIS OFFICE behind a locked door as he dialed Anthony's number with trembling fingers. The phone was answered on the third ring.

"What is it that you want from me?" Jonah asked.

The bone-chilling laughter seemed to echo throughout the universe as Anthony explained his plan to Jonah. The two agreed to meet as soon as Anthony could get away.

Jonah had held the phone so tightly his knuckles lost their color. His heart leapt into his throat at the knock on the door.

CHAPTER FIFTY-SIX

"Ms. Hawkins?" The faint voice gently nudged Catherine awake.

Catherine's eyes fluttered open as she tried to remember where she was. Then the smell and sound hit her at once, bringing on a wave of nausea. "How long have I been asleep?"

"For about an hour." Brenda, Catherine's dialysis technician, answered with a bright smile. "But you're all done for today. Can I get you anything?"

"Got a spare kidney?" Catherine asked sarcastically.

"I wish I had one hundred to give." Brenda helped her from the lounge chair. "All of this takes some getting used to."

"It's harder than you can ever imagine from the other side of that machine." Catherine winced as she tried to put her arm into her jacket.

Brenda noticed the pain on Catherine's face and asked, "How long has your arm been sore?"

"A couple of days, I guess."

"Have you called your doctor?"

"I'm scheduled to see him tomorrow."

"Ms. Hawkins, you know you're supposed to report any soreness in your arm right away," Brenda chastised.

"Yeah, yeah, yeah." Catherine tried to dismiss her. "I'll tell him all about my woes tomorrow."

"Are you seeing your social worker and psychologist?"

"Look, Brenda!" Catherine snapped. "I come in here to see you three times a week. Your job is to hook me up to this damned machine, pump all the blood from my body, clean it and put it back. I don't need your dime-store psychology. I'm a strong black woman. We don't need social workers and shrinks—we solve our own problems."

Unfazed by Catherine's outburst Brenda simply said, "I can see how well you're handling it all."

"F—" Catherine caught the word in her mouth. "I'll see you on Friday." Catherine grabbed her purse and moved toward the door. Her normal, confident stride was held hostage by fatigue and weakness. Jonathan appeared almost miraculously with the car. He rushed around to her side to open the door, and Catherine wearily slid inside.

As she settled in the back for the journey home, she decided to see what crisis had found its way into her world in the three hours she was locked inside the hell called the dialysis center. She had eight messages.

Three of them were from Claire with trivial questions she should have bothered Jonah with. With that thought Catherine realized she hadn't seen much of Jonah since the announcement of Rahid's appointment two weeks before. He always seemed busy with some task or other, but she knew he was hurt. Her faithful puppy was away, licking his wounds; he'd be back soon enough.

She had one message from Rahid with his daily report from Italy and Anthony's latest antics. As soon as she got her strength back she was going to take a little trip to Rome, and when she left, Anthony Esposito would be unemployed.

She deleted the messages from the doctor's office, social worker and psychologist. The last message made her sit up straight—it was from Terrance. He was in Los Angeles and wanted to meet with her immediately. She was almost angry to think he hadn't made an appointment but was too hopeful that he came bearing news that Alisa had changed her mind.

She dialed the number he'd left on the voice mail. The automated attendant answered, giving instructions for dialing guest rooms. She pressed the numbers for his room.

Terry answered on the first ring. "This is Terry Winston."

"This is Catherine." Her tone was even, though her pulse raced. "Why are you in Los Angeles?"

"To meet with you," Terry stated flatly. "We need to talk."

"You took a hell of a chance that I was even in town. What's so important that you couldn't discuss it over the phone?"

"I need to talk to you face-to-face."

"Has Alisa changed her mind?"

"What time is good for you?" Terry liked having Catherine at a disadvantage.

"No time like the present. I'm about twenty minutes from where you are."

Terry held on to a newfound confidence as he said, "Make it an hour and I'll meet you in the lobby." He hung up the phone.

Catherine stared at the cell phone in disbelief. Where had he found balls on sale? She smiled to herself as she thought, *This should be interesting.* Terry fell back on the bed with a smile. When he'd returned home from his road trip Jackie had met him with a hot breakfast and forgiveness. The six hours of driving had given him more than enough time to understand the torment she must have experienced.

He'd explained to her that nothing could change his love for Ariana and Alisa, but she convinced him for a multitude of reasons that he needed to know if he was their biological father. He refused to take the necessary test, but he did agree that he would ask Catherine if there was even a possibility that he wasn't their father.

After a few days of tormenting thoughts, he'd decided he needed to pay Catherine a visit. He had checked Catherine's schedule with Claire and knew that she would be in the L.A. office all week. Jackie had wanted to make the trip with him, but he knew this was one trip he had to make alone. He liked the element of surprise that Roland and Mercedes suggested. After hearing the frustration in Catherine's voice, he knew he had done the right thing.

This hour was probably going to be the longest of his forty-one years. He decided to fill it with a call to Jackie.

"Hey, baby." Jackie's voice immediately relaxed him.

"Hey, yourself. She's on her way."

"Are you nervous?"

"Not as much as I thought I would be. I need to confront her. I need to get things off my chest that have lived there for more than eighteen years."

"We'll be praying for you. Roland and Mercedes are coming over for dinner."

"Good. I'll call you when it's over." Terry started to hang up, then added, "Jackie?"

"Yes, Terry?"

"Thank you."

"Whatever for?"

"Just loving me like you do."

Terry could feel her smile across the miles that separated them. "Talk to you soon."

Terry decided to shower and change. He'd brought a suit and a casual ensemble. He opted for the suit because he meant business.

TERRY WATCHED THROUGH THE GLASS wall with sliding doors that made up the entrance to the LAX Hilton as Catherine stepped from the back of a car that could best be described as a mini limousine. Terry stood, smoothed his tie and buttoned his jacket.

Catherine's appearance shocked him as she approached him through the sliding glass doors. She seemed to have aged ten years. She was even thinner this time than when he'd last seen her. *"When God fixes a thing, it is truly fixed."* Momma C.'s words were so clear Terry turned quickly to see if she was standing nearby.

"Terrance." Catherine extended her hand, which felt very warm.

"Catherine." Despite the anger that had built inside him, he had to ask, "How are you feeling?"

"How do I look like I feel?"

"I've seen you look better."

"Why are we here?" Catherine positioned herself in the corner of a plush sofa. "Has Alisa decided to do the right thing by me?"

Terry sat adjacent in a well-padded armchair. His eyes met

hers and he felt sorry for her, not because of her illness but because of the emptiness he saw there. "Alisa hasn't changed her mind. She's steadfast. She wants nothing to do with you."

"Then what could you possibly need to discuss with me? Don't you know how busy I am?"

"I assure you this won't take long." Terry leaned forward. His first instinct was to look at the floor, but he knew how important it was to look Catherine in the eyes when he talked to her.

"Good."

"As you're aware, Ariana went through extensive testing to see if she was a compatible donor. The initial test was to see if your blood types were compatible, which they were."

"What else did you expect?" Catherine's patience grew thinner by the second. "I gave birth to her."

"Indeed you did." Terry continued at a snail's pace on purpose. He sat back and crossed his legs. "The test also revealed that it is next to impossible that I am the twins' father." There, he said it out loud!

Of all the possibilities of what news Terrance Winston came to L.A. bearing, this would have been below Catherine's last choice. She batted her eyelashes and pulled at her jacket sleeve. "What?"

"You heard me. I'm type O. The twins shouldn't be type AB. Their father could only be type A, B or AB."

"Son of a bitch," Catherine said, lost in her thoughts.

"I think 'daughters of' is more accurate," Terry chided. "I need to know if there is any possibility that I'm not their biological father."

For a long moment Catherine only stared. Then she threw her head back, laughing. Terry refused to believe that she mocked him with laughter. "What's so damned funny?"

"I guess I picked the wrong guy." Catherine continued to laugh. "As the kids would say, my bad."

Terry stood and began pacing the hotel lobby. He suddenly turned to her and yelled, " 'My bad'? That's all you have to say for yourself?"

"Look, you never thought you and I were exclusive. I tried to figure out who I'd slept with closest to the time I thought I got pregnant, and you were so willing to do the responsible thing. I just went along for the ride because I had no intention of keeping it anyway."

"It? The same *it* from whom you now want a kidney?"

Catherine stopped smiling.

"If I'm not their father, then who is?" Terry demanded.

Catherine looked up into his eyes, and for the first time she saw an angry fire that she hadn't known he was capable of igniting. Her first impulse was to crush him even more by telling him that it was his precious friend Roland, but she knew that was impossible since Roland had refused her every advance. For the first time in all the years she'd known Terrance, she feared what he might do to her.

Terry leaned down into her face, just inches from her nose, and demanded, "I want an answer, Catherine!"

She looked first to the left, then to the right for a means of escape. The bellman had turned his attention to them and she suspected she could get his help. "Sit down, Terrance. You're bringing attention to us."

Terry looked to the left and his eyes locked with the bellman's. He backed away and returned to his seat. "Start talking."

"You were the only one who gave me any attention after you slept with me." Catherine's soft tone made her seem small and weak. "Some would call for a second date, while others would see me on campus and not even acknowledge I was alive.

"When I had to tell my Holy-Roller mother that I was pregnant, she of course asked me who the father was. I couldn't tell her I was knocked up but didn't know by whom."

Terry's head involuntarily fell into his hands as he began to chant, "Oh my God."

"I told the lie for so long that even I believed it. After all, it could have been the truth."

Terry raised tear-filled eyes as he opened his mouth to speak. The fragmented words stumbled forth. "And you—you never—you never once thought you should tell me that it was possible that I might not be their father."

"I never cared about you or them. You were willing to take them off my hands and I got on with my life."

"Do you hear yourself?" Terry's feelings of disdain turned to pity as he saw how hate had eaten away at Catherine from the inside.

"What are you going to do? Will you tell them the truth?"

"Are you insane? Sperm donation didn't make me their father. Loving them from the moment I laid eyes on them did. Taking care of them when they were sick, comforting them when they were scared, that's what makes me their father.

"Escorting them down the aisle on their wedding days and holding my grandchildren for the first time makes me their daddy, not my name on a piece of paper." Terry stood. "I don't know why I had to come here. I knew in my heart that whatever you said wouldn't change a thing—not for me anyway."

"So does this mean you're not going to tell them?"

"Never."

Something inside Catherine felt relief, even gratitude. "Terrance, I *am* sorry."

"For what? Giving me a lifetime of happiness? But I'm sure that's not something you can even understand."

Terry turned and walked toward the elevator bank. When he looked back, Catherine was still sitting in the same spot, staring at him.

CHAPTER FIFTY-SEVEN

*T*he pain in Catherine's arm made it impossible to sleep despite the three sleeping pills and three tumblers of vodka she used to wash them down. Her lips felt hot and her eyelids burned—a sure sign she had a fever. She tried to throw the covers off her, but she couldn't lift her arm. She gently slid from between the twelve-hundred-thread-count sheets and stumbled into the bathroom.

The bathroom light assaulted her eyes as she tried to focus. She turned on the cold water and began splashing some on her face. The temperature of the water was a shock to her system and she drew in quick breaths. As she dried her face she caught a glimpse of her reflection. The woman looking back at her made her gasp. Her hue had deepened at least three shades with even darker circles around sunken eyes.

"You can't go on like this," Catherine whispered into the mirror. She opened the medicine cabinet and retrieved two extra-strength aspirin. As she left the bathroom she looked longingly at the toilet. *Oh, the things we take for granted.* She turned off the light.

Catherine slowly walked across the massive space to the pitcher of ice water Dexter had left on the bar. She poured a half glass, swallowed the pills and padded back to the bed. The pain in her arm was so acute she could no longer ignore it. As she sat on the bed she slowly removed her pajama top, taking care not to aggravate her arm. As she looked down at the red and swollen lump in her arm, tears welled in her eyes. Yet another complication had come to plague her. *Alisa, you must change your mind.* With that thought, Catherine drew on a reservoir of strength. Her gaze fell on the envelope on the nightstand. The neat calligraphy of her name and address made her smile. She picked up the envelope and slowly pulled out the engraved card covered with tissue paper. The small card with the name Ariana Winston fell to the floor.

And why shouldn't I accept my daughter's invitation to the commencement exercise? Maybe, just maybe, if Alisa saw her like this she would feel sorry enough to change her mind. She dropped the invitation onto the bed and picked up the phone.

"Adrian Greenwood here," Alex's replacement answered cheerfully despite the early morning hour.

"Captain Greenwood, we're going to Dallas. I'd like to arrive around two this afternoon."

"Very good, Ms. Hawkins. I will see you at nine."

Alex had been stunned when Catherine hadn't renewed his contract. She informed him that she believed it best that he concentrate on his family life. She hired an older, Anglo-American, seasoned pilot who had been happily married to the same woman for more than thirty years. So far, she was pleased with the arrangement; after all, she had Franklin to amuse her once she was well.

CHAPTER FIFTY-EIGHT

*A*fter the commencement ceremony ended, the family and friends of the forty-one seniors of the School for the Talented and Gifted congregated in the lobby outside the school auditorium, trying to find their beloved graduates. Jackie spotted the twins first and began waving frantically to catch their attention. The Winston clan scuttled through the crowd as best they could, reaching Alisa first with outstretched arms. The proud daddy held an arrangement of yellow roses for each of his daughters.

Jackie hugged Alisa first, then Ariana. "I didn't know I could be this proud! I feel like my chest is going to burst!"

Alisa hugged her back tightly. "Oh, Mom, you always say the same thing." She giggled. "But thank you anyhow. I love hearing it."

"What's a dad gotta do to get some of that?" Terry said as he passed them each their roses. "You two are just too much.

The crème de la crème, the cat's meow, the shiz-nit and you're all mine!"

The girls hugged his neck at the same time. T.J. was trying to edge his way between them to get in a hug of his own.

Michael and Michelle stepped up next, to offer their congratulations. "Oh, I can't wait until this is me!" Michelle hugged first Ariana, then Alisa.

Michael, taking the cool-breeze approach, smiled and said, "That was tight. When do we eat?" Everyone laughed. Michael looked perplexed.

In the middle of the revelry Ariana heard someone softly call her name. When she turned, she was face-to-face with Catherine. Ariana's initial reaction was a huge smile, but after a closer look at Catherine's appearance she quickly became concerned.

Jackie, seeing Ariana's expression change, followed her line of sight. Jackie involuntarily gasped at a withered Catherine. "Oh my God," she whispered.

Ariana managed, "Catherine, you came!"

"I wouldn't have missed this for anything. I'm very proud of you." Catherine looked at Alisa. "Both of you."

Ariana moved toward her, to hug her with her free arm. As Catherine leaned down, she winced in pain. "Are you okay?" Ariana asked.

Alisa stood, staring, wondering if this was just another lame attempt by Catherine to manipulate everyone's emotions.

"I haven't felt too well for the past couple of days, but I'll be okay," Catherine answered weakly. "Today is all about you and Alisa."

Catherine caught Terry's and Jackie's eyes before she offered, "I'd love to take everyone out to dinner, if your parents will allow me."

"We're having a party at our house." Michael spoke up before anyone else had the chance.

With pleading eyes Ariana looked to her parents. "Mom, Dad, can Catherine come?" Jackie stared at Ariana. How could she even entertain the thought of Catherine being in their home. She shot a glance to Terry.

The noise that surrounded them seemed drowned out by the pregnant silence.

"It's okay, Ariana. I'm just glad I got to see your commencement. Congratulations on your special recognition." Catherine looked at Jackie and Terry again. "Maybe I can take you to lunch tomorrow?"

How in the hell can we say no to that? Oh, she's good. "No, wait, Catherine," Jackie said, trying to force a smile. "You're welcome to come by the house. We're leaving now."

"I want to take pictures with my friends first," Alisa said with a trace of spite.

"How about you start with your family first, missy," Terry teased. "I don't want to hear that the batteries are dead because you used them all up on your friends."

The cap-and-gowned duo posed for every conceivable combination of picture. Catherine stood by, looking on, feeling as out of place as George W. at a Mensa convention until Ariana asked, "Catherine, would you like to take a picture with us?"

Alisa elbowed her, but Ariana pretended not to notice. Catherine smiled genuinely and said, "I'd love to."

As Catherine watched Ariana and Alisa she felt strange. Not at all physical, but a warmth in her heart. When she saw how beautiful and smart they were she could only imagine what she felt to be maternal pride. A sense of pride for her children was a new and different experience. For the first time in eighteen years she regretted missing so much of their lives. She had achieved great things, but as her mother had promised, she had missed out on what mattered most. Her motives for making the trip had been misguided. She wanted so desperately to make them all understand that she was truly sorry. Sorry for everything.

As Catherine tried to position herself between them, Alisa moved to the other side of Ariana. The only smile captured in this Kodak moment belonged to Ariana.

As the crowd began to thin, Ariana and Alisa returned to a somber group. "We're ready," Alisa said, trying to lighten the mood.

"Would you like to ride in the limo with me," Catherine asked, adding quickly, "if it's okay with your parents?"

"I don't," Alisa said as she walked away.

Ariana searched her father's face for permission, afraid to look at Jackie. Terry smiled. Ariana responded enthusiastically, "I'd love to."

"Can I ride in the limo, too?" T.J. asked, tugging on his mother's arm.

"You're coming with us." Jackie pulled him by the hand.

"Jackie," Catherine began timidly, "I really don't mind if he comes with us. There's actually room for everyone."

"Mom, please," T.J. begged.

Why do I feel like I've just been asked to dance with danger? The hair stood up on the back of Jackie's neck, warning her to say no, but she gave in.

Terry accelerated away from the limo shortly after they left the school parking lot. Michelle talked incessantly about what it would be like when she and Michael graduated from high school. Michael wanted Jackie to repeat the menu for the party for the fourth time and was quite curious about whether there would be anything ready to eat upon their arrival. Alisa stared out the window in silence.

Veronica and Wendell greeted the five of them in the driveway. Roland had a court appearance that day and the Carpenters were expected at seven—thirty-five minutes from now. The five of them spilled from the car just as Wendell and Veronica presented Alisa with balloons and a gift bag. "Where's Ariana?" Veronica asked.

"She's riding with Catherine in her limo." Alisa spat out each word as though her mouth had a bad taste.

Veronica raised an eyebrow and looked incredulously at her brother. "It's a long story," Terry offered.

"I bet it is," Veronica said under her breath as she pasted on a big smile and offered Alisa her arm. "Tell me about the ceremony and don't leave out a thing."

The rest of the crew followed the chummy pair into the kitchen through the garage. The catering staff was busy preparing trays and chafing dishes with a variety of luscious treats.

"Can we eat yet?" Michael asked.

Laughing out loud, Terry said, "Boy, do you have a tapeworm?"

Michael looked at him blankly and said, "A what?"

"Never—" Terry was interrupted by the front door flying open and T.J. rushing in.

"Mommy, Daddy, come quick. Miss Catherine is real sick. The man called nine-one-one."

The group scurried through the kitchen, across the foyer and out the front door as quickly as their legs would carry them. When they arrived at the opened back door of the limo they saw Catherine laid out on the backseat with her body twitching involuntarily. "Mom, Daddy, do something!" Ariana screamed.

"I've called the paramedics." The frightened young limo driver looked as though he thought someone was going to blame him for what was happening. "They should be here shortly."

Wendell moved everyone to the side. "Let me get in here." He placed his hand on her wrist and opened her eyelids with his fingertip. "She's seizing. She's burning up."

Ariana climbed out of limo through the driver's side door and ran around into Veronica's waiting arms. Alisa stood transfixed. Michael, Michelle and T.J. clung to their mother. Terry managed to speak. "Can we do anything until the paramedics get here?"

"Where's your ice bucket?" Wendell asked the driver.

The dumbfounded man simply pointed to the bar. Wendell began scooping ice into Catherine's blouse. Within a minute, the seizing stopped just as the first hint of the paramedics' arrival was heard. Time seemed to stand still as the siren grew louder. The fire truck and paramedic wagon turned the corner and came to a stop just behind the limo. The firefighters and paramedics seemed to leap from their vehicles before they came to a complete stop. Wendell backed away, filled them in on what he had done and let them go to work.

Neighbors appeared on the sidewalk as the Winston family stood by helplessly. In a matter of minutes an ambulance arrived and the paramedics placed a still-unconscious Catherine inside.

Once Catherine was on her way to the hospital, one of the rescue workers, Captain August, approached Wendell. "You did a good thing here. Her fever is over one hundred and three. She's being transported to the nearest hospital. Are you all her family?"

Ariana spoke up quickly. "Yes."

"I'd get to the hospital as quickly as possible if I were you. She has a very serious infection in the shunt for dialysis. She's let it go way too long." The captain turned to leave.

"Thank you, Captain."

He turned and smiled. "She's going to need you all to take care of her."

"We should go to the hospital." Ariana turned to her father with pleading eyes. "Will you drive us?"

"Us?" Alisa said with indignation. "What about our party?"

"How can you think of a party now?" Ariana began to cry.

"The same way she would think of her plans if this was you or me." Alisa turned and her eyes met her father's sad ones.

Ariana fell into Veronica's arms. Alisa looked at each of the adults. Feeling alone and confused she wondered why she and Ariana never seemed to agree when it came to Catherine. She did know one thing, however: she couldn't stand to see her sister in this much pain. Alisa walked over to where Ariana stood with Veronica and took her sister into her arms. "Let's go. I'll drive us."

Pride, like he'd never felt before, flowed through Terry as he saw his little girl as a real woman, acting unselfishly for the first time. She'd put aside her feelings for those of her sister. "No, I'll drive."

CHAPTER FIFTY-NINE

*B*ecause the guests were already en route to the party, Jackie stayed behind. Terry and the girls disappeared around the corner shortly after the ambulance left.

The only sound in the car was the soft music of Pat Metheny's guitar. Terry's thoughts traveled back to the day he first found out that he would become a father and how afraid he'd been. He'd felt so ill equipped to handle the responsibility, but had been determined to make the best of a difficult situation. What would he have done had he known then that there was even the slightest possibility that he might not have been their father? Would he have missed out on all this?

"Do you think Catherine will be okay, Daddy?" Ariana twisted the tissue in her hands.

She's way too ornery to die. "All we can do is pray for her," Terry said, glancing over at Ariana, then in the rearview mirror at Alisa. "It may look a lot worse than it is."

Ariana looked up, suddenly hopeful. "You really think so?"

"I don't want you to get your hopes up, so let's just wait and see."

Terry stole another glance at Alisa, who sat stoically in the backseat, looking out of the window. As Terry pulled into the emergency parking area he noticed the paramedics standing in the ambulance bay, talking. He quickly parked, and the three of them emerged from the car and moved to where they stood.

"You're Ms. Hawkins's family, right?" the younger of them asked.

"Yes," Ariana answered.

"They'll need you to stop at the admitting desk. The doctors are working on her and they'll let you know as soon as they can what's going on."

"Did she regain consciousness?" Terry asked this time.

"No, sir," the senior member of the team responded.

"Thank you," Terry said as he took Ariana's arm. "We'll go into the admitting office."

The three of them moved quickly through the automatic doors into an overflowing waiting room. There were people who coughed, while others held their heads. One man held a pan up to his mouth like he was going to throw up. The scene made Terry want to turn and run.

A pleasant woman sat at a small desk, taking names like they were in an overcrowded restaurant. "We're here to register a patient brought in by ambulance," Terry announced.

The aging woman looked down at a piece of paper, then said, "Is that for Catherine Hawkins?"

Ariana rushed to answer, "Yes!"

"Please have a seat and an admitting clerk will be right with you."

There were no three seats together, so Terry suggested the twins find seats while he stepped outside to call Jackie. Before Terry reached the door, a young Asian man wearing green scrubs, with the name Dr. Lim embroidered on it, caught his attention. "Is there anyone here with Catherine Hawkins?"

Terry, Ariana and Alisa all seemed to freeze in place. Terry spoke. "Right here."

"Please follow me."

The three obediently followed the man through the double doors. They quickly came to a stop at a small room with a desk and two chairs. "We can talk in here," Dr. Lim suggested. "I'll get another chair."

"I'll stand," Terry said.

Ariana and Alisa took seats in front of the desk, holding hands. "I am Dr. Lim and I've examined Ms. Hawkins." He looked at Terry and asked, "Is she your wife?"

Not hardly. "No, she is my daughters' birth mother. She was here visiting for their graduation."

"I see." Dr. Lim continued, "She is very sick. The shunt in her arm for dialysis is severely infected and while we're still waiting for some blood tests to come back, we fear that the infection has spread throughout her body."

"That doesn't sound good," Terry said.

"You are correct. This is very serious. We've already moved her to the intensive care unit. We're also going to have to replace the shunt. Who's her primary physician?"

They each looked from one to the other before Terry answered, "We're not sure. She lives in Los Angeles."

"Do you know when she was last dialyzed?"

"No, we don't. She only arrived this afternoon."

"Is she going to die?" Ariana asked as she squeezed Alisa's hand a little tighter.

"We're going to do everything we can to prevent that, but right now I cannot say for certain."

Terry took a long breath. "Do you know what caused the infection and how long she's had it?"

"Many renal failure patients' bodies reject the shunt as a foreign object. We have no way of knowing for sure what causes this." Dr. Lim looked quickly at Ariana and Alisa. "As for how long, that's hard to say, too. But she must have been feeling sick for days, and the site where the shunt is must have been very painful. Pain is the body's early warning system that something's definitely wrong."

"So if someone donated her a kidney, she wouldn't have these problems anymore?" Ariana asked.

"Our first priority is to get rid of the infection. She's not a candidate for a transplant as long as she has an infection of any kind."

"And after she's well?" Ariana pressed.

"Absolutely. A successful transplant would prevent this kind of thing from happening in the future."

Ariana took Alisa's hand and fell on her knees in front of her sister and began crying. " 'Lisa, please. You have to do this. Please don't let her suffer like this."

Alisa stared at her sister until her own eyes began to fill with tears. "Ari, please don't beg me to do this. You know how I feel. Suppose you need a kidney one day. Then what will we do?"

"But the doctors have all said the same thing. I'm fine. The one kidney I have works fine and there is no reason that it won't keep on doing that." The tears came harder and faster. "Please, 'Lisa. If you don't do it for Catherine, then do it for me."

Silence was Alisa's only response as she leaned over to hold her sister.

Dr. Lim cleared his throat. "Do you have any more questions?"

Ariana wiped her eyes with the back of her hand and tried to speak, but no words would come. Alisa, as had been their way for more than eighteen years, spoke for her. "When can we see her?"

"You'll have to clear that with the nurses in the intensive care unit." Dr. Lim smiled. "But I'm sure it won't be too long."

Dr. Lim stood, shook Terry's hand and smiled at the girls. "If there is anything else we can do in the emergency department, please be sure to let us know."

"Thank you, Dr. Lim," Terry said as they prepared to leave.

WHEN TERRY RETURNED to the waiting room after an update call to Jackie he found the girls huddled together and Ariana still crying. He forced a smile and made his way across the large room.

Ariana sat up, wiping her eyes. "Can we go to the intensive care unit now?"

"Your mother, I mean Jackie, wanted to know if you guys wanted to come home for a while. Your guests have arrived and it's not much of a party if you aren't there."

"How can we have a party when Catherine is so sick?" Ariana stood suddenly.

"Ari, there is nothing we can do here." Alisa pulled at her sister's hand, trying to get her to return to her seat.

"Alisa's right. They're going to be working on her for a while, I'm sure, so the most we could do is sit in the waiting room."

"We're never going to graduate from high school again, Ari. Our friends are at the house and some really good food."

"Suppose something happens while we're away?"

Terry thought quickly for a solution that would make everyone happy. "Let's do this. We'll go up to the ICU, leave our number and tell them to call if there is any change and we can be back here in ten minutes."

Ariana was ready to object, but the plan did make sense. "And if they call, no matter when, we'll come right back?"

Terry crossed his chest with his right index finger. "Cross my heart."

"Okay," Ariana said quietly. "But we're going upstairs first, right?"

Terry fought back the urge to hug her. "Yes, ma'am."

Ariana smiled at her father and gave him a hug. The father and daughters left the emergency department hand in hand. Ariana's sadness weighed down her steps. Alisa's confusion crowded her head. Terry's worries for his daughters made his head ache.

CHAPTER SIXTY

Jackie was loading the last of the glasses into the dishwasher when the phone rang. She glanced at the clock before she answered. A phone call at fifteen minutes before midnight was never good news.

"Hello."

"This is Ms. Wright from Zale Lipshy University Hospital ICU." The woman's no-nonsense tone made Jackie's heart skip a beat.

"I'll get Ariana." Jackie didn't want to have to translate any information.

Ariana, who had been sitting, watching, from the first ring of the telephone, rose slowly and moved toward Jackie. She held the phone for several seconds before she said hello.

"Ms. Winston, we have you as the contact for Catherine Hawkins. Is that correct?"

Ariana's breath didn't seem to know what to do. "Yes."

"Ms. Hawkins's fever has spiked and we're doing everything we can at this point, but if we can't get the temperature under control, we fear there may be brain damage."

Ariana dropped the phone and Alisa rushed to her side. She picked up the phone from the floor and said, "This is Alisa Winston—Ariana's twin. Did Catherine die?"

The questions temporarily stunned the nurse. "No, no. She is gravely ill, however. There's a note on the chart that said we're to notify you, or actually your sister, of any significant changes."

"Should we come to the hospital?"

"That might be a good idea."

"We're on our way." Alisa hung up the phone without any further conversation. "Daddy," she yelled as she walked toward the stairs, "we need to go to the hospital."

Terry appeared at the top of the stairs with his shoes in hand. "What's wrong?"

"Catherine's fever is so high they think it might cause brain damage," Ariana said through her tears.

"Let's go." He kissed Jackie and headed for the garage.

The drive to the hospital was quick with no traffic and Terry pulled into the parking lot in fifteen minutes. Ariana was out of the car first and headed for the entrance. Terry caught up with them and they entered the lobby together. The lack of activity made the place seem eerie. The security officer gave them passes and they were on their way in short order.

When they arrived at the nurses' station, Ms. Wright acknowledged them immediately. "You must be Ms. Winston."

"Yes, I'm Ariana and this is Alisa." She turned to Terry and added, "This is our dad."

"We've had Ms. Hawkins in ice blankets all evening, but

the fever is just so stubborn. The doctor is in with her now. But if you have a seat in the waiting room, I'll get you in to see her as soon as I can."

Neither of the girls said anything but stood transfixed staring at the nurse who seemed to be in charge. Terry decided he'd answer for them. "Thank you. We'll be here," was all he could manage.

He escorted the girls down the short hall and, much to their surprise, there were others in the waiting room. They found a comfortable seat on a slightly worn sofa.

Terry wanted to do something, anything to relieve the tension he felt mounting. "Would you two like some coffee?"

Ariana shook her head. Alisa answered, "No thanks, Daddy."

Ariana turned quickly toward Alisa, startling her. " 'Lisa, you have to promise me something."

Without giving it any thought Alisa said, "Anything."

"Remember you promised me, okay?"

Alisa nodded.

"We both know that Catherine might die. And if she doesn't she may have brain damage." Ariana looked at the floor. "I've prayed and I believe that she is going to get better."

Alisa rubbed her sister's back. "I believe God answers prayers, too. And Daddy always says that God cares about what we want. I know you want her to get better very badly."

"And you don't?"

"Of course I want her to get better."

"You really mean that?"

"I'm not that cold. I care about Catherine. But I just don't feel safe with her."

Looking confused, Ariana asked, "What do you mean, you don't feel safe?"

"Not like she's going to hurt me physically." Alisa shot a glance at her dad and shifted uneasily in the chair. "When we were growing up, every time I expected something, something as simple as a phone call, she disappointed me. That frustration *always* turned to hurt. So after that day in court I promised myself I would never let her hurt me again. I was determined to stay a safe distance from her."

"Does that mean you love her?"

Alisa looked at Terry again. "I don't know. Sometimes I think I do, and then I get mad at myself for feeling that way."

" 'Lisa, I know exactly what you feel. I guess I just did it in reverse. When we were young and she never came around I'd be scared to hope." A lone tear fell from her cheek. "I always thought we had done some terrible thing to make her stay away."

"*I never cared about you or them. You were willing to take them off my hands and I got on with my life.*" Catherine's words echoed in Terry's head. The twins were in a world that had temporarily closed him out. He wanted to jump in somewhere in the middle and tell them they needn't ever worry because he'd always be there for them, but decided to sit in silence instead.

"I've always thought the same thing. But when I look back over the years, I knew it wasn't us. That's when I got so angry and didn't want to have anything to do with her."

"So you do love her?" Ariana locked eyes with Alisa.

Alisa wanted to break the gaze but couldn't. She also couldn't lie. "Who I love is you. And if you love her like I think you do, I'm fine with that."

"Remember you promised me you'd do what I asked?"

"Yes."

"If Catherine gets better"—Ariana hesitated—"I want you to give her a kidney."

"Ari, please don't make me promise that. If this were you, then we'd have already done the damn thing." 'Lisa realized she'd used a curse word in front of her father. Fear struck her soul as she looked in his direction, but he pretended not to have heard.

"The doctor said my one kidney is perfect. There's nothing to worry about with me. I want you to do this, please 'Lisa."

Alisa looked at her dad, around the room and finally back to Ariana. "I just can't take that chance."

"You're not taking any chances. It's me and I know this is a sure thing. I won't need your kidney and on the very off chance I do, medical science will have advanced so much by then, it won't even be an issue like it is now. You may be Catherine's only hope."

"Then this is pretty hope*less*."

"But you promised me."

Alisa let out a long sigh and turned to her father. "Dad, talk to her! Tell her how unreasonable this is."

"I can't help you," Terry said with a heavy heart. "Only *you* can make this decision."

This time Alisa began to cry. She felt like a ball of confusion. How was she ever going to live with herself if she gave Catherine a kidney and later her sister needed one? But that same sister had made her promise she *would* do it. They had never broken a promise to each other.

Ariana grabbed her hands and forced her to look at her. "Please, Alisa."

Alisa wanted to escape, but she felt trapped—not by walls

and doors but by love and dedication. If Ariana felt this strongly about Catherine, then she saw no way out. It was what they did. They lived for and through each other. She finally whispered, "Okay."

Astounded, Ariana asked her, "What did you say?"

With a little more confidence this time, Alisa said, "I'll do it."

Ariana threw her arms around her sister's neck, hugging her tightly as she pulled her off the chair. "Thank you, thank you, thank you! You'll be so happy you did this, 'Lisa, I promise. Catherine will change. I know she will! She just has to now."

Disillusionment encompassed Terry. *Oh my God. This child thinks this gesture will make Catherine love her!* "Alisa, are you sure you want to do this?"

"No, Daddy. I'm not," Alisa said slowly. "But like Ari says, it's the right thing to do. You've taught us that we have to treat people the way Jesus wants us to."

Terry tried to think of a rebuff, but there was nothing he could say. Ariana glowed with happiness.

Meanwhile, down the hall it was as though Catherine had heard the conversation. Sweat began to seep from her every pore as her temperature dropped.

Within an hour she was awake. At ten minutes past two Ms. Wright entered the waiting room with a smile. "We don't know how it happened so quickly, but Ms. Hawkins's temperature is down to one hundred point two, and though she's in and out, she's awake. The doctor said you can see her for a few minutes."

Ariana shot from her seat, moving toward the door. She turned to see if Alisa and Terry were behind her. They were both still seated. "Aren't you coming?"

Terry answered. "No, sweetie, you and your sister go. I'll be right here."

Alisa slowly rose and followed her sister as though she were walking the last mile. She prayed silently that Catherine wouldn't make her live to regret her decision.

CHAPTER SIXTY-ONE

*J*onah's eyes adjusted to the dimly lit restaurant as he searched the small room. Just as the maître d' approached the desk, he saw Anthony wave at him.

"May I help you, sir?" the man dressed all in black asked with a smile.

"I see my dining companion over there. Thank you," Jonah said as he moved toward the back of the restaurant.

"*Saluti! È buono da vederli ancora.*" (Greetings! It's good to see you again.) Anthony stood, extending his hand.

"Thank you for meeting me here." Jonah looked around nervously. "I'm sure I wasn't followed."

"Good." Anthony was relaxed and poised. "I've ordered a bottle of the house's best wine."

Jonah removed a handkerchief and wiped sweat from his brow, taking a moment to look around the restaurant once more, as he sat down and placed a brown envelope in front of him.

"Relax, my friend," Anthony consoled. "You are as safe in

this place as you were in your mother's womb. They serve some of the best pasta on earth here. I want you to enjoy your meal. There's plenty of time to talk business."

You've got to be kidding me. "I just want to get this over with and get back on a plane to Los Angeles." Jonah pulled nervously at his collar.

The wine arrived. Anthony tasted it and signaled that it was acceptable. The waiter poured two half glasses and left. Another server arrived with bread and olive oil.

"Drink up," Anthony admonished.

Jonah removed the envelope from the table and took a long swig of the wine. It warmed him through and through and he relaxed just a little.

"Now isn't that much better?" Anthony asked with a smile.

Jonah tried to fake a smile, but nothing in him felt jovial. Catherine had forced his hand with her betrayal. When she brought in Rahid MacDonald behind his back after stringing him along until all the dirty work was done, she had overestimated her grasp on him.

Even though he knew Catherine was in the hospital in Dallas, he still feared she was having him watched. Surely she was not such a fool as to trust him now. He wanted to complete his business with Anthony and be gone. "Anthony, I'd like to get on with the business at hand."

Setting his glass down, he leaned back in the chair. "Very well, then."

Jonah placed the brown envelope on the table again, letting his hand purposely rest there. "This contains everything you've asked for and a few things you didn't but that I thought would be useful."

"You've done well by me, Jonah." Anthony smiled with satisfaction.

Jonah looked down at the red tablecloth as he spoke. "Understand something, Anthony. This is not as much for you as it is against Catherine."

"But correct me if I'm wrong—the results are much the same?"

Jonah sat staring at the man that reminded him of Michael Corleone from *The Godfather*. He believed him to be ruthless and unstoppable, even by Catherine the Great. "I guess you're right."

Jonah looked down at the brown package one last time. Once he'd passed it to Anthony, there would be no turning back. No bell could be unrung. When the waiter appeared to take their orders, Anthony quickly dismissed him. In slow motion Jonah slid the envelope across the table.

Anthony quickly retrieved the envelope and placed it in his briefcase, which had sat on the floor beside him. For a brief moment Jonah's life passed before him as he thought Anthony would shoot him, that he in fact worked for Catherine and had set Jonah up. When Anthony pulled a white, very thick envelope of his own from his breast pocket, Jonah exhaled. He'd watched one too many episodes of *The Sopranos*.

Anthony slid the envelope across the table to Jonah, who stared down at it before he placed his hand on top of Anthony's for a moment. He then quickly pulled his hand back. Anthony stared at him curiously.

"I don't want your money," Jonah began. "I've done many things in my life of which I am not proud. I didn't care whom I hurt to get what I wanted. Though it was all very suspect, I never broke the law. This is my way of doing penance for what I've done. Catherine did to me what I've helped her do to so many others. But you know what they say?"

Anthony shook his head. "What's that?"

"What goes around . . ."

MARY MONROE

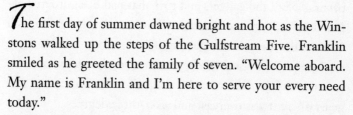

CHAPTER SIXTY-TWO

*T*he first day of summer dawned bright and hot as the Winstons walked up the steps of the Gulfstream Five. Franklin
smiled as he greeted the family of seven. "Welcome aboard.
My name is Franklin and I'm here to serve your every need
today."

Terry involuntarily whistled as he took in the elegant appointments throughout the cabin. The children scurried about,
looking at and touching everything in their path. Jackie tried
hard not to be impressed but she failed.

"You all may sit wherever you like." Franklin carried a tray
of freshly squeezed orange juice and piping hot coffee. "You're
our only passengers today. Mr. and Mrs. Winston, might I
suggest you sit here." Franklin had pointed to the front of the
cabin normally reserved for Catherine. "Ms. Hawkins has impressed upon me that I'm to do whatever it takes to make this
a pleasant trip for you and your family."

Jackie ran her hand across the leather seat that was as soft as her cashmere coat. She turned to Terry and said, "You know we could have taken SWA."

Terry threw his head back, laughing as he hugged her. "Girl, pull in those fangs. You know this is the double-dip chocolate chip with coconut sprinkles."

"Yeah it may be all that, but how many calories does it have?" Jackie said as she settled in the seat that seemed to reach up and grab her behind, surrounding it in luxury. She had never sat in an airplane seat with such comfort. Despite herself she relished the experience.

The twins smiled and took in all that was happening around them. Their focus was more on each other as it had been since the day Alisa had agreed to give Catherine her life back. They watched with amusement as the other children partook of all the gadgets and toys that had been ordered especially for their entertainment. They took seats next to each other as they sipped orange juice.

The pilot announced they were ready for departure and for them to fasten their seat belts. Their next stop was Los Angeles where it was overcast and sixty-three degrees.

As the Winstons exited the limousine in front of Catherine's home, this time even Jackie was impressed. The estate nestled in the Hollywood Hills must have been built for a movie star. There was marble and granite everywhere. Prisms and stained glass cast rainbows of color as the evening sun kissed the house. Catherine had truly pulled out all the stops. The penthouse suite at the hotel was larger than the Winston house. Jackie didn't know how much the suite cost per night, but she did believe that for the two-week stay, they could have paid off their mortgage and maybe one of their cars.

Dexter greeted them in a butler's uniform at the massive front door. "Please come in. Ms. Hawkins is awaiting your arrival."

As they stepped inside, Michael said, "Now this is dope!"

Jackie and Terry laughed as the other young people agreed. Catherine, though still thin with a deeper brown complexion than usual, emerged slowly from a marble-pillared entryway, extending her hand. "Welcome to my home."

Terry took it first, then Jackie. Ariana hugged her while the other children watched. Catherine seemed unsure of what to do with Alisa as she only smiled, making no attempt to embrace Catherine. "Please follow me. Dinner is about to be served."

T.J. grabbed his father's hand while the others fell into step. They walked into a dining room befitting any European castle. The table was dressed with the finest crystal, china and silver. Exquisite candelabras with even more beautiful flowers adorned the center of the table.

"Please sit wherever you like."

They moved about the room quietly as they found seats as if they did this every night. When everyone was finally settled, Catherine spoke. "I can't tell you how much it means to me to have you all in my home. These walls have not seen a lot of what you bring—love.

"I wanted to be sure that you had everything you needed both before and after the surgery." Catherine smiled at Alisa. "Are you all ready for tomorrow?"

"Yes, I believe so. This has all happened so fast. It's only been three weeks since we graduated and all that testing stuff just made the time fly by."

"Are you nervous?"

"No." Alisa looked quickly at Ariana, then at her parents. "Well, maybe a little."

"If it makes you feel any better, I'm terrified. But all the doctors assure me that I'm strong enough and that there is no more perfect match than you."

"I hope you're right," Ariana said.

"And for you, Alisa, this will be a piece of cake. You'll be up and around in just a couple of days." Catherine looked down the length of the table and smiled at Alisa.

Jackie stared at Catherine in disbelief. Had she found Jesus? Or was this an act until she got what she wanted? Jackie thought back to why they had even accepted the invitation in the first place and remembered Ariana and Terry had thought it was a good idea.

Catherine turned her attention back to the adults. "I hope that your accommodations are satisfactory."

Terry laughed. "You're kidding me, right?"

They all laughed. The staff entered and the feast began.

MEANWHILE ACROSS TOWN and down the freeway, the FBI, armed with search warrants and drawn guns, had stormed Hawkins International. Despite the protest of the security guards and the secretaries working late, the assault was swift and thorough.

Somewhere between the main course and dessert with gourmet coffee the doorbell rang. Dexter was quickly pushed aside as the FBI entered the palatial dwelling nestled high above Los Angeles.

*A*riana and Alisa sat next to each other with arms locked. They were each second-guessing their decision to attend different colleges. The Thanksgiving holiday break had seemed like it would never come. Jackie had worried Alisa hadn't totally recovered from the organ donor surgery before she headed off to Hampton University. She had suggested that she wait until the winter semester, but Alisa, with the doctor's blessing, had assured her parents she was strong enough to take on the new challenges college offered.

Ariana had fussed over Alisa during the entire time she recuperated. Despite Catherine's arrest on the eve of the surgery, her lawyers had been able to get her released in time to go under the knife as scheduled. The flawless operation had successfully replaced one of Catherine's failed kidneys and she was well on the road to recovery.

Her health was of little concern these days as Catherine Hawkins was put on trial for alleged violation of the Foreign Corrupt Practice Act. Apparently, it's not just illegal to accept a bribe but equally punishable by federal law to offer one, even to someone in a foreign land. Catherine's dealings in India and her means of having her request expedited had come to the attention of the Federal Bureau of Investigation.

Roland fell back on the sofa as he loosened his belt. "Jackie, I would have sworn Momma C. had been off in that kitchen. You put your foot off in that."

"Everything really was good, Mom." Ariana smiled.

"Thanks, everyone. There's plenty left so we can do the leftover thing later tonight," Jackie said as she sat the tray of coffee and fixings on the coffee table.

T.J. bounced into the den and asked, "Can we watch a movie?"

"Boy, don't you know that it would be un-American on Thanksgiving not to watch football after a meal like that," Terry teased. T.J. bounced out of the room and headed for the basement where the Carpenter boys were already in a heated battle of PlayStation.

"So how are things going with Catherine's legal troubles these days?" Mercedes asked as she slid in next to her husband.

"I know you didn't miss the segment on CNN!" Jackie poured and passed coffee. "She was outside the federal courthouse in Los Angeles, preaching about her persecution or some such nonsense."

"Do tell." Roland sat back and crossed his legs.

"Well, the grand jury indicted her," Terry said. "She's going to trial. Hawkins International is floundering at best. She's appointed some hotshot with a Harvard MBA to run a sinking ship."

"The last I read, they had some pretty damning evidence provided from players on her own team. Her former assistant turned over information to one of the division heads that would incriminate Catherine, and that person took it straight to the feds." Jackie sipped coffee.

"I didn't know it was illegal to bribe someone in another country," Ariana added. "Do you think she'll go to jail?"

"Who knows." Roland went on to ask, "Do we know why she was bribing folks in India?"

"As best as I can figure, she wanted to outsource labor to India to cut costs here in America. The process takes years to put into place, so she thought with paying the right people she'd be able to shave some time off the wait. Apparently, she could save millions a year by doing this."

"So who turned her in?" Mercedes was more than a little intrigued.

"As is her way, Catherine pissed off a lot of people when she was making all these acquisitions and mergers. Someone she screwed decided to screw back."

"That's a trip."

"Do we still have the news report on DVR, honey?" Jackie touched Terry on his left thigh.

"Oh, yeah, I plan to keep that one for a while." Terry laughed. "You guys want to see it. It's actually kinda funny in a sad sort of way."

They each agreed and Terry brought the entertainment center to life with the push of a single button. With a few clicks of the remote control he fast-forwarded through several other reports until he came to the one that showed a healthy Catherine smartly dressed, talking to a news reporter with a team of white men behind her holding umbrellas, presumed to be her lawyers.

The interviewer asked, "So, Ms. Hawkins, why do you think you've been singled out in this most unusual case?"

"Like Martha Stewart I have done nothing more than anyone else, but they are trying to make an example of me."

"Will you appeal?" One reporter pushed a microphone into Catherine's face.

"No comment." Catherine turned quickly, moving away from the onslaught of questions.

The reporter broke away from Catherine to speak directly into the camera. As Catherine descended the courthouse steps en route to her waiting limo, an old brown Buick sped past, splashing dirty rainwater all over her beautiful off-white suit just as a bird flew overhead and crapped on her shoulder.

Away from the crowd and out of the sight of the cameras, two men watched in silence at all that transpired. They hadn't spoken since they'd walked down the courthouse steps.

"What is it you Americans say?" Anthony turned to Jonah. "What goes around . . ."

"Comes around," Jonah finished Anthony's sentence.

"Indeed."

*R*eaders have been asking for a sequel since they first read *The Shirt off His Back*. *Everyone* wanted to see Catherine *get hers*. Though I fought the urge for years, the fans won out. One evening while chatting online with someone who proclaimed *The Shirt off His Back* was her favorite book of all time, I was presented with such a compelling argument for the sequel that I sat up and paid attention. Visiting the character again was like going home to family. When I came to the end I felt like I did when my firstborn graduated from high school. It had all come full circle.

As is my way, I feel it our responsibility to enlighten while we entertain. My mother and cousin both died from kidney disease at a young age, and I wanted readers to know and understand how serious the condition can be. I also wanted readers to think about organ donation. If one person reads this book and decides to become an organ donor, my purpose has been fulfilled.

What Goes Around

A READER'S GUIDE

Parry "EbonySatin" Brown

1. What are three main themes of *What Goes Around*?

2. Are Terry Winston's expectations reasonable regarding his twins' ability to cope with Catherine's demands and choose for themselves how to respond to her?

3. Ariana and Alisa seem to think that being eighteen means that they should be able to do whatever they want because they're adults, legally speaking. Do either of them demonstrate the maturity required to be treated as such? Why or why not?

4. Should Jackie be involved in decisions concerning the twins' real mother? How might she be a better advocate for the twins' best interests than Terry and how might she be worse?

5. Is there any other way Catherine Hawkins, the twins' birth mother, could have more effectively dealt with the family in order to better secure a kidney?

6. We know that deep down inside, Catherine Hawkins, as evil as she is, has her own issues with love and sex to work out. Should we feel sorry for her at all during this time when she is essentially alone with her illness?

7. Catherine continuously tries to buy affection from everyone around her, as well as control them with her wealth. Is it reasonable to hope that her two daughters will not be seduced by this ploy?

8. Jackie says to Terry: "What the hell do you mean, my insecurities? . . . I know I've been a good mother to Ariana and Alisa. I know they love and respect me. . . . Catherine can't change any of that. What you're failing to see is that this isn't only about Catherine. You seem to have forgotten the havoc she leaves in her wake" (p. 42). What is it that Jackie is trying to explain to Terry regarding what happens when he acquiesces to Catherine's manipulations?

9. Jackie goes to Catherine behind Terry's back in an attempt to convince her to leave the family alone. Was she right or wrong to keep this from Terry? Was she right or wrong to go and speak to Catherine?

10. Catherine finds herself alone while dealing with her kidney disease. Is there anything in *What Goes Around* that would make you reevaluate the way you treat others in order to ensure that you are not all alone when dealing with illness? Does this seem like a selfish reason to treat others with respect?

11. Should the twins give up a kidney? Why or why not?

12. Does Catherine Hawkins deserve to benefit from Alisa's sense of obligation to her?

13. How might Alisa's decision to be a donor affect her relationship in the long run with the rest of her family?

14. Does anyone in *What Goes Around* get what s/he deserves? Explain your reasoning.

To learn more about kidney disease please visit the National Kidney Foundation website at www.kidney.org.

If you haven't told your loved ones that you want to be an organ donor, do it today. Do the research, make a difference and give someone the gift of tomorrow.

Visit www.livingbank.org.

Parry "EbonySatin" Brown is the author of national best-sellers *The Shirt off His Back*, *Sexy Doesn't Have a Dress Size*, *Sittin' in the Front Pew*, and, most recently, *Fannin' the Flames*. She is also a contributor to the anthologies *Love Is Blind* and *Destiny's Daughters*. She is a motivational speaker and a radio talk-show host with a special concern for underprivileged children. She lives in the Los Angeles area. Visit her website at www.parryabrown.com.

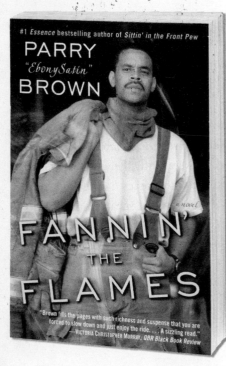